For Connor and Bridger,
chasers of the Olympic dream – M.S.

PRIVATE
GAMES

JAMES PATTERSON is one of the best-known and biggest-selling writers of all time. He is the author of some of the most popular series of the past decade – the Alex Cross, Women's Murder Club and Detective Michael Bennett novels – and he has written many other number one bestsellers including romance novels and stand-alone thrillers. He lives in Florida with his wife and son.

James is passionate about encouraging children to read. Inspired by his own son who was a reluctant reader, he also writes a range of books specifically for young readers. James has formed a partnership with the National Literacy Trust, an independent, UK-based charity that changes lives through literacy. In 2010, he was voted Author of the Year at the Children's Choice Book Awards in New York.

JAMES PATTERSON
AND MARK SULLIVAN

PRIVATE GAMES

arrow books

Published by Arrow Books in 2012

5 7 9 10 8 6 4

First published in Great Britain in 2012 by Century

Arrow Books
Random House, 20 Vauxhall Bridge Road,
London SW1V 2SA

www.randomhouse.co.uk

Addresses for companies within The Random House Group Limited can be found
at: www.randomhouse.co.uk/offices.htm

The Random House Group Limited Reg. No. 954009

A CIP catalogue record for this book
is available from the British Library

Penguin Random House is committed to a sustainable future for
our business, our readers and our planet. This book is made from
Forest Stewardship Council® certified paper.

Typeset in Berkeley (12/16 pt) by SX Composing DTP, Rayleigh, Essex

Printed and bound in Great Britain by Clays Ltd, St Ives plc

It is not possible with mortal mind to search out the purposes of the gods
– Pindar

For then, in wrath, the Olympian thundered and lightninged, and confounded Greece
– Aristophanes

Acknowledgements

We would like to thank Jackie Brock-Doyle, Neil Walker and Jason Keen at the London Organising Committee of the Olympic Games for their willingness to be helpful, candid and yet understandably circumspect regarding a project like this one. The tour of the park construction site was incredibly instructive. We would not have got anywhere without Alan Abrahamson, Olympic expert and operator of 3Wire.com, the world's best source of information about the Games and the culture that surrounds it. Special thanks go out as well to Vikki Orvice, Olympic reporter at the *Sun* and a wealth of knowledge, humour and gossip. We are also grateful to the staff at the British Museum, One Aldwych and 41 for their invaluable aid in suggesting settings for scenes outside the Olympic venues. Ultimately, this is a fictional story of hope and an affirmation of the Olympic ideals, so please forgive us a degree of licence regarding the various events, venues and characters likely to dominate the stage during the London 2012 Summer Games.

Prologue

Wednesday, 25 July 2012: 11:25 p.m.

THERE ARE SUPERMEN and superwomen who walk this Earth.

I'm quite serious about that and you can take me literally. Jesus Christ, for example, was a spiritual superman, as was Martin Luther, and Gandhi. Julius Caesar was superhuman as well. So were Genghis Khan, Thomas Jefferson, Abraham Lincoln, and Adolf Hitler.

Think scientists like Aristotle, Galileo, Albert Einstein, and J. Robert Oppenheimer. Consider artists like da Vinci, Michelangelo – and Vincent Van Gogh, my favourite, who was so superior that it drove him insane. And above all, don't forget athletically superior beings like Jim Thorpe, Babe Didrikson Zaharias and Jesse Owens.

Humbly, I include myself on this superhuman

spectrum as well – and deservedly so, as you shall soon see.

In short, people like me are born for great things. We seek adversity. We seek to conquer. We seek to break through all limits, spiritually, politically, artistically, scientifically and physically. We seek to right wrongs in the face of monumental odds. And we're willing to suffer for greatness, willing to embrace dogged effort and endless preparation with the fervour of a martyr, which to my mind are exceptional traits in any human being from any age.

At the moment I have to admit that I'm certainly feeling exceptional, standing here in the garden of Sir Denton Marshall, a snivelling, corrupt old bastard if there ever was one.

Look at him on his knees, his back to me and my knife at his throat.

Why, he trembles and shakes as if a stone has just clipped his head. Can you smell it? Fear? It surrounds him, as rank as the air after a bomb explodes.

'Why?' he gasps.

'You've angered me, monster,' I snarl at him, feeling a rage deeper than primal split my mind and seethe through every cell. 'You've helped ruin the Games, made them an abomination and a mockery of their intent.'

'What?' Marshall cries, acting bewildered. 'What are you talking about?'

I deliver the evidence against him in three damning sentences whose impact turns the skin of his neck livid and his carotid artery a sickening, pulsing purple.

'No!' he sputters. 'That's . . . that's not true. You can't do this. Have you gone utterly mad?'

'Mad? Me?' I say. 'Hardly. I'm the sanest person I know.'

'Please,' he says, tears rolling down his face. 'Have mercy. I'm to be married on Christmas Eve.'

My laugh is as caustic as battery acid: 'In another life, Denton, I ate my own children. You'll get no mercy from me or my sisters.'

As Marshall's confusion and horror become complete, I look up into the night sky, feeling storms rising in my head, and understanding once again that I *am* superior, a superhuman imbued with forces that go back thousands of years.

'For all true Olympians,' I vow, 'this act of sacrifice marks the beginning of the end of the modern Games.'

Then I wrench the old man's head back so that his back arches.

And before he can scream, I rip the blade furiously back with such force that his head comes free of his neck all the way to his spine.

Part One

THE FURIES

Chapter 1

Thursday, 26 July 2012: 9:24 a.m.

IT WAS MAD-DOG hot for London. Peter Knight's shirt and jacket were drenched with sweat as he sprinted north on Chesham Street past the Diplomat Hotel and skidded around the corner towards Lyall Mews in the heart of Belgravia, one of the most expensive areas of real estate in the world.

Don't let it be true, Knight screamed internally as he entered the Mews. Dear God, don't let it be true.

Then he saw a pack of newspaper jackals gathering at the yellow tape of a Metropolitan Police barricade that blocked the road in front of a cream-coloured Georgian town house. Knight lurched to a stop, feeling as though he was going to retch up the eggs and bacon he'd had for breakfast.

What would he ever tell Amanda?

Before Knight could compose his thoughts or quieten his stomach, his mobile rang and he snatched it from his pocket without looking at the caller ID.

'Knight,' he managed to choke. 'That you, Jack?'

'No, Peter, it's Nancy,' a woman with an Irish brogue replied. 'Isabel has come down sick.'

'What?' Knight groaned. 'No – I just left the house an hour ago.'

'She's running a temperature,' his full-time nanny insisted. 'I just took it.'

'How high?'

'One hundred. She's complaining about her stomach, too.'

'Lukey?'

'He seems fine,' Nancy said. 'But—'

'Give them both a cool bath, and call me back if Isabel's temp hits one oh one,' Knight said. He snapped shut the phone, swallowed back the bile burning at the base of his throat.

A wiry man about six foot tall, with an appealing face and light brown hair, Knight had once been a special investigator assigned to the Old Bailey, England's Central Criminal Court. Two years ago, however, he had joined the London office of Private International at twice the pay and prestige. Private has been called the Pinkerton Agency of the twenty-first century, with premises in every major city in the world, its offices staffed by top-notch forensics scientists, security specialists, and investigators such as Knight.

Compartmentalise, he told himself. Be professional. But this felt like the last straw breaking his back. Knight had already endured too much grief and loss, both personally and professionally. Just the week before, his boss, Dan Carter, and three of his other colleagues had perished in a plane crash over the North Sea that was still under investigation. Could he live with another death?

Pushing that question and his daughter's sudden illness to one side, Knight forced himself to hurry on through the sweltering heat towards the police barrier, giving the newspaper crowd a wide berth, and in so doing spotted Billy Casper, a Scotland Yard inspector he'd known for fifteen years.

He went straight to Casper, a blockish, pock-faced man who scowled the second he saw Knight. 'Private's got no business in this, Peter.'

'If that's Sir Denton Marshall dead in there, then Private does have business in this, and I do too,' Knight shot back forcefully. 'Personal business, Billy. Is it Marshall?'

Casper said nothing.

'Is it?' Knight demanded.

Finally the inspector nodded, but he wasn't happy about it, and asked suspiciously, 'How are you and Private involved?'

Knight stood there a moment, feeling stunned by

the news, and wondering again how the hell he was going to tell Amanda. Then he shook off the despair, and said, 'London Olympic Organising Committee is Private London's client. Which makes Marshall Private's client.'

'And you?' Casper demanded. 'What's your personal stake in this? You a friend of his or something?'

'Much more than a friend. He was engaged to my mother.'

Casper's hard expression softened a bit and he chewed at his lip before saying, 'I'll see if I can get you in. Elaine will want to talk to you.'

Knight felt suddenly as if invisible forces were conspiring against him.

'Elaine got this case?' he said, wanting to punch something. 'You can't be serious.'

'Dead serious, Peter,' Casper said. 'Lucky, lucky you.'

Chapter 2

INSPECTOR ELAINE POTTERSFIELD, in charge of the crime scene, was one of the finest detectives working for the Metropolitan Police, a twenty-year veteran of the force with a prickly, know-it-all style that got results. Pottersfield had solved more murders in the past two years than any other detective at Scotland Yard. She was also the only person Knight knew who openly despised his presence.

An attractive woman in her forties, the inspector always put Knight in mind of a borzoi dog, with her large round eyes, aquiline face and silver hair that cascaded round her shoulders. When Knight entered Sir Denton Marshall's kitchen, Pottersfield eyed him down her sharp nose, looking ready to bite him if she got the chance.

'Peter,' she said coldly.

'Elaine,' Knight said.

'Not exactly my idea to let you into the crime scene.'

'No, I imagine not,' replied Knight, fighting to control his emotions, which were heating up by the second. Pottersfield always seemed to have that effect on him. 'But here we are. What can you tell me?'

The inspector did not reply for several moments, then finally said, 'The maid found him an hour ago out in the garden. Or what's left of him, anyway.'

Thinking of Marshall, the learned and funny man he'd come to know and admire over the past two years, Knight felt dizzy and he had to put his vinyl-gloved hand on the counter to steady himself. 'What's left of him?'

Pottersfield gestured grimly at the open French window.

Knight absolutely did not want to go out into the garden. He wanted to remember Marshall as he'd been the last time he'd seen him, two weeks before, with his shock of startling white hair, scrubbed pink skin, and easy, infectious laugh.

'I'll understand if you'd rather not,' Pottersfield said. 'Inspector Casper said your mother was engaged to Marshall. When did that happen?'

'Last New Year,' Knight said. He swallowed, and moved towards the door, adding bitterly: 'They were to be married on Christmas Eve. Another tragedy. Just what I need in my life, isn't it?'

Pottersfield's expression twisted in pain and

anger, and she looked at the kitchen floor as Knight went past her and out into the garden.

The air in the garden was motionless, growing hotter, and stank of death and gore. On the flagstone terrace, about five litres of blood, the entire reservoir of Sir Denton Marshall's life, had run out and congealed around his decapitated corpse.

'The medical examiner thinks the job was done with a long curved blade that had a serrated edge,' Pottersfield said.

Knight once more fought off the urge to vomit and tried to take in the entire scene, to burn it into his mind as if it were a series of photographs and not reality. Keeping everything at arm's length was the only way he knew how to get through something like this.

Pottersfield said: 'And if you look closely, you'll see that some of the blood's been sprayed back toward the body with water from the garden hose. I'd expect the killer did it to wash away footprints and so forth.'

Knight nodded. Then, by sheer force of will, he moved his attention beyond the body, deeper into the garden, bypassing forensics techs gathering evidence from the flower beds, to a crime-scene photographer snapping away near the back wall.

Knight skirted the corpse by several feet and from that new perspective saw what the photographer was focusing on. It was ancient Greek and one of Marshall's prized possessions: a headless limestone statue of an Athenian senator cradling a book and holding the hilt of a broken sword.

Marshall's head had been placed in the empty space between the statue's shoulders. His face was puffy, lax. His mouth was twisted to the left as if he were spitting. And his eyes were open, dull, and, to Knight, shockingly forlorn.

For an instant, the Private operative wanted to break down. But then he felt himself filled with a sense of outrage. What kind of barbarian would do such a thing? And why? What possible reason could there be to behead Denton Marshall? The man was more than good. He was . . .

'You're not seeing it all, Peter,' Pottersfield said behind him. 'Take a look at the grass over there.'

Knight clenched his hands into fists and walked off the terrace onto the grass, which scratched against the paper slip-ons he wore over his shoes. Then he saw what Pottersfield had indicated and stopped cold.

Five interlocking rings – the symbol of the Olympic Games – had been spray-painted on the grass in front of the statue.

Across the symbol, partially obscuring it, an X had been smeared in blood.

14

Chapter 3

WHERE ARE THE eggs of monsters most likely to be laid? What nest incubates them until they hatch? What are the toxic scraps that nourish them to adulthood?

So often during the headaches that irregularly rip through my mind like gale-driven thunder and lightning I ponder those kinds of questions, and others.

Indeed, as you read this, you might be asking your own questions, such as 'Who are you?'

My real name is irrelevant. For the sake of this story, however, you can call me Cronus. In old, old Greek myths, Cronus was the most powerful of the Titans, a digester of universes, and the Lord God of Time.

Do I think I am a god?

Don't be absurd. Such arrogance tempts fate. Such hubris mocks the gods. And I have never been guilty of that treacherous sin.

I remain, however, one of those rare beings to appear on Earth once a generation or two. How else would you explain the fact that, long before the storms began in my head, hatred was my oldest memory and wanting to kill was my very first desire?

Indeed, at some point in my second year of life I became aware of hatred, as if it and I were linked spirits cast into an infant's body from somewhere out there in the void. And for some time that was what I thought of as me: this burning singularity of loathing thrown on the floor in a corner, in a box filled with rags.

Then one day I began instinctively to crawl from the box, and within that movement and the freedom I gained thereby I soon understood that I was more than anger, that I was a being unto myself, that I starved and went thirsty for days, that I was cold and naked and left to myself for hours on end, rarely cleaned, rarely held by the monsters that walked all around me as if I were some kind of alien creature landed among them. That was when my first direct thought occurred: *I want to kill them all.*

I had that ruthless urge long, long before I understood that my parents were drug addicts, crackheads, unfit to raise a superior being such as me.

When I was four, shortly after I sunk a kitchen knife into my comatose mother's thigh, a woman came to where we lived in squalor and she took me away from my parents for good. They put me in a home where I was forced to live with abandoned little monsters, hateful and distrustful of any other beings but themselves.

Soon enough I grasped that I was smarter, stronger, and more visionary than any of them. By the age of nine I did not know exactly what I was yet, but I sensed that I might be some sort of different species – a super-creature, if you will – who could manipulate, conquer, or slay every monster in his path.

I knew this about myself for certain after the storms started in my head.

They started when I was ten. My foster-father, whom we called 'Minister Bob', was whipping one of the little, little monsters, and I could not stand to hear it. The crying made me feel weak and I could not abide that sensation. So I left the house and climbed the back fence and wandered through some of the worst streets in London until I found quiet and comfort in the familiar poverty of an abandoned building.

Two monsters were inside already. They were older than me, in their teens, and they were members of a street gang. They were high on something, I could tell that about them right away; and they said I'd wandered onto their turf.

I tried to use my speed to get away, but one of them threw a rock that clipped my jaw. It dazed me and I fell, and they laughed and got angrier. They threw more stones that cracked my ribs and broke blood vessels in my thigh.

Then I felt a hard blow above my left ear, followed by a Technicolor explosion that crackled through my brain like lightning bolts ripping through a summer sky.

Chapter 4

PETER KNIGHT FELT helpless as he glanced back and forth, from the Olympic symbol crossed out in blood to the head of his mother's fiancé.

Inspector Pottersfield stepped up beside Knight. In a thin voice, she said, 'Tell me about Marshall.'

Choking back his grief, Knight said, 'Denton was a great, great man, Elaine. Ran a big hedge fund, made loads of money, but gave most of it away. He was also an absolutely critical member of the London Organising Committee. A lot of people think that without Marshall's efforts, we never would have beaten Paris in our bid for the Games. He was also a nice guy, very modest about his achievements. And he made my mother very happy.'

'I didn't think that was possible,' Pottersfield remarked.

'Neither did I. Neither did Amanda. But he did,' Knight said. 'Until just now, I didn't think Denton Marshall had an enemy in the world.'

Pottersfield gestured at the bloody Olympic symbol. 'Maybe it has more to do with the Olympics than who he was in the rest of his life.'

Knight stared at Sir Denton Marshall's head and returned his gaze to the corpse before saying, 'Maybe. Or maybe this is just designed to throw us off track. Cutting off someone's head can easily be construed as an act of rage, which is almost always personal at some level.'

'You're saying this could be revenge of some kind?' Pottersfield replied.

Knight shrugged. 'Or a political statement. Or the work of a deranged mind. Or a combination of the three. I don't know.'

'Can you account for your mother's whereabouts last evening between eleven and twelve-thirty?' Pottersfield asked suddenly.

Knight looked at her as if she was an idiot. 'Amanda loved Denton.'

'Spurned love can be a powerful motive to rage,' Pottersfield observed.

'There was no spurning,' Knight snapped. 'I would have known. Besides, you've seen my mother. She's five foot five and weighs just under eight stone. Denton weighed nearly sixteen. There's no way she'd have had the physical or emotional strength to cut off his head. And she had no reason to.'

'So you're saying you *do* know where she was?' Pottersfield asked.

'I'll find out and get back to you about it. But first I have to tell her.'

'I'll do that if you think it might help.'

'No, I'll do it,' Knight said, studying Marshall's head one last time and then focusing on the way his mouth seemed twisted as if he'd been trying to spit something out.

Knight fished in his pocket for a pen-sized torch, stepped around the Olympic symbol and directed the beam into the gap between Marshall's lips. He saw a glint of something, and reached back into his pocket for a pair of forceps that he always kept there in case he wanted to pick something up without touching it.

Refusing to look at his mother's dead fiancé's eyes, he began to probe between Marshall's lips with the forceps.

'Peter, stop that,' Pottersfield ordered. 'You're—'

But Knight was already turning to show her a tarnished bronze coin that he'd plucked from Marshall's mouth.

'New theory,' he said. 'It's about money.'

Chapter 5

WHEN I RETURNED to consciousness several days after the stoning, I was in hospital with a fractured skull and the nauseating feeling that I had been rewired somehow, made more alien than ever before.

I remembered everything about the attack and everything about my attackers. But when the police came to ask me what had happened, I told them I had no idea. I said I had memories of entering the building, but nothing more; and their questions soon stopped.

I healed slowly. A crablike scar formed on my scalp. My hair grew back, hiding it, and I began to nurture a dark fantasy that became my first obsession.

Two weeks later, I returned home to the little monsters and Minister Bob. Even they could tell I'd changed. I was no longer a wild child. I smiled and acted happy. I studied and developed my body.

Minister Bob thought that I'd found God.

But I admit to you that I did it all by embracing hatred. I stroked that crablike scar on my head, and focused my oldest emotional ally on things that I wanted to have and to happen. Armed with a dark heart, I went after them all, trying to show the entire world how different I really was. And though I acted the changed boy, the happy, achieving friend in public, I never forgot the stoning or the storms it had spawned in my head.

When I was fourteen, I began looking secretly for the monsters who'd broken my skull. I found them eventually, selling small twists of methamphetamine on a street corner not far from where I lived with Minister Bob and the little monsters.

I kept tabs on the pair until I turned sixteen and felt big and strong enough to act.

Minister Bob had been a steelworker before he found Jesus. On the sixth anniversary of my stoning, I took one of his heavy hammers and a pair of his old work overalls, and I slipped out at night when I was supposed to be studying.

Wearing the overalls and carrying the hammer in a satchel harvested from a rubbish bin, I found the two monsters who'd stoned me. Six years of their drug use and six years of my evolution had wiped me from their memory banks.

I lured them to an empty lot with the promise of money, and then I beat their brains to bloody pulp.

Chapter 6

SHORTLY AFTER INSPECTOR Pottersfield ordered Marshall's remains bagged, Knight left the garden and the mansion consumed by far worse dread than he'd felt on entering.

He ducked beneath the police tape, avoided the newspaper jackals, and headed out of Lyall Mews, trying to decide how in God's name he was going to tell his mother about Denton. But Knight knew that he had to, and quickly, before Amanda heard it from someone else. He absolutely did not want her to be alone when she learned that the best thing that had ever happened to her was—

'Knight?' a man's voice called to him. 'Is that you?'

Knight looked up to see a tall, athletic man – mid-forties and wearing a fine Italian suit – rushing towards him. Below his thick salt-and-pepper hair, anguish twisted his ruddy, square face.

Knight had met Michael 'Mike' Lancer at Private London's offices twice in the eighteen months since the company had been hired to act as a special security detail during the Olympic Games. But he knew the man largely by his reputation.

A two-time world decathlon champion in the 1980s and 1990s, Lancer had served with and in the Queen's Guard, which had allowed him to train full-time. At the Barcelona Olympics in 1992 he had led the decathlon after the first day of competition but had then cramped in the heat and humidity during the second day, finishing outside the top ten finishers.

Lancer had since become a motivational speaker and security consultant who often worked with Private International on big projects. He was also a member of LOCOG, the London Organising Committee for the Olympic Games, and had been charged with helping to organise security for the mega-event.

'Is it true?' Lancer asked in a distraught voice. 'Denton's dead?'

'Afraid so, Mike,' Knight said.

Lancer's eyes welled with tears. 'Who would do this? Why?'

'Looks like someone who hates the Olympics,' Knight said. Then he described the manner of Marshall's death, and the bloody X.

Rattled, Lancer said, 'When do they think this happened?'

'Shortly before midnight,' Knight replied.

Lancer shook his head. 'That means I saw him only two hours before his death. He was leaving the party at Tate Britain with . . .' He stopped and looked at Knight in sad reappraisal.

'Probably with my mother,' Knight said. 'They were engaged.'

'Yes, I knew that you and she are related,' Lancer said. 'I'm so, so sorry, Peter. Does Amanda know?'

'I'm on my way to tell her right now.'

'You poor bastard,' Lancer said. Then he looked off towards the police barrier. 'Are those reporters there?'

'A whole pack of them, and getting bigger,' Knight said.

Lancer shook his head bitterly. 'With all due loving respect to Denton, this is all we need with the opening ceremony tomorrow night. They'll blast the lurid details all over the bloody world.'

'Nothing you can do to stop that,' Knight said. 'But I might think about upping security on all members of the organising committee.'

Lancer made a puffing noise, and then nodded. 'You're right. I'd best catch a cab back to the office. Marcus is going to want to hear this in person.'

Marcus Morris, a politician who had stood down at the last election, was now chairman of the London Organising Committee.

'My mother as well,' Knight said and together they headed on towards Chesham Street where they thought there'd be more taxis.

Indeed, they'd just reached Chesham Street when a black cab appeared from the south across from the Diplomat Hotel. At the same time, farther away and from the north, a red cab came down the near lane. Knight hailed it.

Lancer signalled the taxi in the northbound lane, saying, 'Give my condolences to your mother, and tell Jack I'll be in touch sometime later today.'

Jack Morgan was the American owner of Private International. He'd been in town since the plane carrying five members of the London office had gone down in the North Sea with no survivors.

Lancer stepped off the kerb, and set off in a confident stride heading diagonally across the street while the red cab came closer.

But then, to Knight's horror, he heard the growl of an engine and the squeal of tyres.

The black cab was accelerating, heading right at the LOCOG member.

27

Chapter 7

KNIGHT REACTED ON instinct. He leaped into the street and knocked Lancer from the cab's path.

In the next instant, Knight sensed the black cab's bumper less than a metre away and tried to jump in the air to avoid being hit. His feet left the ground but could not propel him out of the cab's path. The bumper and radiator grille struck the side of his left knee and lower leg and drove on through.

The blow spun Knight into the air. His shoulders, chest and hip smashed down on the vehicle's bonnet and his face was jammed against the windscreen. He glimpsed a split-second image of the driver. Scarf. Sunglasses. A woman?

Knight was hurled up and over the cab's roof as if he were no more than a stuffed doll. He hit the road hard on his left side, knocking the wind out of him, and for a moment he was aware only of the sight of the black cab speeding away, the smell of car exhaust, and the blood pounding in his temples.

Then he thought: A bloody miracle, but nothing feels broken.

The red taxi screeched towards Knight and he panicked, thinking he'd be run over after all.

But it skidded into a U-turn before stopping. The driver, an old Rasta wearing a green and gold knitted cap over his dreadlocks threw open his door and jumped out.

'Don't move, Knight!' Lancer yelled, running up to him. 'You're hurt!'

'I'm okay,' Knight croaked. 'Follow that cab, Mike.'

Lancer hesitated, but Knight said, 'She's getting away!'

Lancer grabbed Knight under the arms and hoisted him into the back of the red cab. 'Follow it!' Lancer roared at the driver.

Knight held his ribs, still struggling for air as the Rasta driver took off after the black cab, which was well ahead of them by now, turning hard west along Pont Street.

'I catch her, mon!' the driver promised. 'Dat crazy one tried to kill you!'

Lancer was looking back and forth between the road ahead and Knight. 'You sure you're okay?'

'Banged and bruised,' Knight grunted. 'And she wasn't trying to run me down, Mike. She was trying to run *you* down.'

29

The driver power-drifted into Pont Street, heading west. The black cab was closer now, its brake lights flashing red before it lurched in a hard right turn into Sloane Street.

The Rasta mashed the accelerator hard. They reached the intersection with Sloane Street so fast that Knight felt sure they'd actually catch up with the woman who'd just tried to kill him.

But then two more black cabs flashed past them, both heading north on Sloane Street, and the Rasta was forced to slam on his brakes and wrench the wheel so as not to hit them. Their cab went into a screeching skid and almost hit another car: a Metropolitan Police vehicle.

Its siren went on. So did its flashing lights.

'No!' Lancer yelled.

'Every time, mon!' the driver shouted in equal frustration as he slowed his vehicle to a stop.

Knight nodded, dazed and angry, staring through the windscreen as the taxi that had almost killed him melted into the traffic heading towards Hyde Park.

Chapter 8

BRIGHTLY FLETCHED ARROWS whizzed and cut through the hot mid-morning air. They struck in and around yellow bullseyes painted on large red and blue targets set up in a long line that stretched across the lime-green pitch at Lord's Cricket Ground near Regent's Park in central London.

Archers from six or seven countries were completing their final appointed practice rounds. Archery would be one of the first sports to be decided after the 2012 London Olympic Games opened, with competition scheduled to start mid-morning on Saturday, two days hence, with the medal ceremony to be held that very afternoon.

Which was why Karen Pope was up in the stands, watching through binoculars, boredom slackening her face.

Pope was a sports reporter for the *Sun*, a London tabloid newspaper with six million readers thanks to a tradition of aggressive bare-knuckle journalism and publishing photographs of young bare-breasted women on page three.

Pope was in her early thirties, attractive in the way that Renée Zellweger was in the film *Bridget Jones's Diary* but too flat-chested ever to be considered for the *Sun*'s page three. Pope was also a dogged reporter, and ambitious in the extreme.

Around her neck that morning hung one of only fourteen full-access media passes granted to the *Sun* for the Olympics. Such passes had been severely limited for the British press because more than twenty thousand members of the global media would also be in London to cover the sixteen-day mega-event. The full-access passes had become almost as valuable as Olympic medals, at least to British journalists.

Pope kept thinking that she should be happy to have the pass and to be here covering the Games at all, but her efforts this morning had so far failed to yield anything truly newsworthy about archery.

She'd been looking for the South Koreans, the gold-medal favourites, but had learned that they had already finished their practice session before she arrived.

'Bloody hell,' she said in disgust. 'Finch is going to kill me.'

Pope decided her best hope was to research a feature that with lively writing might somehow make the paper. But what sort? What was the angle?

Archery: Darts for the Posh?

No – there was absolutely nothing posh about archery.

Indeed, what in God's name did she know about archery? She'd grown up in a football family. Earlier that very morning Pope had tried to explain to Finch that she'd be better off assigned to athletics or gymnastics. But her editor had reminded her in no uncertain terms that she'd only joined the paper from Manchester six weeks before and was therefore low-person on the sports desk.

'Get me a big story and you'll get better assignments,' Finch had said.

Pope prodded her attention back to the archers. It struck her that they seemed so calm. It was almost as though they were in a trance over there. Not like a cricket batsman or a tennis player at all. Should she write about that? Find out how the bowmen got themselves into that state?

C'mon, she thought in annoyance, who wants to read about Zen in sports when you can look at bare boobs on page three?

Pope sighed, set down her binoculars, and shifted her position in one of the blue grandstand seats. She noticed, stuffed down into her handbag, a bundle of mail that she'd grabbed leaving the office and started going through the stack, finding various press releases and other items of zero interest.

Then she came to a thick Manila envelope with her name and title printed oddly in black and blue block letters on the front.

Pope twitched her nose as if she'd sniffed something foul. She hadn't written anything recently to warrant a nutcase letter, most definitely not since she'd arrived in London. Every reporter worth a damn got nutcase letters. You learned to recognise them quickly. They usually came after you'd published something controversial or hinting at diabolical conspiracy.

She slit the envelope open anyway, and drew out a sheaf of ten pages attached by paper clip to a folded plain paper greeting card. She flipped the card open. There was no writing inside. But a computer chip in the card was activated by the movement and flute music began to play, weird sounds that got under her skin and made her think that someone had died.

Pope shut the card and then scanned the first page of the sheaf. She saw that it was a letter addressed to her, and that it had been typed in a dozen different fonts, which made it hard to read. But then she began to get the gist of it. She read the letter three times, her heart beating faster with every line until it felt like it was throbbing high in her throat.

She scanned the rest of the documents attached to the letter and the greeting card, and felt almost faint. She dug wildly in her bag for her phone, and called her editor.

'Finch, it's Pope,' she said breathlessly when he answered. 'Can you tell me whether Denton Marshall has been murdered?'

In a thick Cockney accent, Finch said, 'What? *Sir* Denton Marshall?'

'Yes, yes, the big hedge-fund guy, philanthropist, member of the organising committee,' Pope confirmed, gathering her things and looking for the nearest exit from the cricket ground. 'Please, Finchy, this could be huge.'

'Hold on,' her editor growled.

Pope had made it outside and was trying to hail a cab across from Regent's Park when her editor finally came back on the line.

'They've got the yellow tape up around Marshall's place in Lyall Mews and the coroner's wagon just arrived.'

Pope punched the air with her free hand and cried: 'Finch, you're going to have to get someone else to cover archery and dressage. The story I just caught is going to hit London like an earthquake.'

Chapter 9

'LANCER SAYS YOU saved his life,' Elaine Pottersfield said.

A paramedic prodded and poked at a wincing Knight, who was sitting on the bumper of an ambulance on the east side of Sloane Street, a few feet from the Rasta's parked red cab.

'I just reacted,' Knight insisted, aching everywhere and feeling baked by the heat radiating off the pavement.

'You put yourself in harm's way,' the inspector said coldly.

Knight got annoyed. 'You said yourself I saved his life.'

'And almost lost your own,' she shot back. 'Where would that have left . . .' She paused. 'The children?'

He said, 'Let's keep them out of this, Elaine. I'm fine. There should be footage of that cab on CCTV.'

London had 10,000 closed-circuit security

cameras that rolled twenty-four hours a day, spread out across the city. A lot of them had been there since the 2005 terrorist bombings in the Tube left fifty-six people dead and seven hundred wounded.

'We'll check them,' Pottersfield promised. 'But finding a particular black cab in London? Since none of you got the licence number plate that's going to be near-impossible.'

'Not if you narrow the search to this road, heading north, and the approximate time she got away. And call all the taxi companies. I had to have done some damage to her bonnet or radiator grille.'

'You're sure it was a woman?' Pottersfield asked sceptically.

'It was a woman,' Knight insisted. 'Scarf. Sunglasses. Very pissed-off.'

The Scotland Yard inspector glanced over at Lancer who was being interviewed by another officer, before saying, 'Him and Marshall. Both LOCOG members.'

Knight nodded. 'I'd start looking for people who have a beef with the organising committee.'

Pottersfield did not reply because Lancer was approaching them. He'd wrenched his tie loose around his neck and was patting at his sweating brow with a handkerchief.

'Thank you,' he said to Knight. 'I am beyond simply being in your debt.'

'Nothing that you wouldn't have done for me,' Knight replied.

'I'm calling Jack,' Lancer said. 'I'm telling him what you did.'

'It's not necessary,' Knight said.

'It is,' Lancer insisted. He hesitated. 'I'd like to repay you somehow.'

Knight shook his head. 'LOCOG is Private's client, which means you are Private's client, Mike. It's all in a day's work.'

'No, you . . .' Lancer hesitated and then completed his thought. 'You shall be my guest tomorrow night at the opening ceremonies.'

Knight was caught flat-footed by the offer. Tickets to the opening ceremony were almost as prized as invitations to the marriage of Prince William and Kate Middleton had been the year before.

'If I can get the nanny to cover for me, I'll accept.'

Lancer beamed. 'I'll have my secretary send you a pass and tickets in the morning.' He patted Knight on his good shoulder, smiled at Pottersfield, and then walked off towards the Jamaican taxi driver who was still getting a hard time from the patrol officers who'd pulled them over.

'I'll need you to make a formal statement,' Pottersfield said.

'I'm not doing anything until I've spoken with my mother.'

Chapter 10

TWENTY MINUTES LATER, a Metropolitan Police patrol car dropped Knight in front of his mother's home on Milner Street in Knightsbridge. He'd been offered opiate painkillers by the paramedics, but had refused them. Getting out of the police car was agonising and an image of a beautiful pregnant woman standing on a moor at sunset kept flashing into his mind.

Thankfully, he was able to put her out of his thoughts by the time he rang the doorbell, suddenly aware of how dirty and torn his clothes were.

Amanda would not approve. Neither would—

The door swung open to reveal Gary Boss, his mother's long-time personal assistant: thirties, thin, well groomed and impeccably attired.

Boss blinked at Knight from behind round tortoiseshell glasses, and sniffed. 'I didn't know you had an appointment, Peter.'

'Her son and only child doesn't need one,' Knight said. 'Not today.'

'She's very, very busy,' Boss insisted. 'I suggest—'

'Denton's dead, Gary,' Knight said softly.

'What?' Boss said and then tittered derisively. 'That's impossible. She was with him just last—'

'He was murdered,' Knight said, stepping inside. 'I just came from the crime scene. I need to tell her.'

'Murdered?' Boss said, and then his mouth sloughed open, and he closed his eyes as if in anticipation of some personal agony in the near future. 'Dear God. She'll be . . .'

'I know,' Knight said, and moved past him. 'Where is she?'

'In the library,' Boss said. 'Choosing fabric.'

Knight winced. His mother despised being interrupted when she was looking at samples. 'Can't be helped,' he said, and walked down the hall towards the doors of the library, readying himself to tell his mother that she was now, in effect, twice a widow.

When Knight was three, his father Harry had died in a freak industrial accident, leaving his young widow and son a meagre insurance payout. His mother had turned bitter about her loss, but then turned that bitterness into energy. She'd always liked fashion and sewing, so she took the insurance money and started a clothing company that she named after herself.

Amanda Designs had started in their kitchen. Knight remembered how his mother had seemed to look at life and business as one long protracted brawl. Her pugnacious style succeeded. By the time Knight was fifteen, his mother had built Amanda Designs into a robust and respected company by never being happy, by constantly goading everyone around her to do better. Shortly after Knight graduated from Christ's Church college, Oxford she'd sold the concern for tens of millions of pounds and used the cash to fund the launch of four even more successful clothing lines.

In all that time, however, Knight's mother had never allowed herself to fall in love again. She'd had friends and consorts and, Knight suspected, several short-term lovers. But from the day his father had died, Amanda had erected a solid shield around her heart that no one, except for her son, ever managed to breach.

Until Denton Marshall had come into her life.

They'd met at a cancer fund-raiser and, as his mother liked to say, 'It was everything at first sight.' In that one evening, Amanda transformed from a cold, remote bitch to a schoolgirl giddy with her first crush. From that point forward, Marshall had been her soulmate, her best friend, and the source of the deepest happiness of her life.

Knight flashed on that image of the pregnant

woman again, knocked on the library door, and entered.

An elegant woman by any standards – late fifties, with the posture of a dancer, the beauty of an ageing movie star, and the bearing of a benevolent ruler – Amanda Knight was standing at her work table, dozens of fabric swatches arrayed in front of her.

'Gary,' she scolded without looking up. 'I told you that I was not to be—'

'It's me, Mother,' Knight said.

Amanda turned to look at him with her slate-coloured eyes, and frowned. 'Peter, didn't Gary tell you I was choosing . . .' She stopped, seeing something in his expression. Her own face twisted in disapproval. 'Don't tell me: your heathen children have driven off another nanny.'

'No,' Knight said. 'I wish it were something as simple as that.'

Then he proceeded to shatter his mother's happiness into a thousand jagged pieces.

Chapter 11

IF YOU ARE to kill monsters, you must learn to think like a monster.

I did not begin to appreciate that perspective until the night after the explosion that cracked my head a second time, nineteen years after the stoning.

I was long gone from London in the wake of the thwarting of my first plan to prove to the world that I was beyond different, that I was infinitely superior to any other human.

The monsters had won that war against me by subterfuge and sabotage, and as a result, when I landed in the Balkans assigned to a NATO peace-keeping mission in the late spring of 1995, the hatred I felt had no limits to its depth or to its dimensions.

After what had been done to me I did not want peace.

I wanted violence. I wanted sacrifice. I wanted blood.

So perhaps you could say that fate intervened on my behalf within five weeks of my deployment within the fractured, shifting and highly combustible killing fields of Serbia, Croatia and Bosnia-Herzegovina.

It was July, a late afternoon on a dusty road eighteen miles from the Drina Valley and the besieged city of Srebrenica. I was riding in the passenger seat of a camouflaged Toyota Land Cruiser, looking out the window, wearing a helmet and a flak vest.

I'd been reading about Greek mythology from a book I'd picked up, and was thinking that the war-torn Balkan landscape through which we travelled could have been the setting of some dark and twisted myth; wild roses were blooming everywhere around the mutilated corpses we'd been spotting in the area, victims of one side's or the other's atrocity.

The bomb went off without warning.

I can't recall the sound of the blast that destroyed the driver, the truck and the two other passengers. But I can still smell the explosive and the burning fuel. And I can still feel the aftershock of the invisible fist that struck me full force, hurling me through the windscreen, and setting off an electrical storm of epic proportions inside my skull.

Dusk had blanketed the land by the time I regained consciousness, ears ringing, disorientated, nauseated and thinking at first that I was ten years old and had just been stoned unconscious. But then the tilting and whirling in my mind slowed enough for me to make out the charred skeleton of the Land Cruiser and the corpses of my companions, burned beyond recognition. Beside me lay a sub-machine gun and an automatic pistol, a Sterling and a Beretta that had been thrown from the truck.

It was dark by the time I could stand, pick up the weapons and walk.

I staggered, falling frequently, for several miles across fields and through forests before I came to a village somewhere south-west of Srebrenica. Walking in, carrying the guns, I heard something above and beyond the ringing in my ears. Men were shouting somewhere in the darkness ahead of me.

Those angry voices drew me, and as I went towards them I felt my old friend hatred building in my head, irrational, urging me to slay somebody.

Anybody.

Chapter 12

THE MEN WERE BOSNIANS. There were seven of them armed with old single-barrel shotguns and corroded rifles that they were using to goad three handcuffed teenaged girls ahead of them as if they were driving livestock to a pen.

One of them saw me, shouted, and they turned their feeble weapons my way. For reasons I could not explain to myself until much later I did not open fire and kill them all right there, the men and the girls.

Instead, I told them the truth: that I was part of the NATO mission and that I'd been in an explosion and needed to call back to my base. That seemed to calm them somewhat and they lowered their guns and let me keep mine.

One of them spoke broken English and said I could call from the village's police station, where they were heading.

I asked what the girls were under arrest for, and

the one who spoke English said, 'They are war criminals. They belong to Serbian kill squad, working for that devil Mladic. People call them the Furies. These girls kill Bosnian boys. Many boys. Each of them does this. Ask oldest one. She speak English.'

Furies? I thought with great interest. I'd been reading about the Furies the day before in my book of Greek mythology. I walked quicker so that I could study them, especially the oldest one, a sour-looking girl with a heavy brow, coarse black hair, and dead dark eyes.

Furies? This could not be a coincidence. As much as I believed that hatred had been gifted to me at birth, I came to believe instantly that these girls had been put in front of me for a reason.

Despite the pain that was splitting my head, I fell in beside the oldest one and asked, 'You a war criminal?'

She turned her dead dark eyes on me and spat out her reply: 'I am no criminal, and neither are my sisters. Last year, Bosnian pigs kill my parents and rape me and my sisters for four days straight. If I could, I shoot every Bosnian pig. I break their skulls. I kill all of them if I could.'

Her sisters must have understood enough of what their sister was saying because they too turned their dead eyes on me. The shock of the bombing, the brutal throbbing in my head, my jet-fuelled anger, the Serbian girls' dead eyes, the myth of the Furies, all these things seemed to gather together into something that felt suddenly predestined to me.

The Bosnians handcuffed the girls to heavy wooden chairs bolted to the floor of the police station, and shut and locked the doors. The land-lines were not working. Neither were the primitive mobile-phone towers. I was told, however, that I could wait there until a peacekeeping force could be called to take me and the Serbian girls to a more secure location.

When the Bosnian who spoke English left the room, I cradled my gun, moved close to the girl who'd spoken to me, and said 'Do you believe in fate?'

'Go away.'

'Do you believe in fate?' I pressed her.

'Why do you ask me this question?'

'As I see it, as a captured war criminal your fate is to die,' I replied. 'If you're convicted of killing dozens of unarmed boys, that's genocide. Even if you and your sisters were gang-raped beforehand, they will hang you. That's how it works with genocide.'

She lifted her chin haughtily. 'I am not afraid to die for what we have done. We killed monsters. It was justice. We put back balance where there was none.'

Monsters and Furies, I thought, growing excited before replying: 'Perhaps, but you will die, and there your story will end.' I paused. 'But maybe you have another fate. Perhaps everything in your life has been in preparation for this exact moment, this place, this night, right now when your fates collide with mine.'

She looked confused. 'What does this mean, "fates collide"?'

'I get you out of here,' I said. 'I get you new identities, I hide you, and protect you and your sisters for ever. I give you a chance at life.'

She'd gone steely again. 'And in return?'

I looked into her eyes. I looked into her soul. 'You will be willing to risk death to save me as I will now risk death to save you.'

The oldest sister looked at me sidelong. Then she turned and clucked to her sisters in Serbian. They argued for several moments in harsh whispers.

Finally, the one who spoke English said, 'You can save us?'

The clanging in my head continued but the fogginess had departed, leaving me in a state of near-electric clarity. I nodded.

She stared at me with those dark dead eyes, and said, 'Then save us.'

The Bosnian who spoke English returned to the

room and called out to me, 'What lies are these demons from hell telling you?'

'They're thirsty,' I answered. 'They need water. Any luck with the telephone?'

'Not yet,' he said.

'Good,' I replied, flipping the safety on the sub-machine gun as I swung the muzzle around at the Furies' captors before opening fire and slaughtering every one.

Part Two

LET THE GAMES BEGIN

Chapter 13

AS THE TAXI pulled up in front of a sterile-looking skyscraper deep in the City of London, the UK's main financial district, Peter Knight could still hear his mother sobbing. The only other time he'd ever seen her cry like that had been over his father's body after the accident.

Amanda had collapsed into her son's arms after learning of her fiancé's death. Knight had felt the racking depths of her despair, and had understood them all too well. She'd been stabbed in the soul. Knight wouldn't have wished that sensation on anyone, least of all his own mother, and he held her through the worst of the mental and emotional haemorrhaging, reliving his own raw memories of loss.

Gary Boss had come into her office finally, and had nearly wept himself when he'd seen Amanda's abject sorrow. A few minutes later, Knight received a text from Jack Morgan telling him to come directly to Private London's office because the *Sun* had hired the firm to analyse a letter from someone who claimed to be Marshall's killer. Boss said he would take over Amanda's care.

'No, I should stay,' Knight had replied, feeling horribly guilty about leaving. 'Jack would understand. I'll call him.'

'No!' Amanda said angrily. 'I want you to go to work, Peter. I want you to do what you do best. I want you to find the sick bastard who did this to Denton. I want him put in chains. I want him burned alive.'

As Knight took a lift to the top floors of the sky-scraper, his thoughts were dominated by his mother's command, and despite the steady ache in his side he felt himself becoming obsessed. It was always like this with Knight when he was on a big case – obsessed, possessed – but, with his mother's involvement, this particular investigation felt more like a crusade: no matter what happened, no matter the obstacles, no matter the time needed, Knight vowed to nail Denton Marshall's killer.

The lift door opened into a reception area, a hyper-modern room containing some works of art that depicted milestones in the history of espionage, forensics and cryptography. Though the London office itself was seriously understaffed at the moment due to the recent tragic loss of personnel, the lobby bustled with Private International agents from all over the world, here to pick up their Olympic security passes and assignments.

Knight circled the mob, recognising only a few people, before heading for a tinted bulletproof glass wall, passing on his way a model of the Trojan horse and a bust of Sir Francis Bacon. He looked into a retina scan while touching his right index finger to a print reader. A section of the wall hissed open to reveal a scruffy freckle-faced, carrot-haired man with a scraggly beard and wearing cargo jeans, a West Ham United football jersey, and black slippers.

Knight smiled. 'G'day, Hooligan.'

'What the fuck, Peter?' Jeremy 'Hooligan' Crawford said, eyeing Knight's clothes. 'Been having sex with an orang-utan, have you?'

In the wake of Wendy Lee's death in the plane crash, Hooligan was now the chief science, technology, and forensics officer at Private London. Early thirties, caustic, fiercely independent, and unabashedly foul-mouthed, he was also insanely smart.

Born and raised in Hackney Wick, one of London's tougher neighbourhoods, the son of parents who'd never finished secondary school, by the age of nineteen Hooligan had nevertheless obtained degrees in maths and biology from Cambridge. By twenty, he had earned his third degree in forensics and criminal science from Staffordshire University and had been hired by MI5, where he worked for eight years before coming to work at Private at twice the government salary.

Hooligan was also a rabid football fan with a season ticket to West Ham United's matches. Despite his remarkable intelligence, as a youngster he'd been known to get out of control watching the club's big games, at which point his brothers and sisters had given him his nickname. While many would not boast of such a moniker, he wore it proudly.

'I scuffled with the bonnet and roof of a cab and lived to tell the tale,' Knight told Hooligan. 'The letter from the killer here yet?'

The science officer brushed past him. 'She's bringing it up.'

Knight pivoted to look back through the crowd of agents towards the lift whose door was opening again. *Sun* reporter Karen Pope came out, clutching a large manila envelope to her chest. Hooligan went to her. She seemed taken aback at his scruffy appearance, and shook his hand tentatively. He led her back into the hallway and introduced Knight to her.

Pope instantly turned guarded and studied the investigator with suspicion, especially his torn and filthy coat. 'My editors want this to be done discreetly and quickly, with no more eyes than are necessary. As far as the *Sun* is concerned, that means you and you alone, Mr Crawford.'

'Call me Hooligan, eh?'

Knight had instantly found Pope both abrasive and defensive, but maybe it was because he felt as though his entire left side had been beaten with boat oars and had gone through the emotional wringer of his mother's collapse.

He said, 'I'm working the Marshall murder on behalf of the firm – and on behalf of my mother.'

'Your mother?' Pope said.

Knight explained, but Pope still seemed unsure.

Running out of patience, Knight said, 'Have you considered that I just might know something about this case that you don't? I don't recall your byline. Do you work the city desk? The crime beat?'

Chapter 14

THAT HIT A nerve. Pope's face flushed indignantly. 'If you must know, I work sports normally,' she said, thrusting out her chin. 'What of it?'

'It means I know things about this case that you don't,' Knight repeated.

'Is that so?' Pope shot back. 'Well, I'm the one holding the letter, aren't I, Mr Knight? You know, I really would prefer to deal with Mr, uh, Hooligan.'

Before Knight could reply, an American male voice said: 'It *would* be smart to let Peter in on the examination, Ms Pope. He's the best we've got.'

A tall man with surfer good looks, the American stuck out his hand and shook hers saying, 'Jack Morgan. Your editor arranged through me for the analysis. I'd like to be there as well, if possible.'

'All right,' Pope said without enthusiasm. 'But the contents of this envelope cannot be revealed to anyone unless you've seen it published in the *Sun*. Agreed?'

'Absolutely,' Jack said, and smiled genuinely.

Knight admired the owner and founder of Private. Jack was younger than Knight, and even more in a hurry than Knight. He was also smart and driven, and believed in surrounding himself with smart, driven people and paying them well. He also cared about the people who worked for him. He'd been devastated at the loss of Carter and the other Private London operators and had come across the Atlantic immediately to help Knight pick up the slack.

The foursome went to Hooligan's lab one floor down. Jack fell in beside Knight who was moving much more slowly than the others. 'Good job with Lancer,' he said. 'Saving his ass, I mean.'

'We aim to please,' Knight said.

'He was very grateful, and said I should give you a raise,' Jack said.

Knight did not reply. They had not yet talked about any salary upgrade that might be due in light of his new responsibilities.

Jack seemed to remember and said, 'We'll talk money after the Games.' Then the American shot him a more critical look. 'Are *you* all right?'

'Feel like I've been playing in a rugby scrum, but I remain chipper,' Knight assured him as they entered Private London's science unit, a cutting-edge operation in every respect.

Hooligan led them to a far corner of the area, to

an anteroom off a clean lab where he told them all to don disposable white jumpsuits and hoods. Knight groaned, but once in the suit and hood he followed Hooligan through an airlock and into the clean room. The science officer moved to a work-station that included an electron microscope and state-of-the-art spectrographic equipment. He took the envelope from Pope, opened it, and looked inside.

He asked, 'Did you put these in sleeves or did they come to you like this?'

Knight heard the question over a headset built into his hood, which made all their ensuing conversation sound like transmissions from outer space.

'I did that,' Pope replied. 'I knew right away that they'd need to be protected.'

'Smart,' Hooligan said, wagging a gloved finger at her and looking over at Knight and Jack. 'Very smart.'

Despite his initial dislike of Pope, Knight had to agree. He asked, 'Who touched these before you protected them?'

'Just me,' Pope said as Hooligan removed the sleeve that contained the letter. 'And the killer, I suppose. He has a name. You'll see it there. He calls himself "Cronus".'

Chapter 15

SEVERAL MOMENTS LATER the weird flute music from the card played, irritating Knight and making him feel as though the killer was toying with them. He finished scanning the letter and the documents.

The strange sound must have got to Jack as well because he slammed the card shut, cutting off the music, and then said, 'This guy's off his rocker.'

Pope said, 'Crazy like a fox, then, especially those bits about Marshall and his former partner, Guilder. The documents back his allegations.'

'I don't believe those documents,' Knight said. 'I knew Denton Marshall. He was a supremely honest man. And even if the allegations were true, it's hardly justification for cutting the man's head off. Jack's right. This guy is seriously unbalanced, and supremely arrogant. The tone is taunting. He's telling us that we can't stop him. He's saying this is not over, that it could be just the beginning.'

Jack nodded, and said, 'When you start with a

beheading, you're taking a long walk down Savage Street.'

'I'll start running tests,' Hooligan said. He was looking at the card that played the music. 'These chips are in a lot of greeting cards. We should be able to trace the make and model.'

Knight nodded, saying, 'I want to read through the letter one more time.'

While Pope and Jack watched Hooligan slice out the working components of the musical greeting card, Knight returned to the letter and began to read as the flute music died in the lab.

The first sentence was written in symbols and letters that Knight did not recognise but guessed was ancient Greek. The second and all subsequent sentences in the letter were in English.

The ancient Olympic Games have been corrupted. The modern Games are not a celebration of gods and men. They are not even about goodwill among men. The modern Games are a mockery, a sideshow every four years, and made that way by so many thieves, cheats, murderers, and monsters.

Consider the great and exalted Sir Denton Marshall and his corpulent partner Richard Guilder. Seven years ago, Marshall sold out the Olympic movement as a force for honest competition. From the documents that accompany this letter, you will see that they suggest that in order to ensure that London would be selected to host the 2012 games, Marshall and Guilder cleverly siphoned funds from their clients and secretly moved the money into overseas bank accounts owned by shell corporations that were in turn owned by members of the International Olympic Selection Committee. Paris, runner-up in the selection process, never had a chance.

And so, to cleanse the Games, the Furies and I found it just that Marshall should die for his offences, and so that has come to pass. We are unstoppable beings far superior to you, able to see the corruption when you cannot, able to expose the monsters and slay them for the good of the Games when you cannot.

– Cronus

Chapter 16

AS HE FINISHED READING the letter a second time, Knight felt more upset, more anxious than before. Thinking of the letter in the light of what had been done to Marshall, Cronus came across as a madman – albeit a rational one – who made Knight's skin crawl.

Making it worse, the creepy flute melody would not leave Knight's thoughts. What kind of mind would produce that music and that letter? How did Cronus make it work together to produce such a sense of imminent threat and violation?

Or was Knight too close to the case to feel any other way?

He got a camera and began shooting close-ups of the letter and the supporting documents. Jack came over. 'What do you think, Peter?'

'There's a good chance that one of the Furies, as he calls them, tried to run Lancer down this afternoon,' Knight replied. 'A woman was driving that cab.'

'What?' Pope exclaimed. 'Why didn't you tell me that?'

'I just did,' Knight said. 'But don't quote me.'

Hooligan suddenly brayed, 'Big mistake!'

They all turned. He was holding something up with a pair of tweezers.

'What've you got?' Jack asked.

'Hair,' Hooligan said in triumph. 'It was in the glue on the envelope flap.'

'DNA, right?' Pope asked, excited. 'You can match it.'

'Gonna try, eh?'

'How long will that take?'

'Day or so for a full recombinant analysis.'

Pope shook her head. 'You can't have it for that long. My editor was specific. We had to turn it all over to Scotland Yard before we publish.'

'He'll take a sample and leave them the rest,' Jack promised.

Knight headed towards the door.

'Where are you going?' Pope demanded.

Knight paused, not sure of what to tell her. Then he gave her the truth. 'I'm guessing that first sentence is written in ancient Greek so I'm going to pay a call on that bloke James Daring – you know, the fellow who has that show *Secrets of the Past* on Sky — see if he can decipher it for me.'

'I've seen him,' Pope snorted. 'Nattering boob thinks he's Indiana Jones.'

Hooligan shot back, 'That "nattering boob", as you call him, holds doctorates in anthropology and archaeology from Oxford and is the bloody curator of Greek Antiquities at a famous museum.' The science officer looked at Knight. 'Daring *will* know what that says, Peter, and I'll wager he'll have something to say about Cronus and the Furies too. Good call.'

Through the glass plate of her hood Knight could see the reporter twist her lips, as if she was tasting something tart. 'And then?' Pope asked at last.

'Guilder, I suppose.'

'His partner?' Pope cried. 'I'm coming with you!'

'Not likely,' Knight said. 'I work alone.'

'I'm the client,' she insisted, looking at Jack. 'I can trot along, right?'

Jack hesitated, and in that hesitation Knight saw the weight of concern carried by the owner of Private International. He'd lost five of his top agents in a suspicious plane crash. All had been integral players overseeing Private's role in security at the Olympics. And now Marshall's murder and this lunatic Cronus.

Knight knew he was going to regret it but he said,

'No need for you to be on the spot, Jack. I'll change my rules this once. She can *trot* along.'

'Thanks, Peter,' the American said, with a tired smile. 'I owe you once again.'

Chapter 17

IN THE DEAD of night, forty-eight hours after I opened fire and slaughtered seven Bosnians sometime in the summer of 1995, a shifty-eyed and swarthy man who smelled of tobacco and cloves opened the door of a hovel of a workshop in a battle-scarred neighbourhood of Sarajevo.

He was the sort of monster who thrives in all times of war and political upheaval, a creature of the shadows, of shifting identity and shifting allegiance. I'd learned of the forger's existence from a fellow peacekeeper who'd fallen in love with a local girl who was unable to travel on her own passport.

'Like we agree yesterday,' the forger said when I and the Serbian girls were inside. 'Six thousand for three. Plus one thousand rush order.'

I nodded and handed him an envelope. He counted the money, and then passed me a similar envelope containing three fake passports: one

German, one Polish and one Slovenian.

I studied them, feeling pleased at the new names and identities I'd given the girls. The oldest was now Marta. Teagan was the middle girl, and Petra the youngest. I smiled, thinking that with their new haircuts and hair colours, no one would ever recognise them as the Serbian sisters that the Bosnian peasants called the Furies.

'Excellent work,' I told the forger as I pocketed the passports. 'My gun?'

We'd left my Sterling with him as a good-faith deposit when I'd ordered the passports. 'Of course,' he said. 'I was thinking just that.'

The forger went to a locked upright safe, opened it, and took out the weapon. He turned and aimed it at us. 'On your knees,' he snarled. 'I read about a slaughter at a police barracks near Srebrenica and three Serbian girls wanted for war crimes. There's a reward out. A large one.'

'You stinking weasel,' I sneered, keeping his attention on me as I slowly went to my knees. 'We give you money, and you turn us in?'

He smiled. 'I believe that's called taking it coming and going.'

The silenced 9mm round zipped over my head and caught the forger between the eyes. He crashed backward and sprawled dead over his desk, dropping my gun. I picked it up and turned to

Marta, who had a hole in her right-hand jacket pocket where a bullet had exited.

For the first time I saw something other than deadness in Marta's eyes. In its place was a glassy intoxication that I understood and shared. I had killed for her. Now she had killed for me. Our fates were not only completely entwined, we were both of us drunk on the sort of intoxicating liquor that ferments and distils among members of elite military units after each mission, the addictive drink of superior beings who wield the power over life and death.

Leaving the forger's building, however, I was acutely aware that more than two days had passed since the bomb had hurled me from the Land Cruiser. People were hunting for the Furies. The forger had said so.

And someone had to have found the blown-up and burned vehicle I'd been thrown from. Someone had to have counted and examined the charred bodies and figured out that I was missing.

Which meant that people were hunting for me.

Maybe, I decided, they should find me sooner rather than later.

Chapter 18

AT THREE-TWENTY that Thursday afternoon, Karen Pope and Peter Knight crossed the courtyard and climbed the granite front steps of the venerable British Museum in central London. As they entered the museum, Knight was grinding his teeth. He liked to work alone because it gave him enough silence to think things through during the course of an investigation.

Pope, however, had been talking almost non-stop since they'd left Private London, feeding him all sorts of trivial information he really had no need to know, including her career highlights, the creep Lester she'd dated in Manchester, and the travails of being the only woman currently working on the *Sun*'s sports desk.

'Got to be tough,' he said, wondering if he could somehow ditch her without adding to Jack's problems.

Instead, Knight led them to an older woman at the information desk, where he produced his identification and said that someone from Private had called ahead to arrange a brief interview with Dr James Daring.

The woman had sniffed something about the curator being very busy, what with his exhibit about to open that very evening, but then she gave them directions.

They climbed to an upper floor and walked towards the rear of the massive building. At last they came to an archway above which hung a large banner that read *The Ancient Olympic Games: Relics & Radical Retrospective.*

Two guards stood in front of a purple curtain stretched across the archway. Caterers were setting up for a reception to celebrate the opening, with tables for food and a bar in the hallway. Knight showed his Private badge and asked for Daring.

The guard replied, 'Dr Daring has gone to take a—'

'Late lunch, but I'm back, Carl,' called a harried male voice from back down the hallway. 'What's going on? Who are these people? I clearly said no one inside before seven!'

Knight pivoted to see hurrying towards them a familiar handsome, ruggedly built man wearing khaki cargo shorts, sandals and a safari-style shirt. His ponytail bounced on his shoulders. He carried an iPad. His gaze jumped everywhere.

Knight had seen James Daring on television several times, of course. For reasons Knight did not quite understand, his son Luke, almost three years old, loved to watch *Secrets of the Past*, though Knight suspected that the appeal lay in the melodramatic music that accompanied the man in virtually every programme.

'My kids are big fans,' Knight said, extending his hand. 'Peter Knight, with Private. My office called.'

'And Karen Pope. I'm with the *Sun*.'

Daring glanced at her and said, 'I've already invited someone from the *Sun* to view the exhibit along with everyone else – at seven. What can I do for Private, Mr Knight?'

'Actually, Miss Pope and I are working together,' Knight said. 'Sir Denton Marshall has been murdered.'

The television star's face blanched and he blinked several times before saying, 'Murdered? Oh, my God. What a tragedy. He . . .'

Daring gestured at the purple curtains blocking the way into his new exhibit. 'Without Denton's financial support, this exhibit would not have been possible. He was a generous and kind man.'

Tears welled in Daring's eyes. One trickled down his cheek. 'I'd planned to thank him publicly at the reception tonight. And . . . what happened? Who did this? Why?'

'The killer calls himself Cronus,' Pope replied. 'He sent me a letter. Some of it is in ancient Greek. We'd hoped you could translate it for us.'

Daring glanced at his watch and then nodded. 'I can give you fifteen minutes right now. I'm sorry but . . .'

'The exhibition,' Pope said. 'We understand. Fifteen minutes would be brilliant of you.'

After a pause, Daring said, 'You'll have to walk with me, then.'

The museum curator led them behind the curtains into a remarkable exhibition that depicted the ancient Olympic Games and compared them to the modern incarnation. The exhibit began with a giant aerial photograph of the ruins at Olympus, Greece, site of the original Games.

While Pope showed Daring her copy of Cronus's letter, Knight studied the photograph of Olympus and the diagrams that explained the ruins.

Surrounded by groves of olive trees, the area was dominated by the 'Altis', the great Sanctuary of Zeus, the most powerful of the ancient Greek gods. The sanctuary held temples where rituals and sacrifices were performed during the Games. Indeed, according to Daring's exhibit, the entire Olympus site, including the stadium, was a sacred place of worship.

For over a thousand years, in peace and in war, the Greeks had assembled at Olympus to celebrate the festival of Zeus and to compete in the Games. There were no bronze, silver, or gold medals given. A crown of wild olive branches was sufficient to immortalise the victor, his family, and his city.

The exhibit went on to contrast the ancient Games with the modern.

Knight had been highly impressed with the exhibit. But within minutes of reaching the displays that contrasted the old with the new, he began to feel that the ancient Games were heavily favoured over the modern Olympics.

He'd no sooner had that thought than Pope called to him from across the hall. 'Knight, I think you're going to want to hear this.'

Chapter 19

STANDING IN THE exhibition hall in front of a display case featuring Bronze Age discuses, javelins, and terracotta vases painted with scenes of athletic competitions, Dr Daring indicated the first sentence in the text.

'This *is* ancient Greek,' he said. 'It reads, "Olympians, you are in the laps of the gods." That's a term in Greek mythology. It means the fate of specific mortals is in the gods' control. I think the term is most often used when some mortal has committed a wrongdoing grave enough to upset the residents of Mount Olympus. But do you know who it would be better to ask about this sort of thing?'

'Who's that?' Knight asked.

'Selena Farrell,' Daring replied. 'Professor of Classics at King's College, London, eccentric, brilliant. In another life she worked for NATO in the Balkans. That's where I, uh, met her. You should go and see her. Very iconoclastic thinker.'

Writing down Farrell's name, Pope said, 'Who is Cronus?'

The museum curator picked up his iPad and began typing, saying, 'A Titan – one of the gods who ruled the world before the Olympians. Again, Selena Farrell would be better on this point, but Cronus was the God of Time, and the son of Gaia and Uranus, the ancient, ancient rulers of earth and sky.'

Daring explained that, at his enraged mother's urging, Cronus rebelled eventually against his father and ended up castrating him with a scythe.

A long curved blade, Knight thought. Wasn't that how Elaine had described the murder weapon?

'According to the myth, Cronus's father's blood fell into the sea and re-formed as the three Furies,' Daring continued. 'They were Cronus's half sisters – spirits of vengeance, and snake-haired like Medusa.

'Cronus married Rhea and fathered seven of the twelve gods who would become the original Olympians.' Then Daring fell silent, seeming troubled.

'What's the matter?' Pope asked.

Daring's nose twitched as if he smelled something foul. 'Cronus did something brutal when he was told of a prediction that his own son would turn against him.'

'What was that?' Knight asked.

The curator turned the iPad towards them. It

showed a dark and disturbing painting of a dishevelled bearded and half-naked man chewing on the bloody arm of a small human body. The head and opposite arm were already gone.

'This is a painting by the Spanish painter Goya,' Daring said. 'Its title is *Saturn Devouring his Son*. Saturn was the Romans' name for Cronus.'

The painting repulsed Knight. Pope said, 'I don't understand.'

'In the Roman and Greek myths,' the curator replied testily, 'Cronus ate his children one by one.'

Chapter 20

'ATE THEM?' POPE said, her lip curling.

Knight glanced at the painting and envisioned his own children in a playground near his home. He felt even more revolted.

'It's a myth – what can I say?' Daring replied.

The curator went on to explain that Rhea hated her husband for devouring their children and she vowed that no more of her unborn children would suffer the same fate. So she snuck off to have the son she named Zeus, and hid him immediately after birth. Then she got Cronus drunk, and gave him a rock wrapped in a blanket to eat instead of her son.

'Much later,' Daring continued, 'Zeus rose up, conquered Cronus, forced him to vomit up his children, and then hurled his father into the darkest abysmal pits of Tartarus, or something like that. Ask Farrell.'

'Okay,' Knight said, unsure if any of this helped or not, and wondering if this letter could possibly be a ruse designed to take them in a wrong direction. 'You a fan of the modern Olympics, doctor?'

The television star frowned. 'Why?'

'Your exhibit strikes me as a bit slanted in favour of the ancient Games.'

Daring turned coolly indignant. 'I think the work is quite even-handed. But I grant you that the ancient Games were about honour and excelling in celebration of the Greek religion, while the modern version, in my personal opinion, has become too influenced by corporations and money. Ironic, I know, since this exhibit was built with the assistance of private benefactors.'

'So, in a way, you agree with Cronus?' Pope asked.

The curator's voice went chilly. 'I may agree that the original ideals of the Olympics could be getting lost in today's Games, but I certainly do not agree with killing people to "cleanse" them. Now, if you'll excuse me, I must finish up and change before the reception.'

Chapter 21

SEVERAL HOURS AFTER Marta killed the forger, the four of us were staying in a no-star hotel on the outskirts of western Sarajevo. I handed the sisters envelopes that contained their passports and enough money to travel.

'Take separate taxis or buses to the train station. Then use completely separate routes to the address I put in your passports. In the alley behind that address, you'll find a low brick wall. Under the third brick from the left you'll find a key. Buy food. Go inside and wait there quietly until I arrive. Do not go out if you can avoid it. Do not be conspicuous. Wait.'

Marta translated and then asked, 'When will you get there?'

'In a few days,' I said. 'No more than a week, I should imagine.'

She nodded. 'We wait for you.'

I believed her. After all, where else were she and

her sisters to go? Their fates were mine now, and mine was theirs. Feeling more in control of my destiny than at any other time in my life, I left the Serbian girls and went out into the streets where I found dirt and grime to further soil my torn, bloody clothes. Then I wiped down the guns and threw them in a river.

An hour before dawn I wandered up to the security gate at the NATO garrison, acting in a daze. I had been missing for two and a half days.

I gave my superiors and doctors vague recollections of the bomb that tore apart the Land Cruiser. I said I'd wandered for hours, and then slept in the woods. In the morning, I'd set off again. It wasn't until the previous evening that I'd remembered exactly who I was and where I was supposed to go; and I'd headed for the garrison with the fuzzy navigation of an alcoholic trying to find home.

The doctors examined me and determined that I had a fractured skull for the second time in my life. Two days later, I was on a medical transport: Cronus flying home to his Furies.

Chapter 22

AT FIVE MINUTES to four that Thursday afternoon, Knight left One Aldwych, a five-star boutique hotel in London's West End theatre district, and found Karen Pope waiting on the pavement, looking intently at her BlackBerry screen.

'His secretary wasn't putting you off. The doorman says he does come for drinks quite often, but he's not in there yet,' Knight said, referring to Richard Guilder, Marshall's long-time financial partner. 'Let's go and wait inside.'

Pope shook her head, and then gestured across the Strand to a row of Edwardian buildings. 'That's King's College, right? That's where Selena Farrell works, the classical Greek expert that Indiana Jones wannabe told us to talk to. I looked her up. She *has* written extensively about the ancient Greek playwright Aeschylus and his play *The Eumenides*, which is another name for the Furies. We could go and chat with her and then swing back for Guilder.'

Knight screwed up his face. 'In all honesty, I don't know if understanding more about the myth of Cronus and the Furies is going to help us get any closer to catching Marshall's killer.'

'And now I know something you don't,' she said, shaking her BlackBerry at him haughtily. 'Turns out that Farrell fought against the London Olympics tooth and nail. She sued to have the whole thing stopped, especially the compulsory purchase orders that took all that land in East London for the Olympic Park. The professor evidently lost her house when the park went in.'

Feeling his heart begin to race, Knight set off in the direction of the college, saying, 'Denton ran the process that took that land. She had to have hated him.'

'Maybe enough to cut off his head,' Pope said, struggling to keep up.

Then Knight's mobile buzzed. A text from Hooligan:

1st DNA test: hair is female.

Chapter 23

THEY FOUND SELENA Farrell in her office. The professor was in her early forties, a big-bosomed woman who dressed the part of a dowdy Earth child: baggy, faded peasant dress, oval black glasses, no make-up, clogs, and her head wrapped in a scarf held in place by two wooden hairpins.

But it was the beauty mark that caught Knight's eye. Set above her jawline about midway down her right cheek, it put him in mind of a young Elizabeth Taylor and made him think that, given the right circumstances and manner of dress, the professor could have been quite attractive.

As Dr Farrell inspected his identification, Knight glanced around at various framed pictures: one of the professor climbing in Scotland, another of her posing beside some Greek ruins, and a third in which she was much younger, in sunglasses, khaki pants and shirt, posing with an automatic weapon beside a white truck that said NATO on the side.

'Okay,' Farrell said, returning Knight's badge. 'What are we here to discuss?'

'Sir Denton Marshall, a member of the Olympic Organising Committee,' Knight said, watching for her reaction.

Farrell stiffened, and then pursed her lips in distaste. 'What about him?'

'He's been murdered,' Pope said. 'Decapitated.'

The professor appeared genuinely shocked. 'Decapitated? Oh, that's horrible. I didn't like the man, but . . . that's barbaric.'

'Marshall took your house and your land,' Knight remarked.

Farrell hardened. 'He did. I hated him for it. I hated him and everyone who's in favour of the Olympics for it. But I did not kill him. I don't believe in violence.'

Knight glanced at the photo of her with the automatic weapon. But he decided not to challenge her, asking instead: 'Can you account for your whereabouts around ten forty-five last night?'

The classics professor arched back in her chair and took off her glasses, revealing amazing sapphire eyes that stared intently at Knight. 'I *can* account for my whereabouts at that time, but I won't unless it's necessary. I enjoy my privacy.'

'Tell us about Cronus,' Pope said.

The professor drew back. 'You mean the Titan?'

'That's the one,' Pope said.

She shrugged. 'He's mentioned by Aeschylus, especially during the third play in his Oresteia cycle, *The Eumenides*. They were the three Furies of vengeance born from the blood of Cronus's father. Why are you asking about him? All in all, Cronus is a minor figure in Greek mythology.'

Pope glanced at Knight, who nodded. She dug into her bag. She came up with her mobile, which she fiddled with for several seconds as she said to the professor, 'I received a package today from someone who calls himself Cronus and who claims to be Marshall's killer. There's a letter and this: it's a recording of a recording, but . . .'

As the reporter returned to her bag, looking for her copy of Cronus's letter, the weird, irritating flute music began to float from her phone.

The classics professor froze after a few notes had played.

The melody went on and Farrell stared at her desk, becoming agitated. Then she looked around wildly as if she was hearing hornets. Her hands shot up as though to cover her ears, dislodging the hairpins and loosening her headscarf.

She panicked and raised her hands to hold the scarf in place. Then she leaped to her feet and bolted for the door, choking: 'For God's sake turn it off! It's giving me a migraine! It's making me sick!'

Knight jumped to his feet and went out after Farrell, who clopped at high speed down the hall before barging into a women's loo.

'That set off something big,' Pope said. She'd come up behind him.

'Uh-huh,' Knight said. He went back into the office, headed straight to the classics professor's desk and plucked a small evidence bag from his pocket.

He turned the bag inside out before picking up one of the hairpins that had fallen before Farrell bolted. He wrapped the bag around the pins and then drew them out before dropping them back on the desk.

'What are you doing?' Pope demanded in a whisper.

Knight sealed the bag and murmured, 'Hooligan says the hair sample from the envelope was female.'

He heard someone approaching the office, slid the evidence into his coat chest pocket and sat down. Pope stood, and was looking towards the door when another woman, much younger than Farrell but with a similar lack of fashion sense, entered and said: 'Sorry. I'm Nina Langor, Professor Farrell's teaching assistant.'

'Is she all right?' Pope asked.

'She said she's suffering from a migraine and is going home. She said if you'll call her on Monday or Tuesday she'll explain.'

'Explain what?' Knight demanded.

Nina Langor appeared bewildered. 'I honestly have no idea. I've never seen her act like that before.'

Chapter 24

TEN MINUTES LATER, Knight followed Pope up the stairs into One Aldwych, looking questioningly at the hotel doorman he'd spoken with earlier and getting a nod in response. Knight slipped the doorman a ten-pound note and followed Pope towards the muffled sounds of happy voices.

'That music got to Farrell,' Pope said. 'She'd heard it before.'

'I agree,' Knight said. 'It threw her hard.'

'Is it possible she's Cronus?' Pope asked.

'And uses the name to make us think she's a man? Sure. Why not?'

They entered the hotel's dramatic Lobby Bar, which was triangular in shape, with a soaring vaulted ceiling, pale marble floor, glass walls and intimate groupings of fine furniture.

While the bar at the Savoy Hotel along the Strand was about glamour, the Lobby Bar was about money. One Aldwych was close to London's legal and financial districts, and exuded enough corporate elegance to make it a magnet for thirsty bankers, flush traders, and celebrating deal-makers.

There were forty or fifty such patrons in the bar, but Knight spotted Richard Guilder, Marshall's business partner, almost immediately: a corpulent, silver-haired boar of a man in a dark suit, sitting at the bar alone, his shoulders and head hunched over.

'Let me do the talking at first,' Knight said.

'Why?' Pope snapped. 'Because I am a woman?'

'How many allegedly corrupt tycoons have you chatted up lately on the sports beat?' he asked her coolly.

The reporter grudgingly made a show of letting him lead the way.

Marshall's partner was staring off into the abyss. Two fingers of neat Scotch swirled in the crystal tumbler he held. To his left, a bar stool stood empty. Knight started to sit on it.

Before he could, an ape of a man in a dark suit got in the way.

'Mr Guilder prefers to be alone,' he said in a distinct Brooklyn accent.

Knight showed him his identification. Guilder's bodyguard shrugged, and showed Knight his. Joe Mascolo worked for Private New York.

'You in as backup for the Games?' Knight asked.

Mascolo nodded. 'Jack called me over.'

'Then you'll let me talk to him?'

The Private New York agent shook his head. 'Man wants to be alone.'

Knight said loud enough for Guilder to hear: 'Mr Guilder? I'm sorry for your loss. I'm Peter Knight, also with Private. I'm working on behalf of the London Organising Committee, and for my mother, Amanda Knight.'

Mascolo looked furious that Knight was trying to work around him.

But Guilder stiffened, turned in his seat, studied Knight and then said, 'Amanda. My God. It's . . .' He shook his head and wiped away a tear. 'Please, Knight, listen to Joe. I'm not in any condition to talk about Denton at the moment. I am here to mourn him. Alone. As I imagine your dear mother is doing, too.'

'Please, sir,' Knight began again. 'Scotland Yard—'

'Has agreed to talk with him in the morning,' Mascolo growled. 'Call his office. Make an appointment. And leave the man in peace for the evening.'

The Private New York agent glared at Knight. Marshall's partner was turning back to his drink, and Knight was growing resigned to leaving him alone until the next morning when Pope said, 'I'm with the *Sun*, Mr Guilder. We received a letter from Denton Marshall's killer. He mentions you and your company and justifies murdering your partner because of certain illegal activities that Marshall and you were alleged to have been involved in at your place of business.'

Guilder swung around, livid. 'How dare you! Denton Marshall was as honest as the day is long. He was never, ever involved in anything illegal during all the time I knew him. And neither was I. Whatever this letter says, it's a lie.'

Pope tried to hand the financier photocopies of the documents that Cronus had sent her, saying, 'Denton Marshall's killer alleges that these were taken from Marshall & Guilder's own records – or, to be more precise, your firm's *secret* records.'

Guilder glanced at the pages but did not take them, as if he had no time for considering such outrageous allegations. 'We have never kept secret records at Marshall & Guilder.'

'Really?' Knight said. 'Not even about foreign currency transactions made on behalf of your high-net-worth clients?'

The hedge fund manager said nothing, but Knight swore that some of the colour had seeped from his florid cheeks.

Pope said, 'According to these documents, you and Denton Marshall were pocketing fractions of the value of every British pound or US dollar or other currency that passed across your trading desks. It may not sound like much, but when you're talking hundreds of millions of pounds a year the fractions add up.'

Guilder set his tumbler of scotch on the bar, doing his best to appear composed. But Knight could have sworn that he saw a slight tremor in the man's hand as it returned to rest on Guilder's thigh. 'Is that all the killer of my best friend claims?'

'No,' Knight replied. 'He says that the money was moved to offshore accounts and funnelled ultimately to members of the Olympic Site Selection Committee before their decision in 2007. He says that your partner bribed London's way into the Games.'

The weight of the allegation seemed to throw Guilder. He looked both befuddled and wary, as if he'd suddenly realised he was far too drunk to be having this conversation.

'No,' he said. 'No, that's not . . . Please, Joe, make them go.'

Mascolo looked torn but said, 'Leave him be until tomorrow. I'm sure that if we call Jack he's going to tell you the same thing.'

Before Knight could reply there was a noise like a fine crystal wine glass breaking. The first bullet pierced a window on the west side of the bar. It just missed Guilder and shattered the huge mirror behind the bar.

Knight and Mascolo both realised what had happened. 'Get down!' Knight yelled, going for his gun, and scanning the windows for any sign of the shooter.

Too late. A second round was fired through the window. The slug hit Guilder just below his sternum with a sound like a pillow being plumped.

Bright red blood bloomed on the hedge fund manager's starched white shirt and he collapsed forward, upsetting a champagne bucket as he fell and crashed to the pale marble floor.

Chapter 25

IN THE STUNNED silence that now briefly seized the fabled Lobby Bar, the shooter, an agile figure in black motorcycle leathers and visor helmet, spun away and jumped off the window ledge to flee.

'Someone call an ambulance,' Pope yelled. 'He's been shot!'

The bar erupted into pandemonium as Joe Mascolo vaulted over his prone client and bulled forward, ignoring the patrons screaming and diving for cover.

Knight was two feet behind the Private New York operator when Mascolo jumped over a glass cocktail table and up onto the back of a plush grey sofa set against the bar's west wall. As Knight tried to climb up beside Mascolo, he saw to his surprise that the American was armed.

Gun laws in the UK were very strict. Knight had had to jump through two years of hoops in order to get his licence to carry a firearm.

Before he could think any more about it, Mascolo shot through the window. The gun sounded like a cannon in that marble and glass room. Real hysteria swept the bar now. Knight spotted the shooter in the middle of the cul-de-sac on Harding Street, face obscured but plainly a woman. At the sound of Mascolo's shot she twisted, dropped and aimed in one motion, an ultra-professional.

She fired before Knight could and before Mascolo could get off another round. The bullet caught the Private New York agent through the throat, killing him instantly. Mascolo dropped back off the sofa and fell violently through the glass cocktail table.

The shooter was aiming at Knight now. He ducked, raised his pistol above the sill and pulled the trigger. He was about to rise when two more rounds shattered the window above him.

Glass rained down on Knight. He thought of his children and hesitated a moment before returning fire. Then he heard tyres squealing.

Knight rose up to see the shooter on a jet-black motorcycle, its rear tyre smoking and laying rubber in a power drift that shot her around the corner onto the Strand, heading west and disappearing before Knight could shoot.

He cursed, turned and looked in shock at

Mascolo, for whom there was no hope. But he heard Pope cry: 'Guilder's alive, Knight! Where's that ambulance?'

Knight jumped off the couch and ran back through the shouting and the gathering crowd towards the crumpled form of Richard Guilder. Pope was kneeling at his side amid a puddle of champagne and a mass of blood, ice and glass.

The financier was breathing in gasps and holding tight to his upper stomach while the blood on his shirt turned darker and spread.

For a moment, Knight had an unnerving moment of déjà vu, seeing blood spreading on a bed sheet. Then he shook off the vision and got down next to Pope.

'They said there's an ambulance on the way,' the reporter said, her voice strained. 'But I don't know what to do. No one here does.'

Knight tore off his jacket, pushed aside Guilder's hands and pressed the coat to his chest. Marshall's partner peered at Knight as if he might be the last person he ever saw alive, and struggled to talk.

'Take it easy, Mr Guilder,' Knight said. 'Help's on the way.'

'No,' Guilder grunted softly. 'Please, listen . . .'

Knight leaned close to the financier's face and heard him whisper a secret hoarsely before paramedics burst into the Lobby Bar. But as Guilder finished his confession he just seemed to give out.

Blood trickled from his mouth, his eyes glazed, and he slumped like a puppet with its strings cut.

Chapter 26

A FEW MINUTES later, Knight stood on the pavement outside One Aldwych, oblivious to patrons hurrying past him to the restaurants and theatres. He was transfixed by the sight and sound of the wailing ambulance speeding Guilder and Mascolo to the nearest hospital.

He remembered standing on another pavement late at night almost three years before, watching a different ambulance race away from him, its siren's fading cry accompanying a feeling of misery that still had not lifted entirely from him.

'Knight?' Pope said. She'd come up behind him.

He blinked and noticed the double-decker buses braking and taxis honking and people hurrying home all around him. Suddenly he felt disjointed in much the same way that he had on that long-ago night when he'd watched the other ambulance speed away from him.

London goes on, he thought. London always went

on even in the face of tragedy and death, whether the victim was a corrupt hedge fund manager or a bodyguard or a young—

A pair of fingers appeared in front of his nose. They clicked and he looked round, startled. Karen Pope was looking at him in annoyance. 'Earth to Knight. Hello?'

'What is it?' he snapped.

'I asked you if you think Guilder will make it?'

Knight shook his head. 'No. I felt his spirit leave him.'

The reporter looked at him sceptically. 'What do you mean, you felt it?'

Knight sighed softly before replying: 'That's the second time in my life I've had someone die in my arms, Pope. I felt it the first time, too. That ambulance might as well slow down. Guilder is as dead as Mascolo is.'

Pope's shoulders sank a little and there was a brief awkward silence before she said, 'I'd better be going back to the office. I've got a nine o'clock deadline.'

'You should include in your story that Guilder confessed to the currency fraud just before he died,' Knight said.

'He did?' Pope said, digging in her pocket for her notebook. 'What'd he say, exactly?'

'He said that the scam was his, and that the money did not go to any member of the Olympic Site

Selection committee. It went to his personal offshore accounts. Marshall was innocent. He died a victim of Guilder's scheming.'

Pope stopped writing, her scepticism back. 'I don't buy that,' she said. 'He's covering for Marshall.'

'They were his last words,' Knight shot back. 'I believe him.'

'You have a reason to, don't you? It clears your mother's late fiancé.'

'It's what he said,' Knight insisted. 'You have to include that in the story.'

'I'll let the facts speak for themselves,' Pope said, 'including what you say Guilder told you.' She glanced at her watch. 'I've got to get going.'

'We're not going anywhere soon,' Knight said, feeling suddenly exhausted. 'Scotland Yard will want to talk with us, especially because there was gunfire. Meanwhile, I need to call Jack and fill him in, and then speak to my nanny.'

'Nanny?' Pope said, looking surprised. 'You have kids?'

'Twins. Boy and girl.'

Pope glanced at his left hand and said in a joking manner, 'No ring. What, are you divorced? Drove your wife nuts and she left you with the brats?'

Knight gazed at her coldly, marvelling at her insensitivity, before saying, 'I'm a widower, Pope. My wife died in childbirth. She bled to death in my arms two years, eleven months and two weeks ago. They took her away in an ambulance with the siren wailing just like that.'

Pope's jaw sagged and she looked horrified. 'Peter, I'm so sorry, I . . .'

But Knight already had his back turned and was walking along the pavement towards Inspector Elaine Pottersfield, who'd only just arrived.

Chapter 27

DARKNESS FALLS ON London, and my old friend hatred stirs at the thought that my entire life has all been a prelude to this fated moment, exactly twenty-four hours before the opening ceremony of the most hypocritical event on Earth.

It heats in my gut as I turn to my sisters. We're in my office. It's the first chance the four of us have had to talk face to face in days, and I take the three of them in at a glance.

Blonde and cool Teagan is removing the scarf, hat and sunglasses she wore while driving the taxi earlier in the day. Marta, ebony-haired and calculating, sets her motorcycle helmet on the floor beside her pistol and unzips her leathers. Pretty Petra is the youngest, the most attractive, the best actor and therefore the most impulsive. She looks in the mirror on the closet door, checking the fit of a chic grey cocktail dress and the dramatic styling of her short ginger hair.

Seeing the sisters like this, they're each so familiar to me that it's hard to imagine a time when we weren't all together, establishing and projecting our own busy lives, while staying completely unaligned in public.

And why wouldn't they still be with me after seventeen years? *In absentia* in 1997, a tribunal in The Hague indicted them for executing more than sixty Bosnians. Ever since Ratko Mladic – the general who oversaw the Serbian kill squads in Bosnia – was arrested last year, the hunt for my Furies has intensified.

I know. I keep track of such things. My dreams depend on it.

In any case, the sisters have lived under the threat of discovery for so long that it pervades their DNA, but that constant cellular-level menace has made them all the more fanatically devoted to me, mentally, physically, spiritually and emotionally. Indeed, ever so gradually over the years, my dreams of vengeance have become theirs, along with a desire to see those dreams realised that burns almost as incandescently as my own.

Over the years, in addition to protecting them, I've educated them, paid for minor plastic surgery, and trained them to be expert marksmen, hand-to-hand fighters, con artists and thieves. These last two skills have paid me back tenfold on my investment, but that is another story altogether. Suffice it to say that, to the best of my knowledge, they are the best at shadow games, superior to anyone save me.

Now the jaded might be wondering whether I am similar to Charles Manson back in the 1970s, an insane prophet who rescued traumatised women and convinced them that they were apostles sent to Earth for homicidal missions designed to trigger Armageddon. But comparing me to Manson and the Furies to the Helter-Skelter girls is deeply misguided, like trying to compare a true story to a myth of heaven. We are more powerful, transcendent and deadly than Manson could ever have imagined in his wildest drug-induced nightmares.

Teagan pours a glass of vodka, gulps it down, and says, 'I could not have anticipated that man jumping in front of my cab.'

'Peter Knight – he works for Private London,' I say, and then push across the coffee table a photograph that I found on the Internet. In it Knight stands, drink in hand, beside his mother at the launch of her most recent fashion line.

Teagan considers the photograph and then nods. 'That's him. I got a good look when his face smashed against my windscreen.'

Marta frowns, picks up the photograph, studies it, and then trains her dark agate eyes on me. 'He was with Guilder too, just now, in the bar, before I shot. I'm sure of it. He shot at me after I killed the one guarding Guilder too.'

I raise an eyebrow. Private? Knight? They've almost foiled my plans twice today. Is that fate, coincidence, or a warning?

'He's dangerous,' says Marta, always the most perceptive of the three, the one whose strategic thoughts are most likely to mirror my own.

'I agree,' I say, before glancing at the clock on the wall and looking at her ginger-haired sister, still primping in front of the mirror. 'It's time to leave for the reception, Petra. I'll see you there later. Remember the plan.'

'I'm not stupid, Cronus,' Petra says, glaring at me with eyes turned emerald green by contact lenses bought just for this occasion.

'Hardly,' I reply evenly. 'But you have a tendency to be impetuous, to ad lib, and your task tonight demands disciplined adherence to details.'

'I know what I have to do,' she says coldly, and leaves.

Marta's gaze has not left me. 'What about Knight?' she asks, proving once again that relentlessness is another of her more endearing qualities.

I reply, 'Your next tasks are not until tomorrow evening. In the meantime, I'd like you both to look into Mr Knight.'

'What are we looking for?' Teagan asks, setting her empty glass on the table.

'His weaknesses, sister. His vulnerabilities. Anything we can exploit.'

Chapter 28

IT WAS ALMOST eight by the time Knight reached home, a restored red-brick town house that his mother had bought for him several years before. He was as exhausted and sore as he'd ever been after a day at work: run over, shot at, forced to destroy his mother's dreams, not to mention being grilled three times by the formidable Inspector Elaine Pottersfield.

The Metropolitan Police inspector had not been happy when she arrived at One Aldwych. Not only were there two corpses as a result of the shoot-out, she'd heard through the grapevine that the *Sun* had received a letter from Marshall's killer and was incensed to learn that Private's forensics lab had had the chance to analyse the material before Scotland Yard.

'I should be arresting you for obstruction!' she'd shouted.

Knight held up his hands. 'That decision was

made by our client, Karen Pope of the *Sun*.'

'Who is where?'

Knight looked around. Pope had gone. 'She was on deadline. I know they plan on turning over all evidence after they go to press.'

'You allowed a material witness to leave the scene of a crime?'

'I work for Private, not the court any more. And I can't control Pope. She has her own mind.'

The Scotland Yard inspector responded by fixing Knight with a glare. 'Seems as if I've heard that excuse before from you, Peter – with deadly consequences.'

Knight flushed and his throat felt heated. 'We're not having this conversation again. You should be asking about Guilder and Mascolo.'

Pottersfield fumed, and then said, 'Spill it. All of it.'

Knight spilled all of it: their meetings with Daring and Farrell as well as a blow-by-blow account of what had happened in the Lobby Bar.

When he finished, the inspector said, 'You believe Guilder's confession?'

'Do dying men lie?' Knight had replied.

As he climbed the steps to his front door, Knight considered Guilder's confession again. Then he thought of Daring and Farrell. Were they part of these killings?

Who was to say that Daring wasn't some kind of

nut behind the scenes, bent on destroying the modern games? And who was to say that Selena Farrell wasn't the gunman in black leather and a motorcycle helmet? She'd been holding an automatic weapon in that picture in her office.

Maybe Pope's instincts were spot on. Could the professor be Cronus? Or at least involved with him? What about Daring? Didn't he say he'd known Farrell from somewhere in his past? The Balkans back in the 1990s?

Then another voice inside Knight demanded that he think less about villains and more about victims. How was his mother? He'd not heard from her all day.

He'd go inside. He'd call her. But before he could get his key into his front lock he heard his daughter Isabel let loose a blood-curdling cry: 'No! No!'

Chapter 29

KNIGHT THREW OPEN the front door into the lower hallway as Isabel's cry turned into a cutting screech: 'No, Lukey! No!'

Her father heard a high-pitched maniacal laugh and the pattering of little feet escaping before he entered the living area of his home, which looked as though a snow tornado had whirled through it. White dust hung in the air, on the furniture, and coated his daughter, about three years old, who saw him and broke into sobs.

'Daddy, Lukey, he . . . ! He . . .'

A dainty little girl, Isabel went into hiccupping hysterics and ran towards her daddy, who tried to bend down to comfort her. Knight gritted his teeth at the throbbing ache all down his left side, but scooped her up anyway, wanting to sneeze at the baby-powder. Isabel's tears had left little streams of baby powder paste on her cheeks and on her eyelashes. Even covered in talc like this, she was as beautiful as her late mother, with curly fawn-coloured hair and wide cobalt-blue eyes that could cleave his heart even when they weren't spilling tears.

'It's okay, sweetheart,' Knight said. 'Daddy's here.'

Her crying slowed to hiccups: 'Lukey, he . . . he put bottom powder on me.'

'I can see that, Bella,' Knight said. 'Why?'

'Lukey thinks bottom powder is funny.'

Knight held onto his daughter with his good arm and moved towards the kitchen and the staircase that led to the upper floors. He could hear his son cackling somewhere above him as he climbed.

At the top of the stairs, Knight turned towards the nursery only to hear a woman's voice yell, 'Owww! You little savage!'

Knight's son came running from the nursery in his nappy, his entire body covered in talc. He carried a bonus-sized container of baby powder and was laughing with pure joy until he caught sight of his father glaring narrowly at him.

Luke turned petrified and began to back away, waving his hands at Knight as if he were some apparition he could erase. 'No, Daddy!'

'Luke!' Knight said.

Nancy, the nanny, appeared in the doorway behind his son, blocking his way, powder all over her, holding her wrist tight, her face screwed up in pain before she spotted Knight.

'I quit,' she said, spitting out the words like venom. 'They're bloody lunatics.' She pointed at Luke, her whole arm shaking. 'And that one's a pant-shitting, biting little pagan! When I tried to get him on the loo, he bit me. He broke skin. I quit, and you're paying for the doctor's bill.'

Chapter 30

'YOU CAN'T QUIT,' Knight protested as the nanny dodged around Luke.

'Watch me,' Nancy hissed as she barged right by him and down the stairs. 'They've been fed, but not bathed, and Luke's crapped his nappy for the third time this afternoon. Good luck, Peter.'

She grabbed her things and left, slamming the door behind her.

Isabel started to sob again. 'Nancy leaves and Lukey did it.'

Feeling overwhelmed, Knight looked at his son and shouted in anger and frustration: 'That's four this year, Luke! Four! And she only lasted three weeks!'

Luke's face wrinkled. He cried: 'Lukey sorry, Daddy. Lukey sorry.'

In seconds his son had been transformed from this force of nature capable of creating a whirlwind to a little boy so pitiful that Knight softened.

Wincing against the pain in his side, still holding Isabel, he crouched down and gestured to Luke with his free arm. The toddler rushed to him and threw his arms so tight around Knight that he gasped with the ache that shot through him.

'Lukey love you, Daddy,' his son said.

Despite the stench that hung around the boy, Knight blew the talc off Luke's cheeks and kissed him. 'Daddy loves you too, son.' Then he kissed Isabel so hard on the cheek that she laughed.

'A change and a shower is in order for Luke,' he said, and put both his children down. 'Isabel, shower too.'

A few minutes later, after dealing with the soiled nappy, they were in the big stall shower in Knight's master bath, splashing and playing. Knight got out his mobile just as Luke picked up a sponge cricket bat and whacked his sister over the head with it.

'Daddy!' Isabel complained.

'Clonk him back,' Knight said.

He glanced at the clock. It was past eight. None of the nanny services he'd used in the past would be open. He punched in his mother's number.

She answered on the third ring, sounding wrung-out, 'Peter, tell me it's just a nightmare and that I'll wake up soon.'

'I'm so sorry, Amanda.'

She broke down in muffled sobs for several

moments, and then said, 'I'm feeling worse than I did when your father died. I think I'm feeling as you must have with Kate.'

Knight felt stinging tears well in his eyes, and a dreadful hollowness in his chest. 'And still often do, Mother.'

He heard her blow her nose, and then say: 'Tell me what you know, what you've found out.'

Knight knew his mother would not rest until he'd told her, so he did, rapidly and in broad strokes. She'd gasped and protested violently when he'd described Cronus's letter and the accusations regarding Marshall, and now she wept when he told her of Guilder's confession and his exoneration of her late fiancé.

'I knew it couldn't be true,' Knight said. 'Denton was an honest man, a great man with an even greater heart.'

'He was,' his mother said, choking.

'Everywhere I went today, people talked about his generosity and spirit.'

'Tell me,' Amanda said. 'Please, Peter, I need to hear these things.'

Knight told her about Michael Lancer's despair over Marshall's death and how he'd called the financier a mentor, a friend, and one of the guiding visionaries behind the London Olympics.

'Even James Daring, that guy at the British

Museum with the television show,' Knight said. 'He said that without Denton's support, the show and his new exhibit about the ancient Olympics would never have got off the ground. He said he was going to thank Denton publicly tonight at the opening reception.'

There was a pause on the line. 'James Daring said that?'

'He did,' Knight said, hoping that his mother would take comfort from it.

Instead, she snapped, 'Then he's a bald-faced liar!'

Knight startled. 'What?'

'Denton did give Daring some of the seed money to start his television show,' Amanda allowed. 'But he most certainly did not support his new exhibit. In fact, they had a big fight over the tenor of the display, which Denton told me was slanted heavily against the modern Olympics.'

'It's true,' Knight said. 'I saw the same thing.'

'Denton was furious,' his mother told him. 'He refused to give Daring any more money, and they parted badly.'

Definitely not what Daring told me, Knight thought, and then asked, 'When was this?'

'Two, maybe three months ago,' Amanda replied. 'We'd just got back from Crete and . . .'

She began to choke again. 'We didn't know it, but Crete was our honeymoon, Peter. I'll always think of it that way,' she said, and broke down.

Knight listened for several agonising moments, and then said, 'Mother, is anyone there with you?'

'No,' she said in a very small voice. 'Can you come, Peter?'

Knight felt horrible. 'Mother, I desperately want to, but I've lost another nanny and . . .'

She snorted in disbelief. 'Another one?'

'She just up and quit on me half an hour ago,' Knight complained. 'I've got to work every day of the Olympics, and I don't know what to do. I've used every nanny agency in the city, and now I'm afraid that none of them will send anyone over.'

There was a long silence on the phone that prompted Knight to say, 'Mother?'

'I'm here,' Amanda said, sounding as composed as she'd been since she'd learned of Marshall's death. 'Let me look into it.'

'No,' he protested. 'You're not . . .'

'It will give me something to do besides work,' she insisted. 'I need something to do that's outside myself and the company, Peter, or I think I'll turn mad, or to drink, or to sleeping pills and I can't stand the thought of any of those options.'

Chapter 31

AT THAT SAME MOMENT, inside the British Museum, upstairs in the reception hall outside his new exhibit about the ancient Olympics, Dr James Daring felt like dancing to his good fortune as he roamed triumphantly among the crowd of London's high and mighty gathered to see his work.

It has been a good night. No, a *great* night!

Indeed, the museum curator had received high praise from the critics who'd come to see the installation. They'd called it audacious and convincing, a reinterpretation of the ancient Olympics that managed to comment in a completely relevant way about the state of the modern Games.

Even better, several impressed patrons had told him that they wanted to sponsor and buy advertising on *Secrets of the Past*.

What did that dead arsehole Sir Denton Marshall know? Daring thought caustically. *Absolutely nothing.*

Feeling vindicated, basking in the glow of a job

well done, a job that had gone better than according to plan, Daring went to the bar and ordered another vodka Martini to celebrate his exhibit – and more.

Much more.

Indeed, after getting the cocktail – and fretting sympathetically yet again with one of the Museum's big benefactors about Marshall's shocking and horrible passing – Daring eagerly cast his attention about the reception.

Where was she?

The television star looked until he spotted a delightfully feline woman. Her hair was ginger-coloured and swept above her pale shoulders, which were bared in a stunning grey cocktail dress that highlighted her crazy emerald eyes. Daring had a thing for redheads with sparkling green eyes.

She *did* rather look like his sister in several respects, the curator thought. The way she tilted her head when she was amused, like now, as she held a long-stemmed champagne glass and flirted with a man much older than her. He looked familiar. Who was he?

No matter, Daring thought, looking again at Petra. She was saucy, audacious, a freak. The curator felt a thrill go through him. Look at her handling that man, making what were obviously scripted moves seem effortless in their spontaneity. Saucy. Audacious. Freak.

Petra seemed to hear his thoughts.

She turned from her conversation, spotted Daring across the crowd, and flashed him an expression so filled with hunger and promise that he shuddered as if in anticipation of great pleasure. After letting her gaze linger on him for a moment longer, Petra batted her eyelids and returned her attention to the other man. She put her hand on his chest, laughed again, and then excused herself.

Petra angled her way towards Daring, never once looking at him. She got another drink and moved back to the dessert table, where Daring joined her, trying to seem interested in the crème brûlée.

'He's drunk and taking a taxi home,' Petra murmured in a soft Eastern European accent as she used tongs to dig through a pile of kiwi fruit. 'I think it's time we left too, don't you? Lover?'

Daring glanced at her. A freak with green eyes! The television star flushed with excitement and whispered, 'Absolutely. Let's say our goodbyes and go.'

'Not together, silly goose,' Petra cautioned as she plucked two fruit slices onto her plate. 'We don't want to draw attention to ourselves, now, do we?'

'No, no, of course not,' Daring whispered back, feeling wonderfully illicit and deceitful. 'I'll wait for you down the street, near Bloomsbury Square.'

Chapter 32

JUST AFTER NINE that evening, not long after Karen Pope's article appeared on the *Sun*'s website, London radio stations began to pick up the story, focusing on the Cronus angle and rebroadcasting the flute music.

By ten, shortly after Knight had read the twins a story, changed Luke's nappy, and tucked them both into bed, the BBC was whipped into a frenzy, reporting on the allegations about Sir Denton Marshall and the Olympic site-selection process, as well as Guilder's dying confession that it had all been his swindle.

Knight cleaned and vacuumed talcum powder until eleven, and then poured himself a beer and a whisky, swallowed more pain medication, and crawled into bed. Jack Morgan called, distraught over Joe Mascolo's death, and insisted on Knight describing in detail the gunfight that had unfolded at One Aldwych.

'He was fearless,' Knight said. 'Went right after the shooter.'

'That was Joe Mascolo all the way,' Jack said sadly. 'One of Brooklyn's finest before I hired him away to run protection for us in New York. He only got here a couple of days ago.'

'That's brutal,' Knight replied.

'It is, and it's about to get worse,' Jack said. 'I have to call his wife.'

Jack hung up. Knight realised that he had not told Private's owner that he, Knight, had lost his nanny. Better that way, he decided after several moments' worry. The American already had too much on his plate.

He turned on the television to find the Marshall and Guilder slayings splashed all over the nightly news and cable outlets, which were luridly portraying the broader narrative as a scandalous murder-mystery, a shocking allegation about the Byzantine world behind the Olympics site-selection process, as well as a slap against London and indeed the entire UK on the eve of the Games.

Despite Guilder's dying words to the contrary, the French in particular were said to be very unhappy with Cronus's allegation about Olympic corruption.

Knight switched off the television and sat there in the silence. He picked up his whisky glass and drank deeply from it before looking at the framed photograph on his dresser.

Very pregnant and sublimely beautiful, his late wife Kate stood in profile on a Scottish moor lit by a June sunset. She was looking across her left shoulder, seeming to peer out from the photograph at him, radiating the joy and love that had been so cruelly taken from him almost three years before.

'Tough day, Katie girl,' Knight whispered. 'I'm badly beaten up. Someone's trying to wreck the Olympics. My mother is destroyed. And the kids have driven another nanny from the house and . . . I miss you. More than ever.'

He felt a familiar leadenness return to his heart and mind, which triggered a sinking sensation in his chest. He wallowed in that sensation, indeed let himself drown in it for a minute or two, and then did what he always did when he was openly grieving for Kate late at night like this.

Knight turned off the television, took his blankets and pillows and padded into the nursery. He lay down on the couch looking at the cots, smelling the smells of his children, and was at last comforted into sleep by the gentle rhythm of their breathing.

Chapter 33

Friday, 27 July 2012

THE PAINKILLERS STARTED to wear off and Knight felt the throbbing return to his right side around seven the next morning. Then he heard a squeaking noise and stirred where he lay on the couch in the twins' nursery. He looked over and saw Isabel on her belly, eyes closed and still. But Luke's cot was swaying gently.

His son was on his knees, chest and head on the mattress, sucking his thumbs, rocking side to side, and still asleep. Knight sat up to watch. For much of the last two years, Luke had been doing this before waking up in the morning.

After a few minutes, Knight sneaked out of the nursery, wondering if his son's rocking must have something to do with REM sleep. Was it disturbed? Did he have apnoea? Was that why Luke was so wild and Bella so calm? Was it what made his son's language development delayed, and kept him from being toilet-trained when his sister was months ahead of the norm? Was that why Luke was a biter?

Knight came to no solid conclusions as he showered and shaved while listening to the radio, which was reporting that Denton Marshall's murder and the threats from Cronus had resulted in Michael Lancer and representatives of Scotland Yard and MI5 jointly announcing a dramatic tightening of security at the opening ceremonies. Those lucky enough to have tickets were being told to try to arrive at the Olympic Park during the afternoon in order to avoid an expected crush at the security stations.

After hearing that Private would be given a role in the increased security, Knight tried to call Jack Morgan. No answer, but the American was probably going to need him soon.

He knew that his mother had promised to help, but he needed a nanny now. He got a bitterly familiar file from a drawer and opened it, seeing a list of every nanny agency in London, and began calling. The woman who'd found Nancy and the nanny before her laughed at him when he explained his plight.

'A new nanny?' she said. 'Now? Not likely.'

'Why not?' he demanded.

'Because your kids have a terrible reputation and

the Olympics are starting tonight. Everyone I've got is working for at least the next two weeks.'

Knight heard the same story at the next three agencies, and his frustration began to mount. He loved his kids, but he'd vowed to find Marshall's killer, and Private was being called on to contribute more to Olympic security. He was needed. Now.

Rather than getting angry, he decided to hope that his mother would have better luck at finding someone to care for the twins and started doing what he could from home. Remembering the DNA material he'd taken off Selena Farrell's hairpin, he called a messenger to come and take the evidence to Private London and Hooligan.

Then he thought about Daring and Farrell, and decided that he needed to know more about them – about where their lives had crossed, anyway. Hadn't Daring said something about the Balkans? Was that where the photo of Farrell holding the gun had been taken? It had to be.

But when Knight went online and started searching for Farrell, he came up only with references to her academic publishing, and, seven years back, her opposition to the Olympic Park.

'This decision is flat-out wrong,' Farrell had stated in one piece published in *The Times*. 'The Olympics have become a vehicle to destroy neighbourhoods and uproot families and businesses. I pray that the people behind this decision are made to pay some day for what they've done to me and to my neighbours at the public's expense.'

Made to pay, professor? Knight thought grimly. Made to pay?

Chapter 34

ALMOST TWENTY-FOUR HOURS after the flute music had triggered a brutal migraine and a violent bout of nausea, the melody still played as a cruel soundtrack to Selena Farrell's thoughts as she lay in bed, the curtains of her bedroom drawn.

How was it possible? And what did Knight and Pope think of her? She had all but given them a reason to suspect her of something when she'd fled the scene like that. What if they started digging?

For what seemed like the thousandth time since bolting from her office and fleeing home to her tidy little flat in Wapping, Farrell swallowed hard against a burning in her throat that would not leave her. She'd drunk water all afternoon, and taken a handful of antacid tablets. They had only helped a bit.

She'd been dealing with migraines since she was a child, however, and a prescription medicine had blunted the agony of the electric head-clamp, leaving a dull aching at the back of her skull.

Farrell tried to fight the urge to ease that feeling. Not only was it a bad idea, given the medicine she was on, but when she drank alcohol she tended to become another personality, an almost completely different one.

I'm not going there tonight, she thought before the image of an exotic woman sitting deep in the corner of a pink tufted couch flashed into her head. At that, the decision was made for her. Farrell got out of bed, padded to the kitchen, opened the freezer and took out a bottle of Grey Goose vodka.

Soon the classics professor was on her second Martini, the ache at the back of her head was gone, and she believed she'd erased the memory of the flute melody. It was a syrinx melody, actually. The syrinx or Pan pipes featured seven reeds bound side by side. Along with the lyre, the Pan pipes were one of the oldest musical instruments in the world. But their eerie, breathy tonality had been banned from the ancient Olympics because it sounded too funereal.

'Who cares?' Farrell grumbled, and then gulped at her drink. 'To hell with the Olympics. To hell with Denton Marshall. To hell with the lot of them.'

Buzzing on the vodka now, becoming another person, Farrell vowed that with the migraine behind her she wasn't going to dwell on loss or injustice, or oppression. It was Friday night in London. She had places to go. People to see.

The professor felt a thrill go through her that deepened into a hunger when she swayed down the hall, went into her bedroom closet and unzipped a garment bag hanging there.

Inside was a dramatic hip-hugging A-line black skirt slit provocatively up its right flank, and a sexy sleeveless maroon satin blouse designed to show plenty of abundant cleavage.

Chapter 35

AT FIVE O'CLOCK that Friday afternoon, Knight was in his kitchen making the twins dinner, resigned to the fact that he would not witness the opening ceremony of the Games live and in person.

Knight felt spent, anyway. All day long, from the moment Luke had awoken crying, he had been consumed by the needs of his children, his frustration with the nanny issue, and his inability to push the Cronus investigation forward.

Around noon, while the twins were playing, he had called his mother and asked her how she was holding up.

'I slept two hours,' she replied. 'I'd nod off and all I could see in my dreams was Denton, and every time I'd feel such joy that I'd wake up and then face heartbreak all over again.'

'God, how horrible, mother,' said Knight, remembering the insomnia and anguish he'd suffered in the immediate weeks after the birth of the twins and

Kate's death. Many nights he'd thought he was going crazy.

He thought to change the conversation. 'I forgot to tell you: Mike Lancer invited me as his guest to sit in the organising committee's box for the opening ceremonies. If you find me a nanny, we can go together.'

'I don't know if I'm ready for that volume of pity quite yet. Besides, no memorial service has been planned. It would be unseemly for me to look as if I'm celebrating.'

'The Olympics are part of Denton's legacy,' Knight reminded her. 'You'd be honouring him. Besides, it would do you good to get out of the house and help me defend Denton's reputation to one and all.'

'I'll consider it.'

'And by the way: no nanny, no work on Denton's murder investigation.'

'I'm not a nincompoop, Peter!' his mother snapped.

Then Amanda Knight hung up on her son.

Around three, when the children were napping, Knight reached Jack Morgan. Private's owner was usually laid back and very cool, but even over the phone Knight could sense the pressure that Jack was under.

'We're doing everything we can to find a nanny,' Knight said.

'Good,' Jack said. 'Because we need you.'

'Bollocks,' Knight fumed after he'd hung up.

His doorbell rang at around five-thirty. Knight looked through the security peephole and saw his mother in stylish black slacks, shoes and blouse, grey pearl necklace and earrings. Dark sunglasses. He opened the door.

'I arranged a nanny for the evening,' Amanda said, and then stepped aside to reveal a very unhappy Gary Boss, resplendent in pedal-pusher khaki trousers, argyle socks, loafers, and a bow tie with barber-pole stripes.

His mother's personal assistant sniffed at Knight as if he were the purveyor of all things distasteful, and said: 'Do you know that I personally spoke with Nannies Incorporated, Fulham Nannies, the Sweet & Angelic Agency, and every other agency in the city? Quite the reputation, I'd say, Peter. So where are they? The little brutes? I'll need to know their schedules, I suppose.'

'They're in the living room, watching the telly,' Knight said. Then he looked at his mother as Boss disappeared inside. 'Is he up for this?'

'At triple his exorbitant hourly wage, I'm sure he'll figure out a way,' Amanda said, taking off her sunglasses to reveal puffy red eyes.

Knight ran up the stairs to his bedroom and changed quickly. When he came down he found the twins hiding behind the couch, eyeing Boss warily. His mother was nowhere to be seen.

'Her highness is in the car,' Boss said. 'Waiting.'

'I done one, Daddy,' Luke said, patting the back of his nappy.

Why couldn't he just use the loo?

'Well, then,' Knight said to Boss. 'Their food is in the fridge in plastic containers. Just a bit of heating-up to do. Luke can have a taste of ice cream. Bella's allergic, so digestive biscuits for her. Bath. Story. Bed by nine, and we'll see you by midnight, I'd think.'

Knight went to his children and kissed them. 'Mind Mr Boss, now. He's your nanny for tonight.'

'I done one, Daddy,' Luke complained again.

'Right,' Knight said to Boss. 'And Luke's had a BM. You'll need to change it straight away or you'll be bathing him sooner rather than later.'

Boss became distressed. 'Change a shitty nappy? Me?'

'You're the nanny now,' Knight said, stifling a laugh as he left.

Chapter 36

AS KNIGHT AND his mother made their way to St Pancras Station and the high-speed train to Stratford and the Olympic Park, Professor Selena Farrell was feeling damn sexy, thank you very much.

Dusk was coming on in Soho. The air was sultry, she'd got vodka in her, and she was dressed to kill. Indeed, as she walked west from Tottenham Court Road towards Carlisle Street, the classics professor kept catching glimpses of herself in the shop windows she passed, and in the eyes of men and women who could not help but notice every sway of her hips and every bounce of her breasts in the skirt and sleeveless blouse that clung to her like second skins.

She wore alluring make-up, startling blue contact lenses, and the scarf was gone, revealing dark-dyed hair cut in swoops that framed her face and drew the eye to that little dark mole on her right jawline. But for the mole no one, not even her research assistant, would ever have recognised her.

Farrell loved feeling like this. Anonymous. Sexual. On the prowl.

When she was like this she was far from who she was in her everyday life, truly someone else. The illicitness of it all excited the professor yet again, empowered her yet again, and made her feel magnetic, hypnotic and, well, downright irresistible.

When she reached Carlisle Street, she found number four, its sign lit in pink neon, and entered. The Candy Club was the oldest and largest lesbian nightclub in London, and was Farrell's favourite place to go when she needed to let off steam.

The professor headed towards the long bar on the ground floor and the many beautiful women milling around in it. A petite woman, quite exquisite in her loveliness, caught sight of Farrell, spun in her seat, mojito in hand, and threw her a knowing smile. 'Syren St James!'

'Nell,' Farrell said, and kissed her on the cheek.

Nell put her hand on Farrell's forearm and studied her outfit. 'My, my, Syren. Look at you: more brilliant and delicious than ever. Where have you been lately? I haven't seen you in almost a month.'

'I was here the other night,' Farrell said. 'Before that I was in Paris. Working. A new project.'

'Lucky you,' Nell said. Then she turned conspiratorial and added, 'You know, we could always leave and . . .'

'Not tonight, lover,' Farrell said gently. 'I've already made plans.'

'Pity,' Nell sniffed. 'Your "plan" here yet?'

'Haven't looked,' Farrell replied.

'Name?'

'That's a secret.'

'Well,' Nell said, miffed. 'If your secret is a no-show, come back.'

Farrell blew Nell a kiss before setting off, feeling anticipation make her heart beat along with the dance music thudding up from the basement. She peered into the nooks and crannies of the ground floor before heading upstairs where she scanned the crowd gathered around the pink pool table. No luck.

Farrell was beginning to think she'd been stood up until she went to the basement where a femme kink performer was pole dancing to the riffs and dubs of a disc jockey named V. J. Wicked. Pink sofas lined the walls facing the stripper.

The professor spotted her quarry on one of those sofas in the far corner of the room, nursing a flute of champagne. With jet-black hair pulled back severely, she was elegantly attired in a black cocktail frock and a pill hat with a black lace veil that obscured the features of her face except for her dusky skin and ruby lips.

'Hello, Marta,' Farrell said, sliding into a chair beside her.

Marta took her attention off the dancer, smiled and replied in a soft East European accent. 'I had faith I'd see you here, my sister.'

The professor smelled Marta's perfume and was enthralled. 'I couldn't stay away.'

Marta ran her ruby fingernails over the back of Farrell's hand. 'Of course you couldn't. Shall we let the games begin?'

Chapter 37

BY SEVEN THAT evening the world's eyes had turned to five hundred-plus acres of decaying East London land that had been transformed into the city's new Olympic Park, which featured a stadium packed with ninety thousand lucky fans, a teeming athletes' village, and sleek modern venues for cycling, basketball, handball, swimming and diving.

These venues were all beautiful structures, but the media had chosen British sculptor Anish Kapoor's *ArcelorMittal Orbit* as the park's and, indeed, the Games's signature design achievement. At three hundred and seventy-seven feet, the Orbit was taller than Big Ben, taller than the Statue of Liberty, and soared just outside the east flank of the stadium. The Orbit was rust red and featured massive hollow, steel arms that curved, twisted and wove together in a way that put Knight in mind of DNA helices gone mad. Near the top, the structure supported a circular observation deck and restaurant. Above the deck, another of those DNA helices was curved into a giant arch.

From his position high on the west side of the stadium, at the window of a lavish hospitality suite set aside for LOCOG, Knight trained his binoculars on the massive Olympic cauldron, which was set on a raised platform on the roof of the observation deck. He wondered how they were going to light it, and then found himself distracted by a BBC broadcaster on a nearby television screen saying that nearly four billion people were expected to tune in to the coverage of the opening ceremonies.

'Peter?' Jack Morgan said behind him. 'There's someone here who would like to talk to you.'

Knight lowered his binoculars and turned to find the owner of Private standing next to Marcus Morris, the chairman of LOCOG. Morris had been a popular Minister of Sport in a previous Labour government.

The two men shook hands.

'An honour,' Knight said as he shook Morris's hand.

Morris said, 'I need to hear from you exactly what Richard Guilder said before he died regarding Denton Marshall.'

Knight told him, finishing with, 'The currency scam had nothing to do with the Olympics. It was greed on Guilder's part. I'll testify to that.'

Morris shook Knight's hand again. 'Thank you,' he said. 'I didn't want there to be any hint of impropriety hanging over these Games. But it does nothing to make any of us feel any better about the loss of Denton. It's a tragedy.'

'In too many ways to count.'

'Your mother seems to be holding up.'

Indeed, upon their arrival Amanda had been showered with sympathy and was now somewhere in the crowd behind them.

'She's a strong person, and when this Cronus maniac claimed that Denton was crooked she got angry, very angry. Not a good thing.'

'No, I suppose not,' Morris said, and smiled at last. 'And now I've got a speech to give.'

'And an Olympics to open,' Jack said.

'That too,' Morris said, and walked away.

Jack looked out the window at the huge audience, his eyes scanning the roofline.

Knight noticed and said, 'Security seems brilliant, Jack. It took more than an hour for my mother and I to get through screening at Stratford. And the blokes with the weapons were all Gurkhas.'

'World's most fearsome warriors,' Jack said, nodding.

'Do you need me somewhere?'

'We're fine,' Jack said. 'Enjoy the show. You've earned it.'

Knight looked around. 'By the way, where's Lancer? Poor form to miss his own party.'

Jack winked. 'That's a secret. Mike said to thank you again. In the meantime, I think you should introduce me to your mother so I can offer my condolences.'

Knight's mobile buzzed in his pocket. 'Of course. One second, Jack.'

He dug out the phone, saw that Hooligan was calling and answered just as the lights in the stadium dimmed and the audience began to cheer.

'I'm at the stadium,' Knight said. 'The opening ceremony's starting.'

'Sorry to bother you, but some of us have to work,' Hooligan snapped. 'I got results on that hair sample you sent over this morning. They're—'

A trumpet fanfare erupted from every speaker in the stadium, drowning out what Hooligan had just said.

'Repeat that,' Knight said, sticking his finger in his ear.

'The hair in Cronus's envelope and Selena Farrell's hair,' Hooligan yelled. 'They fuckin' match!'

Chapter 38

'WE'VE GOT CRONUS!' Knight said in a hoarse whisper as he hung up. A powerful spotlight broke the darkness, fixing on a lone figure crouched in the middle of the stadium floor.

'What?' Jack Morgan said, surprised.

'Or one of his Furies, anyway,' Knight said, and then described the match. 'Farrell's house was razed to make way for this stadium. She said publicly that the people who did it to her were going to pay, and she completely flipped when we played the flute music for her.'

'Call Pottersfield,' Jack advised. 'Have her go to Farrell's house. Put her under surveillance until they can get a warrant.'

Out in the stadium a clarinet solo started and from the corner of his eye, Knight saw the figure on the stadium floor rise. He wore green and carried a bow. A quiver of arrows was slung across his back. Robin Hood?

'Unless Farrell's in the stadium,' Knight said, anxiety rising in his chest.

'They've got names attached to every ticket somewhere,' Jack said. He started moving away from the window towards the exit, with Knight trailing after him.

Behind them the crowd roared as a spectacle designed by British film-maker Danny Boyle moved into high gear, depicting through song and dance the rich history of London. Knight could hear drums booming and music echoing in the long hallway outside the heavily guarded hospitality suite. He speed-dialled Elaine Pottersfield, got her on the third ring, and explained the DNA evidence linking Selena Farrell to Cronus's letter.

Beside him, he heard Jack giving the same information to whoever was the watch commander of the moment inside the Olympic Park.

'How did you come by Farrell's DNA?' Pottersfield demanded.

'Long story,' Knight said. 'We're looking for her inside the Olympic stadium at the moment. I suggest you start doing the same at her home.'

He and Jack Morgan both hung up at the same time. Knight glanced at the four armed Private operatives guarding the entrance to LOCOG's hospitality suite.

Reading his thoughts, Jack said: 'No one's getting in there.'

Knight almost nodded, but then thought of Guilder and Mascolo, and said, 'We can't consider LOCOG members as the only targets. Guilder proved that.'

Jack nodded. 'We have to think that way.'

The pair entered the stadium in time to see Mary Poppins launch off the Orbit, umbrella held high as she floated over the roof and the delirious crowd towards a replica of the Tower of London that had been moved onto the floor. She landed near the Tower, but disappeared in smoke when lights began flashing red and white and kettledrums boomed to suggest the London blitz during the Second World War.

The smoke cleared and hundreds of people dressed in a multitude of costume styles danced around the replica of the Tower, and Knight thought he heard someone say that they were depicting modern London and the diverse citizenry of the most cosmopolitan city in the world.

But Knight was not interested in the spectacle: he was looking everywhere in the stadium, trying to anticipate what a madwoman might do in a situation like this. He spotted an entryway on the west side of the venue.

'Where does that go?' he asked Jack.

'The practice track,' Jack replied. 'That's where the teams are getting ready for the parade of nations.'

For reasons that Knight could not explain he felt drawn to that part of the stadium. 'I want to take a look,' he said.

'I'll walk with you,' Jack said. They crossed the stadium as the lights dimmed yet again except for a spotlight aimed at that Robin Hood figure who was now perched high above the stage at the venue's south end.

The actor was pointing up at the top of the Orbit, above the observation deck where more spotlights revealed two armed members of the Queen's Guard marching stiffly towards the cauldron from opposite sides of the roof. They pivoted and stood at rigid attention in their red tunics and black bearskin hats, flanking the cauldron.

Two more guardsmen appeared in the stadium at either side of the main stage. The music faded and an announcer said, 'Ladies and Gentlemen, Mesdames et Messieurs: Queen Elizabeth and the Royal Family.'

Chapter 39

THE LIGHTS ON the stage came up to reveal Queen Elizabeth the Second in a blue suit. She was smiling and waving as she moved to a microphone while Prince Philip, Charles, William, Kate, and various other members of the Windsor family flanked and followed her.

Knight and Jack slowed to gawk for several moments while the queen gave a short speech welcoming the youth of the world to London. But then they moved on towards that entryway.

As more dignitaries gave speeches, the two Private operatives reached the grandstand above the tunnel entry and had to show their corporate badges and IDs to get to the railing. Teams of armed Gurkhas flanked both sides of the tunnel below them. Several of the Nepalese guards immediately began studying Knight and Jack, gauging their level of threat.

'I absolutely would not want one of those guys

pissed-off at me,' Jack said as athletes from Afghanistan started to appear in the entryway.

'Toughest soldiers in the world,' Knight said, studying the traditional long, curved and sheathed knives several of the Gurkhas wore at their belts.

A long curved knife cut off Denton Marshall's head, right?

He was about to mention this fact to Jack when Marcus Morris shouted in conclusion to his speech: 'We welcome the youth of the world to the greatest city on Earth!'

On the stage at the south end of the stadium, the rock band The Who appeared, and broke into 'The Kids Are Alright' as the parade of athletes began with the contingent from Afghanistan entering the stadium.

The crowd went wild and wilder still when The Who finished and Mick Jagger and the Rolling Stones appeared with Keith Richards' guitar wailing the opening riff of 'Can't You Hear Me Knocking?'

With a thousand camera flashes, London went into full Olympic frenzy.

Below Jack and Knight, the Cameroon team filed into the stadium.

'Which one's Mundaho?' Jack asked. 'He's from Cameroon, right?'

'Yes, indeed,' Knight said, searching among the contingent dressed in green and bright yellow until he spotted a tall, muscular and laughing man with his hair done up in beads and shells. 'There he is.'

'Does he honestly reckon he can beat Shaw?'

'He certainly thinks so,' Knight said.

Filatri Mundaho had appeared out of nowhere on the international track scene at a race in Berlin only seven months before the Olympics. Mundaho was a big, rangy man built along the same lines as the supreme Jamaican sprinter Zeke Shaw.

Shaw had not been in Berlin, but many of the world's other fastest men had. Mundaho ran in three events at that meet: the 100-metre, 200-metre, and 400-metre sprints. The Cameroonian won every heat and every race convincingly, which had never been done before at a meet that big.

The achievement set off a frenzy of speculation about what Mundaho might be able to accomplish at the London Games. At the 1996 Atlanta Games, American Henry Ivey gold-medalled and set world records in both the 400-metre and 200-metre sprints. At Beijing in 2008, Shaw won the 100 and 200-metre sprints, also setting world records in both events. But no man, or woman for that matter, had ever won all three sprint events at a single Games.

Filatri Mundaho was going to try.

His coaches claimed that Mundaho had been discovered running in a regional race in the eastern part of their country after he'd escaped from rebel forces who had kidnapped him as a child and turned him into a boy soldier.

'Did you read that article the other day where he attributed his speed and stamina to bullets flying at his back?' Jack asked.

'No,' Knight said. 'But I can see that being a hell of a motivator.'

Chapter 40

TWENTY MINUTES LATER, with The Who and the Stones still counterpunching with songs from their greatest-hits collections, the contingent from the United States entered the stadium led by their flag-bearer Paul Teeter, a massive bearded man whom Jack knew from Los Angeles.

'Paul went to UCLA,' Jack said. 'Throws the shot and discus – insanely strong. A really good guy, too. He does a lot of work with inner-city youth. He's expected to go big here.'

Knight took his eyes off Teeter and caught sight of a woman he recognised walking behind the flag-bearer. He'd seen a picture of her in a bikini in *The Times* of all places the week before. She was in her late thirties and easily one of the fittest women he'd ever seen. And she was even better-looking in person.

'That's Hunter Pierce, isn't it?' Knight said.

Jack nodded in admiration. 'What a great story she is.'

Pierce had lost her husband in a car accident two years before, leaving her with three children under the age of ten. Now an emergency-room doctor in San Diego, she'd once been a twenty-one-year-old diver who'd almost made the Atlanta Olympic team, but had then quit the sport to pursue a career in medicine and raise a family.

Fifteen years later, as a way to deal with her husband's death, she began diving again. At her children's insistence, Pierce started competing again at the age of thirty-six. Eighteen months later, with her children watching, she'd stunned the American diving community by winning the ten-metre platform competition at the US Olympic qualifying meet.

'Absolutely brilliant,' Knight said, watching her waving and smiling as the team from Zimbabwe entered the stadium behind her.

Last to enter was the team from the UK – the host country. Twenty-three-year-old swimmer Audrey Williamson, a two-time gold medallist at Beijing, carried the Union Jack.

Knight pointed out to Jack the various athletes from the British contingent who were said to have a chance to win medals, including marathon runner Mary Duckworth, eighteen-year-old sprint sensation Mimi Marshall, boxer Oliver Price, and the nation's five-man heavyweight crew team.

Soon after, 'God Save the Queen' was sung. So was the Olympic Hymn. The athletes recited the Olympic creed, and a keen anticipation descended over the crowd, many of whom were looking towards the tunnel entry below Knight and Jack.

'I wonder who the cauldron lighter will be,' Jack said.

'You and everyone else in England,' Knight replied.

Indeed, speculation about who would receive the honour of lighting the Olympic cauldron had only intensified since the flame had come to Britain from Greece earlier in the year and been taken to Much Wenlock in Shropshire, where Pierre de Coubertin, the father of the modern Olympics, had been guest of honour at a special festival in 1890.

Since then, the torch had wound its way through England, Wales and Scotland. At every stop, curiosity and rumour had grown.

'The odds-makers favour Sir Cedric Dudley, the UK's five-times gold medallist in rowing,' Knight told Jack. 'But others are saying that the one to light the cauldron should be Sir Seymour Peterson-Allen, the first man to run a mile in under four minutes.'

But then a roar went up from the crowd as the theme from the movie *Chariots of Fire* was played and two men ran into the stadium directly below Knight and Jack, carrying the torch between them.

It was Cedric Dudley running beside . . .

'My God, that's Lancer!' Knight cried.

It *was* Mike Lancer, smiling and waving joyously to the crowd as he and Dudley ran along the track towards the spiral staircase that climbed the replica of the Tower of London at the bottom of which stood a waiting figure in white.

Chapter 41

AT THAT VERY moment, Karen Pope was in the *Sun*'s newsroom on the eighth floor of a modern office building on Thomas More Square near St Katharine Docks on the Thames's north bank. She wanted to go home to get some sleep, but could not break away from the coverage of the opening ceremonies.

Up on the screen, Lancer and Dudley ran towards that figure in white standing at the bottom of a steep staircase that led up onto the tower. Seeing the joy on the faces all over the stadium, Pope's normal cynicism faded and she started to feel weepy.

What an amazing, amazing moment for London, for all of Britain.

Pope looked over at Finch, her editor. The crusty sports veteran's eyes were glassy with emotion. He glanced at her and said, 'You know who that is, don't you? The final torch-bearer?'

'No idea, boss,' Pope replied.

'That's goddamn—'

'You Karen Pope?' a male voice behind her said, cutting Finch off.

Pope turned to see – and smell – a scruffy bicycle messenger who looked at her with a bored expression on her face.

'Yes,' she said. 'I'm Pope.'

The messenger held out an envelope with her name on it, spelled out in odd block letters of many different fonts and colours. Pope felt her stomach yawn open like an abysmal pit.

Chapter 42

AS THE FINAL torch-bearer climbed the Tower of London replica, the entire crowd were cheering and whistling and stamping their feet.

Knight frowned and glanced up at the roof of the Orbit and the guardsmen flanking the cauldron. How the hell were they going to get the flame from the top of the Tower of London replica to the top of the Orbit?

The final torch-bearer raised the flame high overhead as the applause turned thunderous and then cut to a collective gasp.

Holding his bow, an arrow strung, Robin Hood leaped into the air off the scaffolding above the south stage and flew out over the stadium on guy wires, heading for the raised Olympic torch.

As the archer whizzed past, he dipped the tip of his arrow into the flame, igniting it. Then he soared on, higher and higher, drawing back his bowstring as he went.

When he was almost level with the top of the Orbit, Robin Hood twisted and released the fiery arrow, which arced over the roof of the stadium, split the night sky, and passed between the Queen's guardsmen, inches over the cauldron.

A great billowing flame exploded inside the cauldron, turning the stadium crowd thunderous once more. The voice of Jacques Rogge, the chairman of the International Olympic Committee rang out over the public address system:

'I declare the 2012 London Games open!'

Fireworks erupted off the top of the Orbit and exploded high over East London while church bells all over the city began to ring. Down on the stadium floor, the athletes were all hugging each other, trading badges, and taking pictures and videos of this magical moment when each and every dream of Olympic gold seemed possible.

Looking at the athletes, and then up at the Olympic flame while chrysanthemum rockets burst in the sky, Knight got teary-eyed. He had not expected to feel such overwhelming pride for his city and for his country.

Then his mobile rang.

Karen Pope was near-hysterical: 'Cronus just sent me another letter. He takes credit for the death of Paul Teeter, the American shot-putter!'

Knight grimaced in confusion. 'No, I just saw him – he's . . .'

Then Knight understood. 'Where's Teeter?' he shouted at Jack and started running. 'Cronus is trying to kill him!'

Chapter 43

KNIGHT AND JACK fought their way down through the crowd. Jack was barking into his mobile, informing the stadium's security commander of the situation. They both showed their Private badges to get onto the stadium floor.

Knight spotted Teeter holding the US flag and talking to Filatri Mundaho, the Cameroonian sprinter. He took off across the infield just as the American flag began to topple. The flag-bearer went with it and collapsed to the ground, convulsing, bloody foam on his lips.

By the time Knight reached the US contingent, people were screaming for a doctor. Dr Hunter Pierce broke through the crowd and went to the shot-putter's side while Mundaho watched in horror.

'He just falls,' the ex-boy soldier said to Knight.

Jack looked as stunned as Knight felt. It had all happened so fast. Three minutes' warning. That's all they'd been given. What more could they have done to save the American?

Suddenly, the public address system crackled and Cronus's weird flute music began playing.

Panic surged through Knight. He remembered Selena Farrell turning crazed in her office, and then realised that many of the athletes around him were pointing up at the huge video screens around the Olympic venue, all displaying the same three red words:

OLYMPIC SHAME EXPOSED

Part Three

THE FASTEST MAN ON EARTH

Chapter 44

KNIGHT WAS INFURIATED. Cronus was acting with impunity, not only managing to poison Teeter but somehow hacking into the Olympic Park's computer system and taking over the scoreboard.

Could Professor Farrell do such a thing? Was she capable?

Mike Lancer ran up to Knight and Jack, looking as if he had aged ten years in the past few moments. He pointed at the screens. 'What the hell does that mean? What's that infernal music?'

'It's Cronus, Mike,' Knight said. 'He's taking credit for the attack.'

'What?' Lancer cried, looking distraught. Then he spotted Dr Pierce and the paramedics gathered around the US shot-putter. 'Is he dead?'

'I saw him before Dr Pierce got to him,' Knight said. 'He had bloody foam around his mouth. He was convulsing and choking.'

Shaken, bewildered, Lancer said, 'Poison?'

'We'll have to wait for a blood test.'

'Or an autopsy,' Jack said as paramedics put an unconscious Teeter on a gurney and rushed towards the ambulance with Dr Pierce in tow.

Some in the remaining crowd at the Olympic stadium were softly clapping for the stricken American. But more were heading for the exits, holding their hands to their ears to block out the baleful flute music, and shooting worried glances at Cronus's message still glowing up there on the screens.

OLYMPIC SHAME EXPOSED

Jack's voice shook as the ambulance pulled away: 'I don't care what claim Cronus might have. Paul Teeter was one of the good guys, a gentle giant. I went to see one of his clinics in LA. The kids adored him. Absolutely adored him. What kind of sick bastard would do such a thing on a night like this to such a good person as him?'

Knight recalled Professor Farrell fleeing her office the day before. Where was she? Did Pottersfield have her in custody? Was she Cronus? Or one of the Furies? And how did they poison Teeter?

Knight went to Mundaho, introduced himself, and asked him what had happened. The Cameroonian sprinter said in broken English that

Teeter was sweating hard and had looked flushed in the minutes before he collapsed.

Then Knight grabbed other American athletes and asked whether they'd seen Teeter drink anything before the start of the opening ceremony. A high-jumper said he had seen the shot-putter drinking from one of the thousands of plastic water bottles that London Olympic volunteers, or Game Masters, were handing out to athletes as they lined up for the parade of nations.

Knight told Jack and Lancer who went ballistic and barked into his radio, ordering all Game Masters held inside the Olympic Park until further notice.

The security commander, who had arrived on the scene a few minutes earlier, glared up at the glowing screens and bellowed into his radio, 'Shut down the PA system and end that goddamn flute music! Get that message off the scoreboards, too. And I want to know how in the bloody hell someone cracked our network. Now!'

Chapter 45

Saturday, 28 July 2012

PAUL TEETER, LEADING field athlete and tireless advocate for disadvantaged youth, died en route to hospital shortly after midnight. He was twenty-six.

Hours later, Knight suffered a nightmare that featured the flute music, the severed head of Denton Marshall, the blood blooming on Richard Guilder's chest, Joe Mascolo crashing through the cocktail table at the Lobby Bar, and the bloody foam on the shot-putter's lips.

He awoke with a start, and for several heart-racing moments the Private investigator had no idea where he was.

Then he heard Luke sucking his thumb in the darkness and knew. He began to calm down and pulled the sheets up around his shoulders, thinking of Gary Boss's face when Knight had arrived home at three in the morning.

The place had been a shambles and his mother's personal assistant vowed to never, ever babysit Knight's insane children again. Even if Amanda quintupled his salary he would not do it.

His mother was upset with Knight as well. Not only had he cut out on her the night before, he hadn't responded to her calls after Teeter's death had been announced. But he'd been swamped.

Knight tried to doze again, but his mind lurched between worry about finding a new nanny for his kids, his mother, and the contents of Cronus's second letter. He, Jack and Hooligan had examined the letter in the clean room at Private London shortly after Pope brought them the package at around one a.m.

'What honour can there be in a victory that is not earned?' Cronus had written at the start of the letter. 'What glory in defeating your opponent through deceit?'

Cronus claimed that Teeter was a fraud 'emblematic of the legions of corrupt Olympic athletes willing to use any illegal drug at their disposal to enhance their performance.'

The letter had gone on to claim that Teeter and other unnamed athletes at the London Games were using an extract of deer and elk antler 'velvet' to increase their strength, speed, and recovery time. Antler is the fastest growing substance in the world because the nutrient-rich sheathing, or velvet, that surrounds it during development is saturated with IGF-1, a super-potent growth hormone banned under Olympic rules. Under careful administration, however, and delivered by mouth spray rather than direct injection, the use of antler velvet was almost impossible to detect.

'The illicit benefits of IGF-1 are enormous,' Cronus wrote. 'Especially to a strength athlete like Teeter because it gives him the ability to build muscle faster, and recover faster from workouts.'

The letter had gone on to accuse two herbalists – one in Los Angeles and another in London – of being involved in Teeter's elaborate deception.

Documents that accompanied the letter seemed to shore up Cronus's claims. Four were receipts from the herbalists showing sales and delivery of red-deer velvet from New Zealand to the post-office box of an LA construction company that belonged to Teeter's brother-in-law Philip. Other documents purported to show the results of independent cutting-edge tests on blood taken from Teeter.

'They clearly note the presence of IGF-1 in Teeter's system within the last four months,' Cronus wrote before concluding. 'And so this wilful cheat, Paul Teeter, had to be sacrificed to cleanse the Games and make them pure again.'

On the couch in the twins' nursery, several hours

after reading those words, Knight stared at the dim forms of his children, thinking, is this how you make the Olympics pure again? By murdering people? What kind of insane person thinks that way? And why?

Chapter 46

I ROAM THE city for hours after Teeter's collapse on the global stage, secretly gloating over the vengeance we've taken, revelling in the proof of our superiority over the feeble efforts of Scotland Yard, MI5 and Private. They'll never come close to finding my sisters or me.

Everywhere I go, even at this late hour, I see Londoners in shock and newspapers featuring a photo of the Jumbotron in the stadium and our message: *Olympic Shame Exposed!*

And the headlines: *Death Stalks the Games!*

Well, what did they think? That we'd simply let them continue to make a mockery of the ancient rites of sport? That we'd simply let them defile the precepts of fair competition, earned superiority, and immortal greatness?

Hardly.

And now Cronus and the Furies are on the lips of billions upon billions of people around the globe, uncatchable, able to kill at will, bent on exposing and eliminating the dark side of the world's greatest sporting event.

Some fools are comparing us to the Palestinians who kidnapped and murdered Israelis during the 1972 summer Games in Munich. They keep describing us as terrorists with unknown political motives.

Those idiots aside, I feel as though the world is beginning to understand me and my sisters now. A thrill goes through me when I realise that people everywhere are sensing our greatness. They are questioning how it could be that such beings walk among them, holding the power of death over deceit and corruption, and making sacrifices in the name of all that is good and honourable.

In my mind I see the monsters that stoned me, the dead eyes of the Furies the night I slaughtered the Bosnians, and the shock on the faces of the broadcasters explaining Teeter's death.

At last, I think, I'm making the monsters pay for what they did to me.

I'm thinking the same thing as dawn breaks and bathes the thin clouds over London in a deep red hue that makes them look like raised welts.

I knock on the side entrance of the house where the Furies live, and enter. Marta is the only one of the sisters still awake. Her dark agate eyes are shiny with tears and she hugs me joyfully, her happiness as burning as my own.

'Like clockwork,' she says, closing the door behind me. 'Everything went off perfectly. Teagan got the bottle to the American, and then changed and slipped out before the chaos began, as if it were all fated.'

'Didn't you say the same thing when London got the Olympics?' I ask. 'Didn't you say that when we found the corruption and the cheating, just like I said we would?'

'It's all true,' Marta replies, her expression as fanatical as any martyr's. 'We are fated. We are superior.'

'Yes, but make no mistake: they will hunt us now,' I reply, sobering. 'You said we were fine on all counts?'

'All counts,' Marta confirms, all business now.

'The factory?'

'Teagan made sure it's sealed tight. No possibility of discovery.'

'Your part?' I ask.

'Went off flawlessly.'

I nod. 'Then it's time we stay in the shadows. Let Scotland Yard, MI5 and Private operate on high alert long enough for them to tire, to imagine that we're done, and allow themselves to let their guard down.'

'According to plan,' Marta says. Then she

hesitates. 'This Peter Knight – is he still a threat to us?'

I consider the question, and then say, 'If there is one, it's him.'

'We found something, then. Knight has a weakness. A large one.'

Chapter 47

KNIGHT JERKED AWAKE in the twins' nursery. His mobile was ringing. Sun flooded the room and blinded him. He groped for the phone and answered.

'Farrell's gone,' Inspector Elaine Pottersfield said. 'Not at her office. Not at her home.'

Knight sat up, still squinting, and said, 'Did you search both of them?'

'I can't get a warrant until my lab corroborates the match that Hooligan got.'

'Hooligan found something more last night in Cronus's second letter.'

'What?' Pottersfield shouted. 'What second letter?'

'It's already at your lab,' Knight said. 'But Hooligan picked up some skin cells in the envelope. He gave you half the sample.'

'Goddamn it, Peter,' Pottersfield cried. 'Private must not analyse anything to do with this case without—'

'That's not my call, Elaine,' Knight shot back. 'It's the *Sun*'s call. The paper is Private's client!'

'I don't care who the—'

'What about your end?' Peter demanded. 'I always seem to be giving you information.'

There was a pause before she said, 'The big focus is on how Cronus managed to hack into the . . .'

Knight noticed that the twins weren't in their cots and stopped listening. His attention shot to the clock. Ten a.m.! He hadn't slept this late since before the twins were born.

'Gotta go, Elaine! Kids,' he said and hung up.

Every worrying thought that a parent could have sliced through him, and he lurched through the nursery door and out onto the landing above the staircase. What if they've fallen? What if they've mucked around with . . .?

He heard the television spewing coverage of the 400-metre freestyle relay swimming heats, and felt as if every muscle in his body had changed to rubber. He had to hold tight to the railings to get down to the first floor.

Luke and Isabel had pulled the cushions off the sofa and piled them on the floor. They were sitting on them like little Buddhas beside empty cereal and juice boxes. Knight thought he'd never seen anything so beautiful in his life.

He fed, changed and dressed them while tracking

the broadcast coverage of Teeter's murder. Scotland Yard and MI5 weren't talking. Neither was F7, the company hired by LOCOG to run security and scanning at the Games.

But Mike Lancer was all over the news, assuring reporters that the Olympics were safe, defending his actions but taking full responsibility for the breaches in security. Shaken and yet resolved, Lancer vowed that Cronus would be stopped, captured, and brought to justice.

Knight, meanwhile, continued to struggle with the fact that he had no nanny and would not be actively working the Cronus case until he could find one. He'd called his mother several times, but she hadn't answered. Then he called another of the agencies, explained his situation, and begged for a temp. The manager told him she might be able to recruit someone by Tuesday.

'Tuesday?' he shouted.

'It's the best I can do – the Games have taken everyone available,' the woman said and hung up.

The twins wanted to go to the playground around noon. Figuring it would help them to nap, he agreed. He put them in their buggy, bought a copy of the *Sun*, and walked to a playground inside the Royal Hospital Gardens about ten minutes from his house. The temperature had fallen and there wasn't a cloud in the sky. London at its finest.

But as Knight sat on a bench and watched Luke playing on the big-boy slide and Isabel digging in the sandbox, his thoughts weren't on his children or on the exceptional weather for the first full day of Olympic competition. He kept thinking about Cronus and wondering if and when he'd strike again?

A text came in from Hooligan: 'Skin cells in second letter are male, no match yet. Off to Coventry for England-Algeria football match.'

Male? Knight thought. Cronus? So Farrell was one of the Furies?

In frustration, Knight picked up the newspaper. Pope's story dominated the front page under the headline: *Death Stalks The Olympics*.

The sports reporter led with Teeter's collapse and death in a terse, factual account of the events as they had unfolded at the opening ceremony. Near the end of the piece, she'd included a rebuttal of Cronus's charges from Teeter's brother-in-law who was in London for the Games. He claimed that the lab results Cronus had provided were phoney, and that he, in fact, was the person who had bought deer-antler velvet. Working on construction sites all day long as he did, he said it gave him relief from chronic back spasms.

'Hello? Sir?' a woman said.

The sunlight was so brilliant at first that Knight could only see the outline of a female figure standing in front of him holding out a flyer. He was about to say he wasn't interested, but then he put his hand to his brow to block the sun's glare from his eyes. The woman had a rather plain face, short dark hair, dark eyes, and a stocky athletic build.

'Yes?' he said, taking the flyer.

'I am so sorry,' she said with a humble smile, and he heard the soft East European accent for the first time. 'Please, I see you have children and I was wondering do you know someone who needs or do you yourself need a babysitter?'

Knight blinked several times in astonishment and then looked down at her flyer, which read: 'Experienced babysitter/nanny with excellent references available. Undergraduate degree in early-childhood development. Accepted into graduate programme in speech-language pathology.'

It went on, but Knight stopped reading and looked up at her. 'What's your name?'

She sat down beside him, with an eager smile.

'Marta,' she said. 'Marta Brezenova.'

Chapter 48

'YOU'RE AN UNEXPECTED answer to my prayers, Marta Brezenova, and your timing could not have been better,' Knight announced, feeling pleased at his good fortune. 'My name is Peter Knight, and I am actually in desperate need of a nanny at the moment.'

Marta looked incredulous and then happy. Her fingers went to her lips as she said, 'But you are the first person I've handed my flier to! It's like fate!'

'Maybe,' Knight said, enjoying her infectious enthusiasm.

'No, it is!' she protested. 'Can I apply?'

He looked again at her flier. 'Do you have a C.V.? References?'

'Both,' she said without hesitation, then dug in her bag and brought out a professional-looking C.V. and an Estonian passport. 'Now you know who I am.'

Knight glanced at the C.V. and the passport before saying: 'Tell you what. Those are my kids over there. Luke's on the slide and Isabel is in the sandbox. Go and introduce yourself. I'll look this over and give your references a call.'

Knight wanted to see how his kids interacted with Marta as a total stranger. He'd seen them revolt against so many nannies that he did not want to bother calling this woman's references if she and the twins did not click. No matter how badly he needed a nanny it wouldn't be worth the effort if they did not get along.

But to his surprise Marta went to Isabel, the more reserved of his children, and won her over almost immediately, helping her build a sandcastle and generating such enthusiasm that Luke soon left the slide to help. In three minutes, she had Lukey Knight – the big, bad, biting terror of Chelsea – laughing and filling buckets.

Seeing his children fall so easily under Marta's sway, Knight read the C.V. closely. She was an Estonian citizen, mid-thirties, but had done her undergraduate studies at the American University in Paris.

During her last two years at the university, and for six years after graduating, she had worked as a nanny for two different families in Paris. The mothers' names and phone numbers were included.

Marta's C.V. also indicated that she spoke English, French, Estonian and German, and had been accepted into the graduate programme in speech-language pathology at London's City University. She was due to join the course in 2014. In many ways, Knight thought, she was typical of the many educated women streaming into London these days: willing to take jobs beneath their qualifications in order to live and survive in the greatest city in the world.

My luck, Knight thought. He got out his mobile and started calling the references, thinking: Please let this be real. Please let someone answer the—

Petra DeMaurier came on the line almost immediately, speaking French. Knight identified himself and asked if she spoke English. In a guarded tone, she said that she did. When he told her that he was thinking of hiring Marta Brezenova as a nanny for his young twins, she turned effusive, praising Marta as the best nanny her four children had ever had, patient, loving, yet strong-willed if necessary.

'Why did she leave your employ?' Knight asked.

'My husband was transferred to Vietnam for two years,' she said. 'Marta did not wish to accompany us, but we parted on very good terms. You are a lucky man to have her.'

The second reference, Teagan Lesa, was no less positive, saying, 'When Marta was accepted for graduate studies in London, I almost cried. My three children *did* cry, even Stephan who is normally my brave little man. If I were you, I'd hire her before someone else does. Better yet, tell her to come back to Paris. We wait for her with open arms.'

Knight thought for several moments after hanging up, knowing he should check with the universities here and in Paris, something he couldn't do until Monday at the earliest. Then he had an idea. He hesitated, but then called Pottersfield back.

'You hung up on me,' she snapped.

'I had to,' Knight said. 'I need you to check an Estonian passport for me,'

'I most certainly will not,' Pottersfield shot back.

'It's for the twins, Elaine,' Knight said in a pleading tone. 'I've got an opportunity to hire them a new nanny who looks great on paper. I just want to make sure, and it's the weekend and I have no other way to do it.'

There was a long silence before Pottersfield said, 'Give me the name and passport number if you've got it.'

Knight heard the Scotland Yard inspector typing after he read her the number. He watched Marta get onto the slide, holding Isabel. His daughter on the slide? That was a first. They slid to the bottom with only a trace of terror surfacing on Isabel's face before she started clapping.

'Marta Brezenova,' said Pottersfield. 'Kind of a plain Jane, isn't she?'

'You were expecting a supermodel moonlighting as a nanny?'

'I suppose not,' Pottersfield allowed. 'She arrived in the UK on a flight from Paris ten days ago. She's here on an educational visa to attend City University.'

'Graduate programme in speech-language pathology,' Knight said. 'Thanks, Elaine. I owe you.'

Hearing Luke shriek with laughter, he hung up and spotted his son and his sister running through the jungle gym with Marta in hot pursuit, playing the happy monster, laughing maniacally.

You're not much to look at, Knight thought. But thank God for you, anyway. You're hired.

Chapter 49

Monday, 30 July 2012

EARLY THAT AFTERNOON, Metropolitan Police Inspector Billy Casper eyed Knight suspiciously, and said, 'Can't say I think it's proper for you to have access. But Pottersfield wanted you to see for yourself. So go on up. Second floor. Flat on the right.'

Knight mounted the stairs, fully focused on the investigation now that Marta Brezenova had come into the picture. The woman was a marvel. In less than two days she'd put his children under a spell. They were cleaner, better behaved, and happier. He'd even checked with City University. No doubt. Marta Brezenova had been accepted on their speech-language pathology programme. He hadn't bothered to call the American University in Paris. That aspect of his life felt settled at last. He'd even called up the agency that had offered him part-time help and had cancelled his request.

Now Inspector Elaine Pottersfield was waiting for Knight at the door to Selena Farrell's apartment.

'Anything?' he asked.

'A lot, actually,' she said. After he'd put on gloves and slip-ons she led him inside. A full crime-scene unit from Scotland Yard and specialists from MI5 were tearing the place apart.

They went into the professor's bedroom, which was dominated by an oversized dressing table that featured three mirrors and several drawers open to reveal all manner of beauty items: twenty different kinds of lipstick, an equal number of nail-polish bottles, and jars of make-up.

Dr Farrell? It didn't fit with the professor whom Knight and Pope had met in the office. Then he looked around and spotted the open closets, which were stuffed with what looked like high-end expensive women's clothing.

Was she a secret fashionista or something?

Before Knight could express his confusion, Pottersfield gestured past a crime tech examining a laptop on the dressing table towards a filing cabinet in the corner. 'We found all sorts of written diatribes against the destruction the Games caused in East London, including several poisonous letters to Denton—'

'Inspector?' the crime tech interrupted excitedly. 'I think I've got it!'

Pottersfield frowned. 'What?'

The tech struck the keyboard and from the computer flute music began to play, the same haunting melody that had echoed inside the Olympic Stadium on the night Paul Teeter was poisoned, the same brutal tune that had accompanied Cronus's letter accusing him of using an illicit performance-enhancing substance.

'That's on the computer?' Knight asked.

'Part of a simple *.exe* file designed to play the music and to display this.'

The tech turned the screen to show three words centred horizontally:

OLYMPIC SHAME EXPOSED

Chapter 50

WEARING A SURGICAL hair-cap and mask, a long rubber apron and the sort of high-sleeved rubber gloves that butchers use to disembowel cattle, I carefully load the third letter into an envelope addressed to Karen Pope.

More than sixty hours have passed since we slew the monster Teeter, and the initial frenzy that we caused in the global media has subsided considerably because the London Games have gone on, and gold medals have been won.

On Saturday we dominated virtually every broadcast and every written account of the opening ceremonies. On Sunday, the stories about the threat we posed were shorter and focused on law-enforcement efforts to figure out how the Olympic computer system was hacked, as well as insignificant coverage of the impromptu memorial service that the US athletes held for the corrupt swine Teeter.

Yesterday we were merely context for news features that trumpeted the fact that, apart from Teeter's murder, the 2012 Summer Olympics were going off flawlessly. This morning we didn't even make page one, which was dominated by the search of Serena Farrell's home and office where conclusive evidence had been found linking her to the Cronus murders; and by reports that Scotland Yard and MI5 had launched a nationwide manhunt for the classics professor.

This is troubling news at some level, but not unexpected. Nor is the fact that it will take more than a death or two to destroy the modern Olympic movement. I've known that ever since the night when London won the right to host the Games. My sisters and I have had seven years since to work out our intricate plan for vengeance, seven years to penetrate the system and use it to our advantage, seven years to create enough false leads to keep the police distracted and uncertain, unable to anticipate our final purpose until it's much too late.

Still wearing the apron and gloves, I slip the envelope into a plastic Ziploc bag and hand it to Petra, who stands with Teagan, both sisters clad in disguises that render them fat and unrecognisable to anyone but me or their older sister.

'Remember the tides,' I say.

Petra says nothing and looks away from me, as if she is having an internal argument of some sort. The act creates unease in me.

'We will, Cronus,' Teagan says, sliding on dark sunglasses below the official Olympic Volunteer cap she wears.

I go to Petra and say, 'Are you all right, sister?'

Her expression is conflicted, but she nods.

I kiss her on both cheeks, and then turn to Teagan.

'The factory?' I ask.

'This morning,' she replies. 'Food and medicine enough for four days.'

I embrace her and whisper in her ear: 'Watch your sister. She's impulsive.'

When we part, Teagan's face is expressionless. My cold warrior.

Removing the apron and gloves, I watch the sisters leave, and my hand travels to that crablike scar on the back of my head. Scratching it, the hatred ignites almost instantly, and I deeply wish that I could be one of those two women tonight. But, in consolation, I remind myself that the ultimate revenge will be mine and mine alone. The disposable mobile in my pocket rings. It's Marta.

'I managed to put a bug in Knight's mobile before he left for work,' she informs me. 'I'll tap the home computer when the children sleep.'

'Did he give you the evening off?'

'I didn't ask for it,' Marta says.

If the stupid bitch were in front of me right now, I swear I'd wring her pretty little neck. 'What do you mean, you didn't ask?' I demand in a tight voice.

'Relax,' she says. 'I'll be right where I'm needed when I'm needed. The children will be asleep. They'll never even know I was gone. And neither will Knight. He told me not to expect him until almost midnight.'

'How can you be sure the brats will be sleeping?'

'How else would I do it? I'm going to drug them.'

Chapter 51

SEVERAL HOURS LATER, inside the Aquatics Centre in the grounds of the Olympic Park, US diver Hunter Pierce flipped backwards off the ten-metre platform. She spun through the chlorine-tainted air, corkscrewing twice before slicing the water with a cutting sound, leaving a shallow whirlpool on the surface and little else.

Knight joined the packed house, cheering, clapping and whistling. But no one in the crowd celebrated more than the American diver's three children – one boy and two girls – in the front row, stamping their feet and waving their hands at their mother as she surfaced, grinning wildly.

That was Pierce's fourth attempt, and her best in Knight's estimation. After three dives she had been in third place behind athletes from South Korea and Panama. The Chinese were a surprisingly distant fourth and fifth.

She's in the zone, Knight thought. She feels it.

As he'd been for much of the past two hours, Knight was standing in the exit gangway opposite the ten-metre platform, watching the crowd and the competition. Nearly four days had passed since Teeter's death, four days without subsequent attack, and one day since the discovery of the software program in Selena Farrell's computer designed to breach and take over the Olympic Stadium's electronic scoreboard system.

Everyone was saying it was over. Capturing the mad professor was only a matter of time. The investigation was simply a manhunt now.

But Knight was nevertheless concerned that another killing might be coming. He'd taken to studying the Olympic schedule at all hours of the night, trying to anticipate where Cronus might strike again. It would be somewhere high-profile, he figured, with intense media coverage, as there was here in the Aquatics Centre as Pierce tried to become the oldest woman ever to win the platform competition.

The American diver hoisted herself from the pool, grabbed a towel, ran over, and slapped the outstretched hands of her children before heading towards the jacuzzi to keep her muscles supple. Before she got there, a roar went up at the scores that flashed on the board: all high eights and nines. Pierce had just moved herself into the silver medal position.

Knight clapped again with even more enthusiasm. The London Games needed a feel-good story to counteract the pall that Cronus had cast over the Games, and this was it. Pierce was defying her age, the odds, and the murders. Indeed, she'd become something of a spokesman for the US Team, decrying Cronus in the wake of Teeter's death. And now here she was, within striking distance of gold.

I am damn lucky to be here, Knight thought. Despite everything, I'm lucky in many ways, especially to have found that Marta.

The woman felt like a gift from on high. His kids were different creatures around her, as if she were the Pied Piper or something. Luke was even talking about using the 'big-boy loo'. And she was incredibly professional. His house had never looked so organised and clean. All in all, it was as if a great weight had been lifted from Knight's shoulders, freeing him to hunt for the madman stalking the Olympics.

At the same time, however, his mother had begun to retreat into her old pre-Denton Marshall ways. She'd opted to hold a memorial for Marshall after the Olympics, and had then disappeared into her work. And there was a bitterness that crept into her voice every time Knight talked to her.

'Do you ever answer your mobile, Knight?' Karen Pope complained.

Startled, Knight looked round, surprised to see the reporter standing next to him in the entryway. 'I've been having problems with it, actually,' he said.

That was true. For the past day, there'd been an odd static audible during Knight's cellular connections, but he had not had time to have the phone looked at.

'Get a new phone, then,' Pope snapped. 'I'm under a lot of pressure to produce and I need your help.'

'Looks to me like you're doing just fine on your own,' Knight said.

Indeed, in addition to the story about the things found on Farrell's home computer, Pope had published an article detailing the results of Teeter's autopsy: the shot-putter had been given a cocktail not of poisons but of drugs designed to radically raise his blood pressure and heart rate, which had resulted in a haemorrhage of his pulmonary artery, hence the bloody foam that Knight had seen on his lips.

In the same story, Pope had got an inside scoop from Mike Lancer explaining how Farrell must have isolated a flaw in the Olympics' IT system, which had allowed her a gateway into the Games' server and the scoreboard set-up.

Lancer said the flaw had been isolated and fixed and all volunteers were being doubly scrutinised. Lancer also revealed that security cameras had caught a woman wearing a Games Master uniform handing Teeter a bottle of water shortly before the Parade of Athletes but she'd been wearing one of the hats given to volunteers, which had hidden her face.

'Please, Knight,' Pope pleaded. 'I need something here.'

'You know more than me,' he replied, watching as the Panamanian in third place made an over-rotation on her last dive, costing her critical points.

Then the South Korean athlete in first place faltered. Her jump lacked snap and it affected the entire trajectory of her dive, resulting in a mediocre score.

The door was wide open for Pierce now, Knight thought, growing excited. He could not take his gaze off the American doctor as she began to climb to the top of the diving tower for her fifth and final dive.

Pope poked him in the arm and said, 'Someone told me Inspector Pottersfield is your sister-in-law. You have to know things that I don't.'

'Elaine does not talk to me unless she absolutely has to,' Knight said, lowering his binoculars.

'Why's that?' Pope asked, sceptically.

'Because she thinks I'm responsible for my wife's death.'

Chapter 52

KNIGHT WATCHED PIERCE reach the three-storey-high platform, and then he glanced over at Pope to find that the reporter was looking shocked.

'Were you? Responsible?' she asked.

Knight sighed. 'Kate had problems during the pregnancy, but wanted the delivery to be natural and at home. I knew the risks – we both knew the risks – but I deferred to her. If she'd been in hospital, she would have lived. I'll wrestle with that for the rest of my life because, apart from my own feelings of loss and remorse, Elaine Pottersfield won't let me forget it.'

Knight's admission confused and saddened Pope. 'Anyone ever tell you that you're a complicated guy?'

He did not reply. He was focused on Pierce, praying that she'd pull it off. He'd never been a huge sports fan, but this felt . . . well, monumental for some reason. Here she was, thirty-eight, a widow and a mother of three about to make her fifth and final dive, the most difficult in her repertoire.

At stake: Olympic gold.

But Pierce looked cool as she settled and then took two quick strides to the edge of the platform. She leaped out and up into the pike position. She flipped back towards the platform in a gainer, twisted, and then somersaulted twice more before knifing into the water.

The crowd exploded. Pierce's son and daughters began dancing and hugging each other.

'She did it!' Knight cried and felt tears in his eyes and then confusion: why was he getting so emotional about this?

He couldn't answer the question, but he had goose bumps when Pierce ran to her children amid applause that turned deafening when the scores went up, confirming her gold-medal win.

'OK, so she won,' Pope said snippily. 'Please, Knight. Help a girl out.'

Knight had an angry look about him as he yanked out his phone. 'I've got a copy of the complete inventory of items they found at Farrell's flat and her office.'

Pope's eyes grew wide. Then she said, 'Thanks, Knight. I owe you.'

'Don't mention it.'

'It is over, then, really?' Pope said, with more than a little sadness in her voice. 'Just a manhunt from here on out. With all the beefed-up security, it would be impossible for Farrell to strike again. I mean, right?'

Knight nodded as he watched Pierce holding her children, smiling through her tears, and felt thoroughly satisfied. Some kind of balance had been achieved with the American diver's performance.

Of course, other athletes had already shown remarkable fortitude in the last four days of competition. A swimmer from Australia had come back from a shattered right leg last year to win swimming gold in the men's 400-metre freestyle race. A flyweight boxer from Niger, raised in abject poverty and subjected to long periods of malnourishment, had somehow developed a lion's heart that had allowed him to win his first two boxing matches with first-round knockouts.

But Pierce's story and her vocal defiance of Cronus seemed to echo and magnify what continued to be right with the modern Olympic Games. The doctor had shown grace under incredible pressure. She'd shaken off Teeter's death and had won. As a result the Games no longer felt as tainted. At least to Knight.

Then his mobile rang. It was Hooligan.

'What do you know that I don't, mate?' Knight asked in an upbeat voice, provoking a sneer from Pope.

'Those skin cells we found in the second letter?' Hooligan said, sounding shaken. 'For three days, I get no match. But then, through an old friend from MI5, I access a NATO database in Brussels. And I get a hit – a mind-boggling hit.'

Knight's happiness over Pierce's win subsided, and he turned away from Pope, saying, 'Tell me.'

'The DNA matches a hair sample taken in the mid-1990s as part of a drug-screening test given to people applying to be consultants to the NATO peacekeeping contingent that went to the Balkans to enforce the ceasefire.'

Knight was confused. Farrell had been in the Balkans at some point in the 1990s. But Hooligan had said his initial examination indicated that the skin cells in the second letter from Cronus belonged to a male.

'Whose DNA is it?' Knight demanded.

'Indiana Jones,' Hooligan said, sounding very disappointed. 'Indiana Fuckin' Jones.'

Chapter 53

FIVE MILES AWAY, and several hundred yards south of the Thames in Greenwich, Petra and Teagan walked under leaden skies towards the security gate of the O2 Arena, an ultra-modern white-domed structure perforated by and trussed to yellow towers that held the roof in place. The O2 Arena sat at the north end of a peninsula and normally played host to concerts and larger theatrical productions. But for the Olympics it had been transformed into the gymnastics venue.

Petra and Teagan were dressed in official Games Master uniforms, and carried official credentials that identified them as recruited and vetted volunteers for that evening's Olympic highlight event: the women's team gymnastics final.

Teagan looked grim, focused, and determined as they walked towards the line of volunteers and concessionaires waiting to clear security. But Petra appeared uncertain, and she was walking with a hesitant gait.

'I said I was sorry,' Petra said.

Teagan said icily: 'Hardly the actions of a superior being.'

'My mind was elsewhere,' her sister replied.

'Where else could you possibly be? This is the moment we've waited for!'

Petra hesitated before complaining in a whisper: 'This isn't like the other tasks that Cronus has given us. It feels like a suicide mission. The end of two Furies.'

Teagan halted and glared at her sister. 'First the letter and now doubts?'

Petra's attitude hardened. 'What if we get caught?'

'We won't.'

'But—'

Teagan cut her off, asking archly, 'Do you honestly want me to call Cronus and say that now, at the last minute, you are leaving this to me? Do you really want to provoke him like that?'

Petra blinked and then her expression twisted towards alarm. 'No. No, I never said anything like that. Please. I'll . . . I'll do it.' She straightened and brushed her jacket with her fingers. 'A moment of doubt,' she added. 'That's all. Nothing more than that. Even superior beings entertain doubt, sister.'

'No, they don't,' said Teagan, thinking 'impetuous'

and 'lacking in attention to detail' – wasn't that how Cronus had described her younger sister?

Some of that was definitely true. Petra had just now proved it, hadn't she?

As they'd waited on a pavement near King's College, their only stop on the way to the gymnastics venue, the youngest of the Furies had forgotten to keep her gloves on when getting out the latest letter to Pope. Teagan had gone over the package with a disposable wipe, and had then held it with the wipe until she could pass the envelope to a bicycle messenger who gave them a sharp but cursory glance in their fat-women disguises.

As if in reaction to the same memory, Petra raised her chin towards Teagan. 'I know who I am, sister. I know what fate holds for me. I'm clear about that now.'

Teagan hesitated, but then gestured to Petra to lead on. Despite her sister's doubts, Teagan felt nothing but waves of certainty and pleasure. Drugging a man to death was one thing, but there was no substitute for looking the person you were about to kill in the eye, showing them your power.

It had been years since that had happened – since Bosnia, in fact. What she had done back then should have been fuel for nightmares, but it was not so for Teagan.

She often dreamed of the men and boys she'd

executed in the wake of her parents' death and the gang rape. Those bloody dreams were Teagan's favourites, true fantasies that she enjoyed reliving again and again.

Teagan smiled, thinking that the acts she would commit tonight would ensure that she'd have a new dream for years to come, something to celebrate in the dark, something to cling to when times got rough.

At last they reached the X-ray screeners. Stone-faced Gurkhas armed with automatic weapons flanked the checkpoint, and for a moment Teagan feared that Petra might baulk and retreat at the show of force.

But her sister acted like a pro and handed her identification to the guard, who ran her badge through a reader and checked her face against computer records that identified her as 'Caroline Thorson'. Those same records indicated that she was a diabetic and therefore cleared to bring an insulin kit into the venue.

The guard pointed to a grey plastic tub. 'Insulin kit and anything metal in there. Jewellery, too,' he said, pointing at the pitted silver ring she wore.

Petra smiled, tugged the ring off and set it beside the insulin kit in the tray. She walked through the metal-detectors without incident.

Teagan took off a ring identical to her sister's and

put it in the tray after her credentials checked out. 'Same ring?' the guard said.

Teagan smiled and gestured towards Petra. 'We're cousins. The rings were presents from our grandma who loved the Olympics. The poor dear passed on last year. We're wearing them in her honour to every event we work.'

'That's nice,' the guard said, and waved her through.

Chapter 54

THE ORBIT'S OBSERVATION deck revolved slowly clockwise, offering a panoramic view of the interior of the Olympic Stadium where several athletes and coaches were inspecting the track, and of the Aquatics Centre that Knight had only just left.

Standing at the deck's railing in a cooling east wind that sent clouds scudding across a leaden sky, Mike Lancer squinted at Knight and said: 'You mean the television guy?'

'And Greek antiquities curator at the British Museum.'

Jack Morgan said, 'Does Scotland Yard know about this yet?'

Knight had called Jack Morgan and had been told that he and Lancer were up on the Orbit, inspecting security on the Olympic flame. Knight had rushed over. He nodded to Jack's question and said, 'I just spoke with Elaine Pottersfield. She has squads en route to the museum and to his house.'

For several moments there was silence, and all Knight was really aware of was the smell of carbon in the air, coming from the Olympic cauldron burning on the roof above them.

'How do we know for sure that Daring has gone missing?' Jack asked.

Knight replied, 'I called his secretary before I called Elaine, and she told me that the last time anyone saw Daring was last Thursday night around ten o'clock when he left the reception for his exhibit. That was probably six hours after Selena Farrell was last seen as well.'

Lancer shook his head. 'Did you see that coming, Peter? That they could have been in on it together?'

'I didn't even consider the possibility,' Knight admitted. 'But they both served with NATO in the Balkans during the mid-1990s, they both had issues with the modern Olympic Games, and there's no denying the DNA results.'

Lancer said, 'Now that we know who they are, it's only a matter of time until they're caught.'

'Unless they manage to strike again before they're caught,' Jack said.

The LOCOG security adviser blanched, puffed out his lips, and exhaled with worry. 'Where? That's the question I keep asking myself.'

'Somewhere big,' Knight said. 'They killed during the opening ceremony because it gave them a world audience.'

Jack said, 'Okay, so what's the biggest event left?'

Lancer shrugged. 'The sprints have drawn the most interest. Millions of people applied for seats in the stadium this coming Sunday evening – the final of the men's 100-metre sprint – because of the possibility of a showdown between Zeke Shaw and Filatri Mundaho.'

'What about today or tomorrow? What's the ticket everyone wants?' Knight asked.

'Has to be the women's gymnastics, I'd think,' Jack said. 'Carries the biggest television audience in the States, anyway.'

Lancer glanced at his watch and reacted as though his stomach had just soured. 'The women's team final starts in less than an hour.'

Anxiety coiled through Knight as he said, 'If I were Cronus, and wanted to make a big statement, women's gymnastics is where I'd attack next.'

Lancer grimaced and started heading for the lift, saying, 'I hate to say it, but I think you may be right, Peter.'

'What's the fastest way to the gymnastics venue?' Jack demanded, hustling after the LOCOG member.

'Blackwall Tunnel,' Knight said.

'No,' Lancer said. 'Scotland Yard's got it closed during the competitions to prevent a possible car bombing. We'll go by river bus.'

Chapter 55

AFTER CHECKING IN with Petra's immediate supervisors, the sisters scouted out the seats for which she would act as usher. They were low and at the north end of the O2 Arena, just off the vault floor. Teagan left her sister at that point, and found the hospitality suite to which she'd been assigned as a waitress. She told her team leader there that she would return after a quick trip to the loo.

Petra was waiting. They took stalls next to each other.

Teagan opened the seat-cover dispenser in her stall and retrieved two slender, green CO_2 canisters and two sets of plastic tweezers that had been taped there.

She kept one and passed the other under the partition that separated the stalls. In return, Petra handed Teagan two tiny darts, scarcely as long as a bee's sting, with miniature plastic vanes glued to tiny insulin needles and stuck to a small strip of duct tape.

Next came a six-inch length of thin clear plastic tubing with miniature pipe-fitting hardware at either end. Teagan took off her ring and then screwed the male fitting into one of the silver pits on the back of the ring.

Satisfied with the connection, she unscrewed it and coiled the line back to where she'd attached the CO_2 cartridge. She taped the cartridge and coiled gas line to her forearm, and then slid on the ring.

She'd no sooner finished than Petra pushed the vial from the insulin kit under the partition. Teagan used her tweezers to grab one of the darts. She stuck the tip of its needle through the rubber gasket into the vial and the liquid it contained, drew it out, and inserted it vane first into a tiny hole on her ring opposite the gas connection.

After dipping the second tiny dart, she blew on it until the liquid dried, and then stuck it ever so carefully into the lapel of her uniform in case she needed a second shot. With utmost care, she drew down her blouse sleeve before flushing the loo and leaving the stall.

Petra appeared as Teagan washed her hands. She smiled uncertainly at her older sister, but then whispered, 'Aim twice.'

'Shoot once,' Teagan said, thinking that this felt like part of a dream already. 'Do you have your bees?'

'I do.'

Chapter 56

UNDER A SPITTING rain an unseasonal fog crept west up the Thames to meet the river bus as it sped past the Isle of Dogs, heading towards the North Greenwich peninsula and the Queen Elizabeth II Pier. The boat was packed with latecomers holding tickets to the team gymnastics finals, which were just a few minutes from starting.

Knight's attention, however, was not on the other passengers; it roved off the bow of the ferry, looking towards the brilliantly lit O2 Arena dome coming closer, feeling strongly that it could be the scene of Farrell and Daring's next strike.

Beside him, Lancer was talking insistently on his phone, explaining that he was on the way with reinforcements for the security detail, which he ordered to be on highest alert. He had already called Scotland Yard's Marine Unit and had been told that a patrol boat was anchored off the back of the arena.

'There it is,' Jack said, pointing through the mist at a large rigid inflatable craft with dual outboard engines bobbing in the water south of them as they rounded the head of the peninsula.

Five officers in black raincoats and carrying automatic weapons stood in the boat, watching them. A single officer, a woman in a dry suit, rode an ultra-quiet black jet ski that trailed the river bus into the dock.

'Those are primo counter-terror vessels, especially that sled,' Jack said in admiration. 'No chance of entry or escape by water with those suckers around.'

Security around the actual arena was just as tight. There were ten-foot-high fences around the venue with armed Gurkhas every fifty yards. The screening process was tough. There was still a long line waiting to get in. Without Lancer it would have taken them at least half an hour to clear the scanners. But he'd got them inside in less than five minutes.

'What are we looking for?' Knight asked as they heard applause from the entryway in front of them, and a woman's voice on the public address system announcing the first rotation of the women's team finals.

'Anything out of the ordinary,' Lancer said. 'Absolutely anything.'

'When was the last time dogs swept the building?' Jack asked.

'Three hours ago,' Lancer said.

'I'd bring them back,' Jack said as they emerged into the arena itself. 'Are you monitoring mobile traffic?'

'We jammed it,' Lancer said. 'We figured it was easier.'

While LOCOG's security chief gave orders over his radio to recall the canine-sniffer bomb squad, Knight and Jack scanned the arena floor, seeing teams lining up near individual pieces of gymnastics apparatus.

The Chinese were at the south end of the venue, preparing to compete on the uneven parallel bars. Beyond, the Russians were doing stretching exercises beside the balance beam. The UK contingent, which had performed remarkably well in the qualifying rounds thanks to gutsy performances by star gymnast Nessa Kemp, was arranging gear near the floor-exercise mat. At the far end of the arena, the Americans were preparing to vault. Guards, many of them Gurkhas as well, stood at their posts around the floor, facing away from the competitors so they could scan the crowd for threat with zero distraction.

Knight concluded that an attack on one of the athletes down on the floor was virtually impossible.

But what about their safety back in the locker rooms? Or on the way to and from the Olympic Village?

Would the next target even be an athlete?

Chapter 57

AT SIX-FIFTEEN that Tuesday evening, the last of the Chinese gymnasts stuck her dismount off the balance beam, landing on her feet with nary a bobble.

The crowd inside the Chinese Gymnastics Federation's luxury box high in the arena roared with delight. With one round to go, their team was winning handsomely. The Brits were a surprising second, and the Americans sat solidly in third place. The Russians had unexpectedly imploded and were trailing a distant fourth.

Amid the celebration, Teagan set her drinks tray on the bar and then dropped a pen on purpose. She squatted and in seconds had the thin gas line running beneath her wrist, up across her palm, past her little finger and attached to the back of the ring.

She stood to smile at the bartender. 'I'm going to clear glasses for a bit.'

He nodded and returned to pouring wine. As the Chinese team moved to the vaulting pit, Teagan's senses were on fire. She slipped through the crowded luxury box towards a stocky woman in a grey suit who was watching at the window.

Her name was Win Bo Lee. She was chairman of the national committee of the Chinese Gymnastics Association, or CGA. She was also, in her own way, as corrupt as Paul Teeter and Sir Denton Marshall had been. Cronus was right, Teagan thought. People like Win Bo Lee deserved exposure and death.

As she neared the woman, Teagan held her right arm low and by her waist while her left hand slipped into the pocket of her uniform coat and felt something small and bristly. When the distance between her and Win Bo Lee was less than two feet, she snapped her hand sharply upward and squeezed the right side of the ring with her little finger.

With a soft spitting noise rendered inaudible by the joyous conversations in the hospitality suite, the tiny dart flew and stuck in the back of Win Bo Lee's neck. The CGA's chairman jerked, and then cursed. She tried to reach around the back of her neck. But before she could, Teagan slapped her there, dislodging the dart, which fell to the floor. She crushed it with her shoe.

Win Bo Lee twisted around angrily and glared at Teagan, who looked deeply into her victim's eyes, savouring them, imprinting them in her memory, and then said, 'I got it.'

She crouched down before the Chinese woman could reply and acted as if she were picking something up with her left hand. She stood and showed Win Bo Lee a dead bee.

'It's summer,' Teagan said. 'Somehow they get in here.'

Win Bo Lee stared at the bee and then up at Teagan, her temper cooling, and said, 'You are quick, but not quicker than that bee. It stung me hard!'

'A thousand pardons,' Teagan said. 'Would you like some ice?'

The CGA chairman nodded as she reached around to massage her neck.

'I'll get you some,' Teagan said.

She cleared the table in front of the CGA chairman, took one last look into Win Bo Lee's eyes, and then left the glasses at the bar. Heading towards the exit with no intention of returning, Teagan was already replaying every moment of her quiet attack as if it were a slow-motion highlight on a sports reel.

Chapter 58

I AM SUPERIOR, Petra told herself as she moved parallel to the vault pit along the railing and towards the Gurkha with the thin black moustache. I am not like them. I am a weapon of vengeance, a weapon of cleansing.

She carried a stack of towels that hid her right hand when she smiled at the Gurkha with the moustache, and said, 'For the vault station.'

He nodded. It was the third time the fat woman had brought towels to the pit, so he didn't bother to go through them.

I am superior, Petra said over and over in her mind. And then, as it had as a young girl, during the rape and the killings, everything seemed to go strangely silent and slow-motion for her. In that altered state, she spotted her quarry: a slight man in a red sweat-jacket and white trousers, who was starting to pace as the first Chinese woman adjusted the springboard and prepared to vault.

Gao Ping was head coach of the Chinese women's gymnastics team and a known pacer in big competitions. Petra had seen the behaviour in several films of Ping that she'd studied. He was a demonstrative, high-energy man who liked to goad his athletes to big performances. He was also a coach who had committed repeated crimes against the Olympic ideals, thereby sealing his fate.

The assistant coach, a woman named An Wu, and no less a criminal herself, had taken a seat, her face as emotionless as Ping's was expressive. An Wu was an easier target than the ever-moving head coach. But Cronus had ordered Petra to take Ping first, and the assistant coach only if the opportunity followed.

Petra slowed in order to match her movement to Ping's pacing. She handed the towels over the rail to another Game Master, and moved at an angle to the Chinese coach, who was bent over, exhorting his tiny athlete to greatness.

The first Chinese girl took off down the runway.

Ping took two skipping steps after her, and then stopped right in front of Petra, no more than eight feet away.

She rested her hand on the rail, intent on the head coach's neck. When the Chinese girl hit the springboard, Petra fired.

I am a superior being, she thought as the dart hit Ping.

Superior in every way.

Chapter 59

THE CHINESE COACH slapped at the back of his neck just before his athlete nailed her landing and a roar went up from the crowd. Ping winced and looked around, bewildered by what had happened. Then he shook the sting off and ran clapping towards his vaulter, who beamed and shook her clasped hands above her head.

'That little girl crushed that,' Jack said.

'Did she?' Knight said, lowering his binoculars. 'I was watching Ping.'

'The Joe Cocker of gymnastics?' Jack remarked.

Knight laughed, but then saw the Chinese coach rubbing at his neck before starting his histrionic ritual all over again as his next athlete got set to vault.

'I think Joe Cocker got stung,' Knight said, raising his binoculars again.

'By what, a bee? How can you see that from here?'

'I can't see any bee,' Knight said. 'But I saw his reaction.'

Behind them, Knight heard Lancer talking in a strained voice into his radio to the arena's internal and external security forces, fine-tuning how they were going to handle the medal ceremony.

Knight felt uneasy. He raised his binoculars and watched the Chinese coach cheer three more women through their vaults. As his last athlete took off down the runway, Ping danced like a voodoo man. Even his taciturn assistant, An Wu, got caught up in the moment. She was on her feet, hand across her mouth as the last girl twisted and somersaulted off the horse.

An Wu suddenly slapped at her neck as if she'd been stung.

Her athlete stuck her landing perfectly.

The audience erupted. The Chinese had won gold, and the UK silver, the best finish ever for a British gymnastics team. The coaches and athletes from both nations were celebrating. So were the Americans, who'd taken bronze.

Knight was aware of it all while using his binoculars to scan the raucous crowd cheering and aiming cameras above the vaulting pit. With Ping doing a high-step dance and his girls celebrating with him, the attention of virtually everyone at that end of the arena was on the victorious Chinese team.

Except for a heavyset platinum-blonde Game Master. She had her back turned to the celebration and was hurrying with an odd gait up the stairs away from the arena floor. She disappeared along the walkway, heading for the outer halls.

Knight felt suddenly short of breath. He dropped his binoculars and said to Jack and Lancer, 'There's something wrong.'

'What?' Lancer demanded.

'The Chinese coaches. I saw them both slap at their necks, as if they'd been stung. Ping and then Wu. Right after the assistant coach slapped her neck, I saw a chunky platinum-blonde female Game Master hurrying out when everyone else was focused on the Chinese, cheering that last vault.'

Jack closed one eye, as if aiming at some distant target.

Lancer pursed his lips, 'Two slaps, and an overweight usher moving to her post? Nothing more than that?'

'No. It just seemed out of synch with . . . out of synch, that's all.'

Jack asked, 'Where did the volunteer go?'

Knight pointed across the arena. 'Out the upper exit between sections 115 and 116. Fifteen seconds ago. She was moving kind of funny, too.'

Lancer picked up his radio and barked into it. 'Central, do you have a Game Master, female, platinum-blonde hair, heavyset, on camera up there in the hallways off 115?'

Several tense moments passed as Olympic workers moved the medals podium out onto the arena floor.

At last Lancer's radio squawked: 'That's a negative.'

Knight frowned. 'No, she has to be there somewhere. She just left.'

Lancer looked at him again before saying into his radio: 'Tell officers if they see a Game Master in that area, chubby female with platinum-blonde hair, she is to be detained for questioning.'

'We might want to get a medic to look at the coaches,' Knight said.

Lancer replied, 'Athletes frown on being treated by strangers, but I'll alert the Chinese medical teams at the very least. Does that cover it?'

Knight almost nodded before saying, 'Where are those security cameras being monitored?'

Lancer gestured up towards a mirror-faced box in the balcony above them.

'I'm going up there,' Knight said. 'Get me in?'

Chapter 60

PETRA FOUGHT NOT to hyperventilate as she closed the door to the middle stall in the ladies' loo just west of the high north entry to the arena. She took a deep breath and felt like screaming with the sense of power surging through her, a power that she'd long forgotten.

See? I am a superior being. I have slain monsters. I have meted vengeance. I am a Fury. And monsters don't catch Furies. Read the myths!

Shaking with adrenalin, Petra ripped off her platinum-blonde wig, revealing her ginger hair pinned against her scalp. She dug the plastic barrettes out and let her short locks fall free.

Petra reached up and grabbed hold of the outer metal edges of the seat-cover dispenser. She tugged and the entire unit came free of the wall. She set it on the seat, then reached deep into the dark cavity she'd exposed and came up with a knapsack made of dark blue rubber, a dry bag that contained a change of clothes.

She set the bag on top of the dispenser, stripped off her volunteer's uniform, and hung it on a peg on the stall door. Then she peeled off the rubber prostheses that she'd glued to her hips, belly and legs to make herself look chubby. She looked at the dry bag, thinking how much more heavy and cumbersome it would be, given their anticipated escape route, and then dropped the rubber prostheses inside the hollow wall along with the wig.

Four minutes later, the seat-cover dispenser back in place and her uniform concealed in the dry bag, Petra left the loo stall.

She washed her hands and took stock of her outfit: low blue canvas sneakers, snug white jeans, a sleeveless white cotton sweater, a simple gold necklace, and a blue linen blazer. She added a pair of designer spectacles with clear lenses and smiled. She could have been any old posh now.

The stall to Petra's immediate right opened.

'Ready?' Petra asked without looking.

'Waiting on you, sister,' Teagan said, coming to the mirror beside Petra. Her dark wig had gone, revealing her sandy hair. She was dressed in casual attire and carried a similar knapsack-style dry bag. 'Success?'

'Two,' Petra said.

Teagan tilted her head in reappraisal. 'They'll write myths about you.'

'Yes, they will,' said Petra, grinning, and together the two Furies headed for the lavatory door.

Over loudspeakers out in the hall, they heard the arena announcer say, 'Mesdames et Messieurs, Ladies and Gentlemen, take your seats. The medal ceremonies are about to begin.'

Chapter 61

KNIGHT'S ATTENTION ROAMED over various split images on the security monitors in front of him, all showing camera views of the upper hallway off the O2 building's sections 115 and 116, where fans were hurrying back into the arena.

Two women, one slender with stylish sandy hair and the other equally svelte with short ginger hair, came out of the women's lavatory and merged with pedestrian traffic returning to the inner arena. Knight considered them only briefly, still searching for a brassy, beefy blonde in a Games Master uniform.

But something about the way the redhead had walked when she left the toilet nagged at Knight, and he looked back to the feed on which he'd seen them. They were gone. Had she been limping? It had looked that way, but she was slender, not fat, and a redhead, not a blonde.

The medal ceremony began with the awarding of

the bronze medals. Knight trained his binoculars north from the security station, looking for the redhead and her companion among the fans still hurrying back to their seats.

Knight's efforts were hampered by the announcement of the silver-medal award to Great Britain. That sent the host-country crowd up on its feet, clapping, whistling and catcalling. Several lads at the north end of the arena unfurled large Union Jack flags and waved them about wildly, further obscuring Knight's view.

The flags were still waving when the Chinese team was called to the high spot on the podium. Knight temporarily abandoned the search and looked for the Chinese coaches.

Ping and Wu stood off to the side of the floor-exercise mat beside a short, stocky Chinese woman in her fifties.

'Who is she?' Knight asked one of the men manning the video station.

He looked and replied, 'Win Bo Lee. Chairman of the Chinese Gymnastics Association. Bigwig.'

Knight kept his binoculars on Ping and Wu as the Chinese national anthem began and the country's red flag started to rise. He was expecting an emotional outpouring from the Chinese head coach.

To his surprise, however, he thought Ping looked oddly sombre for a man whose team had just won its

Olympic event. Ping was looking at the ground and rubbing the back of his neck, not up at the Chinese flag as it reached the arena rafters.

Knight was about to turn his binoculars north again to look for the two women when Win Bo Lee suddenly wobbled on her feet as if she were dizzy. The assistant coach, Wu, caught the CGA chairman by the elbow and steadied her.

The older woman wiped at her nose and looked at her finger. She appeared alarmed and said something to An Wu.

But then Knight's attention caught jerky movement beside the older woman. As the last few bars of the Chinese national anthem played, Ping lurched up onto the floor-exercise mat. The victorious head coach staggered across the spring-loaded floor toward the podium, his left hand clutching his throat, and his right reaching out to his triumphant team as if they were rope and he was drowning.

The anthem ended. The Chinese girls looked down from the flag, tears flowing down their cheeks, only to see their agonised coach trip and sprawl onto the mat in front of them.

Several girls started to scream.

Even from halfway across the arena, Knight could see the blood dribbling from Ping's mouth and nose.

Chapter 62

BEFORE PARAMEDICS COULD reach the fallen coach, Win Bo Lee complained hysterically of sudden blindness before collapsing with blood seeping from her mouth, eyes, nose, and ears.

The fans began to grasp what was happening and shouts and cries of disbelief and fear pierced the arena. Many started grabbing their things and heading towards the exits.

Up in the arena's security pod, Knight knew that An Wu, the assistant coach, was in mortal danger, but he forced his attention away from the drama developing on the arena floor to watch the camera feeds showing the walkway where the two women had entered the arena. The men manning the security station were inundated with radio traffic.

One of them suddenly roared, 'We've got an explosion immediately south-east of the venue on the riverbank! River Police responding!'

Thank God no one heard the bomb inside the

arena, because more fans were now moving towards the exits and would have caused a stampede. An Wu dropped to the floor suddenly, bleeding also and adding to the building terror.

And then, right there on the nearest screen on the security console, Knight spotted the sandy blonde and the redhead leaving the north arena along with a steady flow of jittery sports fans.

Though he could not make out their faces, the redhead was definitely limping. 'It's her!' Knight shouted.

The men monitoring the security station barely glanced at him as they frantically tried to respond to questions flying at them over radios from all over the arena. Realising they were being overcome by the rapid pace of developments, Knight bolted for the door to the security pod, wrenched it open and started pushing though the shocked crowds, hoping to intercept the women.

But which way had they gone? East or west?

Knight decided they'd head for the exit closest to transportation, and therefore ran down the west hallway, searching among the stream of people coming at him until he heard Jack Morgan shout, 'Knight!'

He glanced to his right and saw Private's owner hustling out of the inner arena.

'I've got them!' Knight cried. 'Two women, a

sandy blonde and a redhead. She's limping! Call Lancer. Have him seal the perimeter.'

Jack ran with him, trying to use his phone while weaving through the crowd that was trying to leave.

'Damn it!' Jack grunted. 'They're jamming mobile traffic!'

'Then it's up to us,' Knight said and ran faster, determined that the two women would not get away.

In moments they reached the section of the north hallway he'd watched on camera. There was no way they could have got past him, Knight thought, cursing himself for not taking the east passage. But then, suddenly, he caught a glimpse of them several hundred feet ahead: two women going out through a fire-exit door.

'Got them!' Knight roared, holding his badge up and yanking out his Beretta. He shot twice into the ceiling, and bellowed, 'Everyone down!'

It was as if Moses had parted the Red Sea. Olympic fans began diving to the cement floor and trying to shield themselves from Knight and Jack who sprinted towards the fire-escape door. And that was when Knight understood.

'They're going for the river!' he cried. 'They set off a bomb as a diversion to pull the River Police away from the arena!'

Then the lights flickered and died, throwing the entire gymnastics venue into pitch darkness.

Chapter 63

KNIGHT SKIDDED TO a halt in the blackness, feeling as if he was tottering at the edge of a cliff and struck with vertigo. People were screaming everywhere around him as he dug out a penlight on the key chain he always carried. He snapped it on just as battery-powered red emergency lights started to glow.

He and Jack sprinted the last seventy feet to the fire-escape door and tried to shoulder it open. Locked. Knight shot out the lock, provoking new chaos among the terrified fans, but the door flew open when they kicked it.

They hurtled down the fire-escape stairs and found themselves above the arena's back area, which was clogged with media production trucks and other support vehicles for the venue. Red lights had gone on here as well, but Knight could not spot the pair of escaping women at first because there were so many people moving around below them, shouting, demanding to know what had happened.

Then he saw them, disappearing through an open door at the north-east end of the arena. Knight barrelled down the staircase, dodged past irate broadcast personnel, and spotted a security guard standing at the exit.

He showed his badge and gasped, 'Two women. Where did they go?'

The guard looked at him in confusion. 'What women? I was—'

Knight pushed past him and ran outside. Every light at the north end of the peninsula was dead, but thunder boomed and lightning cracked all around, giving them flashes of flickering vision.

The unseasonal fog swirled. Rain was pelting down. Knight had to throw up a forearm to shield his eyes. When the next flashes of lightning came, he peered along the nine-foot chain-link fence that separated the arena from a path along the Thames that led east and south to the river-bus pier.

The sandy-blonde Fury was crouched on the ground on the other side of the fence. The redhead had cleared the top and was climbing down.

Knight raised his gun, but it all went dark again and his penlight was no match for the night and the storm.

'I saw them,' Jack grunted.

'I did too,' Knight said.

But rather than go straight after the two women, Knight ran to the barrier where it was closest, pocketing the light and stuffing the gun into the back of his jeans. He clambered up the fence and jumped off the top.

It had been four days since he'd been run over, but Knight's sore ribs still made him hiss with pain when he landed on the paved path. To his left, still well out on the water, he spotted the next ferry coming.

Jack landed beside Knight and together they raced towards the pier, which was lit by several dim red emergency lights. They slowed less than twenty yards from the ramp that led down onto the pier itself. Two Gurkhas lay dead on the ground, their throats slit from ear to ear.

Rain drummed on the surface of the dock. The river bus's engines growled louder as it approached. But then Knight heard another engine start up.

Jack heard it too. 'They've got a boat!'

Knight vaulted the chain that was strung across the entrance to the ramp and ran down onto the dock, sweeping his gun and penlight from side to side, looking for movement.

A Metropolitan Police officer, the woman who'd been riding the jet sled, lay dead on the pier, eyes bulging, her neck at an unnatural angle. Knight ran past her to the edge of the dock, hearing an out-board motor starting to accelerate in the fog and rain.

He noticed the officer's jet sled tied to the pier, ran to it, saw the key in the ignition, jumped on, and started it while Jack grabbed the officer's radio and got on behind Knight, calling, 'This is Jack Morgan with Private. Metropolitan River Police officer dead on Queen Elizabeth II Pier. We are in pursuit of killers on the river. Repeat, we are in pursuit of killers on the river.'

Knight twisted the throttle. The sled leaped away from the pier, making almost no noise, and in seconds they were deep into the fog.

The mist was thick, reducing visibility to less than ten metres, and the water was choppy with a strong current drawn east by the ebbing tide. Radio traffic crackled on Jack's radio in response to his call.

But he did not answer and turned down the volume so they could better hear the outboard coughing somewhere ahead of them. Knight noticed a digital compass on the dashboard of the sled.

The outboard was heading north by north-east in the middle of the Thames at a slow speed, probably because of the poor visibility. Feeling confident that he could catch them now, Knight hit the throttle hard and prayed they did not hit anything. Were there buoys out here? There had to be. Across the river, he could just make out the blinking light at Trinity Buoy Wharf.

'They're heading towards the River Lea,' Knight yelled over his shoulder. 'It goes back through the Olympic Park.'

'Killers heading towards Lea river mouth,' Jack barked into the radio.

They heard sirens wailing from both banks of the Thames now, and then the outboard motor went full throttle. The fog cleared a bit and no more than one hundred metres ahead of them on the river Knight spotted the racing shadow of a bow rider with its lights extinguished, and heard its engine screaming.

Knight mashed his throttle to close the gap at the same moment he realised that the escape boat wasn't heading towards the mouth of the Lea at all; it was off by several degrees, speeding straight at the high cement retaining wall on the east side of the confluence.

'They're going to hit!' Jack yelled.

Knight let go the throttle of the jet sled a split second before the speedboat struck the wall dead on and exploded in a series of blasts that mushroomed into fireballs and flares that licked and seared through the rain and the fog.

Debris and shrapnel rained down, forcing Knight

and Jack to retreat. They never heard the quiet sounds of three swimmers moving eastward with the ebbing tide.

Chapter 64

THE STORM HAD passed and it was four in the morning by the time Knight climbed into a taxi and gave the driver his address in Chelsea.

Dazed, damp, and running on fumes, his mind nevertheless spun wildly with all that had happened since the Furies had run their boat into the river wall.

There were divers in the water within half an hour of the crash, searching for bodies, though the tidal currents were hampering their efforts.

Elaine Pottersfield had been pulled off the search of James Daring's office and apartment, and had come to the O2 Arena as part of a huge Scotland Yard team that had arrived in the wake of the triple murder.

She'd debriefed Knight, Jack and Lancer, who'd been rushing to the arena floor when the lights went out and the venue erupted in chaos. The former decathlon champion had had the presence of mind to order the perimeter of the arena sealed after he'd heard Knight's shots in the hallway, but his action had not come in time to prevent the Furies' escape.

When Lancer ordered electricians to get the lights back on they found that a simple timer-and-breaker system had been attached to the venue's main power line, and that the relay that triggered the backup generators had been disabled. Power was restored within thirty minutes, however, which enabled Knight and Pottersfield to study the security video closely while Lancer and Jack went to help screen the literally thousands of witnesses to the triple slaying.

To their dismay the video of the two Furies showed little of their faces. The women seemed to know exactly when to turn one way or another, depending on the camera angles. Knight remembered spotting them leaving the lavatory after the chubby Game Master disappeared and before the medal ceremony began, and said, 'They had to have switched disguises in there.'

He and Pottersfield went to search the loo. On the way, Knight's sister-in-law said she'd found flute music on Daring's home computer as well as essays – tirades, really – that damned the commercial and corporate aspects of the modern

Olympics. In at least two instances, the television star and museum curator had remarked that the kind of corruption and cheating that went on in the modern Olympics would have been dealt with swiftly during the old Games.

'He said the gods on Olympus would have struck them down one by one,' Pottersfield said as they entered the lavatory. 'He said their deaths would have been a "just sacrifice".'

Just sacrifice? Knight thought bitterly. Three people dead. For what?

As he and Pottersfield searched the lavatory, he wondered why Pope had not called him. She must have received another letter by now.

Twenty minutes into the search, Knight found the loose seat-cover dispensary and tugged it out of the wall. A minute later he fished out a platinum-blonde wig from inside, handed it to Pottersfield, and said, 'That's a big mistake there. There has to be DNA evidence on that.'

The inspector grudgingly slipped the wig into an evidence bag. 'Well done, Peter, but I'd rather that no one else should know about this – at least, not until I can have it analysed. And most certainly not your client, Karen Pope.'

'Not a soul,' he promised.

Indeed, around three that morning, shortly before Knight left the O2 Arena, he'd found Jack again and not mentioned the wig. Private's owner informed him, however, that a guard at the gate where all Game Master volunteers cleared security distinctly remembered the two chunky cousins who came through the scanners early, one with diabetes, both wearing identical rings.

The computer system remembered them as 'Caroline and Anita Thorson', cousins who lived north of Liverpool Street. Police officers sent to the flat found two women called Caroline and Anita Thorson, but both of them were sleeping. They claimed not to have been anywhere near the O2 Arena much less being accredited Game Masters for the Olympics. They were being brought to New Scotland Yard for further questioning, though Knight did not hold much hope for a breakthrough there. The Thorson women had been used, their identities stolen.

The taxi pulled up in front of Knight's house just before dawn with him figuring that Cronus or one of his Furies was a very sophisticated hacker and that they had to have had access at some point to the arena's electrical infrastructure.

Right?

He was so damn tired that he couldn't even answer his own question. He paid the driver and told him to wait. Knight trudged to his front door, went in, and turned on the hallway light. He heard a creaking noise and looked in the playroom. Marta yawned on the couch, dropping the blanket from her shoulders.

'I'm so sorry,' Knight said softly. 'I was at the gymnastics venue and they were jamming mobile traffic. I couldn't get through.'

Marta's hand went to her mouth. 'I saw it on the television. You were there? Did they catch them?'

'No,' he said despairingly. 'We don't even know if they're alive or not. But they've made a big mistake. If they're alive, they'll be caught.'

She yawned again, wider this time, and said, 'What mistake?'

'I can't go into it,' Knight replied. 'There's a taxi waiting for you out front. I've already paid your fare.'

Marta smiled drowsily. 'You're very kind, Mr Knight.'

'Call me Peter. When can you be back?'

'One?'

Knight nodded. Nine hours. He'd be lucky to be able to sleep for four of them before the twins awoke, but it was better than nothing.

As if she were reading his mind, Marta headed towards the door, saying, 'Isabel and Luke were both very, very tired tonight. I think they'll sleep in for you.'

Chapter 65

SHORTLY AFTER DAWN that morning, racked with a headache that felt like my skull was being axed in two, I thundered at Marta: 'What mistake?'

Her eyes exuded the same dead quality I'd first seen the night I rescued her in Bosnia. 'I don't know, Cronus,' she said. 'He wouldn't tell me.'

I looked around wildly at the other two sisters. 'What mistake?'

Teagan shook her head. 'There was no mistake. Everything went exactly according to plan. Petra even got off the second shot on Wu.'

'I did,' Petra said, looking at me with an expression that bordered on delirium. 'I was superior, Cronus. A champion. No one could have executed the task better. And on the river, we jumped off the boat well before it hit the wall and we timed the tides right on the money. We were a perfect ten all round.'

Marta nodded. 'I was back at Knight's home

almost two hours before he came in. We've won, Cronus. They'll shut down the Olympics now, for sure.'

I shook my head. 'Not even close. The corporate sponsors and the broadcasters won't let them stop until it's too late.'

But what mistake could we have made?

I look at Teagan. 'What about the factory?'

'I left it sealed tight.'

'Go and check,' I say. 'Make sure.' Then I go to a chair by the window, wondering again what error we could have made. My mind rips through dozens of possibilities, but the truth is that my information is incomplete. I can't devise countermeasures if I do not know the nature of this supposed error.

Finally I glare at Marta. 'Find out. I don't care what you have to do. Find out what the mistake is.'

Chapter 66

AT TWENTY TO noon that same Wednesday, Knight pushed Isabel in the swing at the playground inside the gardens of the Royal Hospital. Luke had figured out the swing on his own, and was pumping wildly with his feet and hands, trying to get higher and higher. Knight kept slowing him down gently.

'Daddy!' Luke yelled in frustration. 'Lukey goes up!'

'Not so up,' Knight said. 'You'll fall out and crack your head.'

'No, Daddy,' Luke grumbled.

Isabel laughed. 'Lukey already has a cracked head!'

That did not go over well. Knight had to take them off the swings and separate them, Isabel in the sandbox and Luke on the jungle gym. When they'd finally become absorbed in their play, he yawned, checked his watch – another hour and a quarter until Marta was scheduled to return – and went to the bench and his iPad, which he'd been using to track the news coverage.

The country, and indeed the entire world, was in an uproar over the slayings of Gao Ping, An Wu and Win Bo Lee. Heads of state around the globe were condemning Cronus, the Furies, and their brutal tactics. So were the athletes.

Knight clicked on a hyperlink that led him to a BBC news video. It led with reaction to the killings of the Chinese coaches, and featured parents of athletes from Spain, Russia, and the Ukraine who fretted about security and wondered whether to dash their children's dreams and insist that they leave. The Chinese had protested vigorously to the International Olympic Committee, and issued a release stating their frustration that the host nation seemed unable to provide as safe a venue for the Games as Beijing had four years before in Beijing.

But the BBC story then tried to lay blame for the security breaches. There were plenty of targets, including F7, the corporate-security firm hired to run the surveillance equipment at the venues. An F7 spokesman vigorously defended their operation, calling it 'state of the art' and run by 'the most qualified people in the business'. The BBC piece also noted that the computer-security system had been designed by representatives of Scotland Yard and MI5 and had been touted as 'impenetrable' and 'unbeatable' before the start of the Games. But neither law-enforcement organisation was responding to questions about what were obviously serious breaches.

That left the focus on 'an embattled Mike Lancer' who'd faced the cameras after several members of Parliament had called for him to step down or be fired.

'I'm not one to dodge blame when it's warranted,' Lancer said, sounding alternately angry and grief-stricken. 'These terrorists have managed to find cracks in our system that we could not see. Let me assure the public that we are doing everything in our power to plug these cracks, and I know that Scotland Yard, MI5, F7 and Private are doing everything they can to find these murderers and stop them before any other tragedy can befall what should rightly be a global celebration of youth and renewal.'

In response to the calls for Lancer's head, LOCOG chairman Marcus Morris was playing the stiff-upper-lip Brit, adamantly opposed to giving ground to Cronus and positive that Lancer and the web of UK security forces in place would prevent further attacks, find the killers, and bring them to justice.

Despite the overall gloomy tone of the piece, the video closed on something of a positive note. The scene was the Olympic Village, where shortly after dawn hundreds of athletes poured out onto the lawns and pavements. They burned candles in memory of the slain. American diver Hunter Pierce, Cameroonian sprinter Filatri Mundaho, and the girls of the Chinese gymnastics team had spoken, denouncing the murders as an 'insane, unwarranted, and direct assault on the fabric of the games'.

The piece closed with the reporter noting that police divers were continuing to probe the murky depths of the Thames near its confluence with the River Lea. They had found evidence that the speed-boat that had slammed into the river wall had contained explosives. No bodies had turned up.

'These facts do not bode well for an already shaken London Olympics,' he'd intoned, ending the story.

'Knight?'

Sun reporter Karen Pope was coming through the gate into the playground, looking anxious and depressed.

Knight frowned. 'How did you find me here?'

'Hooligan told me you like to come here with your kids,' she replied and her unease deepened. 'I tried your house first, then came here.'

'What's wrong?' Knight asked. 'Are you all right?'

'No, I'm not, actually,' the reporter said in a shaky voice as she sat down on the bench with him. Tears welled in her eyes. 'I feel like I'm being used.'

'Cronus?'

'And the Furies,' she said, wiping angrily at her tears. 'I didn't ask for it, but I have become part of their insanity, their terror. At first, you know, I admit it: I welcomed the story. Bloody brilliant for the career and all that, but now . . .'

Pope choked up and looked away.

'He's written to you again?'

She nodded and in a lost voice said: 'I feel like I've sold my soul, Knight.'

At that he saw the reporter in an entirely new light. Yes, she was abrasive and insensitive at times. But deep down she was human. She had a soul and principles; and this case tore at both. His estimation of Pope rose immeasurably.

'Don't think that way,' Knight said. 'You don't support Cronus, do you?'

'Of course not,' she sniffed.

'Then you're just doing your job: a difficult thing, but necessary. Do you have the letter with you?'

Pope shook her head. 'I dropped it off with Hooligan this morning.' She paused. 'A messenger brought it to me last night at my flat. He said two fat women met him in front of King's College and gave him the letter to deliver. They were wearing official Olympic volunteer uniforms.'

'It fits,' Knight said. 'What reason did Cronus give for killing the Chinese?'

'He claims that they were guilty of state-sponsored child enslavement.'

Cronus claimed that China routinely ignored Olympic age rules, doctoring birth certificates in order to force children into what was effectively athletic servitude. These practices were also fraud. Ping and Wu knew that sixty per cent of the Chinese women's gymnastics team was underage. So did Win Bo Lee, who Cronus claimed was the architect of the entire scheme.

'There are plenty of supporting documents,' Pope said. 'Cronus makes the case quite well. The letter says the Chinese "enslaved underage children for state glory", and that the punishment was death.'

She looked at Knight, crying again. 'I could have published it all last night. I could have called my editor and made the deadline for today's paper. But I couldn't, Knight. I just . . . They know where I live.'

'Lukey wants milk, Daddy,' Luke said.

Knight turned from the distraught reporter to find his son staring at him expectantly. Then Isabel appeared. 'I want milk too!'

'Bollocks,' Knight muttered, and then said apologetically, 'I forgot the milk, but I'll go and get some right now. This is Karen. She works for the newspaper. She's a friend of mine. She'll sit with you until I get back.'

Pope frowned. 'I don't think . . .'

'Ten minutes,' Knight said. 'Fifteen, tops.'

The reporter looked at Luke and Isabel who studied her, and said reluctantly, 'Okay.'

'I'll be right back,' Knight promised.

He ran across the playground and out through the Royal Hospital grounds towards his home in Chelsea. The one-way trip took six minutes exactly and he arrived sweating and breathing hard.

Knight put his key in the lock and was upset to find the door unlocked. Had he forgotten to secure it? It was completely unlike him, but he was operating on limited, broken sleep, wasn't he?

He stepped inside the front hallway. A floorboard creaked somewhere above him. And then a door clicked shut.

Chapter 67

KNIGHT TOOK FOUR quiet steps to the front hall closet and reached up high on a shelf for his spare Beretta.

He heard a noise like furniture moving and slid off his shoes, thinking: My room or the kids'?

Knight climbed the stairs as stealthily as a cat, looking all around. He heard another noise ahead of him. It was coming from his room. He crept down the hallway, gun up, and peered inside, seeing the desk on top of which his laptop lay shut.

He paused, listening intently. For several moments he heard nothing more.

Then the loo flushed. Thieves commonly relieve themselves in the homes of their victims. Knight had known that for years and figured he was dealing with a burglar. Stepping over the threshold into his bedroom, he aimed the pistol at the closed door. The handle twisted. Knight flipped off the safety.

The door swung open.

Marta stepped out and spotted Knight. And the gun.

Gasping, her hand flew to her chest and she screamed, 'Don't shoot!'

Knight's brows knitted, but he lowered his pistol several inches. 'Marta?'

The nanny was gasping. 'You scared me, Mr Knight! My God, my heart feels like the fireworks.'

'I'm sorry,' he said, dropping the pistol to his side. 'What are you doing here? I'm not supposed to see you for another hour.'

'I came early so you can go to work early,' Marta replied breathlessly. 'You left me the key. I came in, saw the buggy gone, and thought you'd gone to the park, so I started to clean the kitchen and then came up to do the nursery.'

'But you're up here in my bedroom,' Knight said.

'I'm sorry,' Marta replied plaintively, and then, in an embarrassed tone, she added: 'I had to pee. Badly.'

After a moment's pause in which he saw no guile on the nanny's part, he pocketed the gun. 'I apologise, Marta. I'm under stress. I overreacted.'

'It's both our faults, then,' Marta said, just before Knight's phone rang.

He snatched it up and immediately heard Isabel and Luke crying hysterically.

'Pope?' he said.

'Where are you?' the reporter demanded in a harried voice. 'You said you'd be right back, and your kids are throwing a world-class shit fit.'

'Two minutes,' he promised and hung up. He looked at Marta, who appeared worried. 'My friend,' he said. 'She's not very good with kids.'

Marta smiled. 'Then it is a very good thing I came early, yes?'

'A very good thing,' Knight said. 'But we're going to have to run.'

He sprang down the stairs and into the kitchen, seeing that the breakfast dishes had been cleaned and put away. He got milk and put it, some biscuits, and two plastic cups in a bag.

He locked the front door and together they hurried back to the park, where Luke was sitting off by himself in the grass, whacking the ground with his shovel, while Isabel knelt in the sandbox, crying and imitating an ostrich.

Pope was just standing there, out of her league, baffled about what to do.

Marta swooped in and gathered up Luke. She tickled his belly, which caused him to giggle and then to cry, 'Marta!'

Isabel heard that, stopped crying, and pulled her hair out of the sand. She spotted Knight coming towards her and broke into a grin. 'Daddy!'

Knight scooped up his daughter, brushed the

sand from her hair, and kissed her. 'Daddy's here. So is Marta.'

'I want milk!' Isabel said, pouting.

'Don't forget the biscuits,' Knight said, handing his daughter and the sack containing the milk to the concerned nanny, who brought the kids over to a picnic table and began to feed them.

'What caused the meltdown?' Knight asked Pope.

Flustered, the reporter said, 'I don't know, actually. It was just like there was a time bomb ticking that I couldn't hear until it went off.'

'That happens a lot,' Knight remarked with a laugh.

Pope studied Marta. 'The nanny been with you long?'

'Not a week yet,' Knight replied. 'But she's bloody fantastic. Best I've—'

Pope's mobile rang. She answered and listened. After several moments she cried, 'No fucking way! We'll be there in twenty minutes!'

The reporter clicked off her phone, and spoke with quiet urgency, 'That was Hooligan. He pulled a fingerprint off the package that Cronus sent me last night. He's run it and wants us at Private London ASAP.'

Chapter 68

SURROUNDED BY A four-day growth of orange beard, the grin on Hooligan's face put Knight in mind of a mad leprechaun. It didn't hurt the image when Private London's chief scientist did a jig out from behind his lab desk, and said, 'We've got a third name and, as Jack might say, it's a whopper that set off alarms. I've had two calls from The Hague in the past hour.'

'The Hague?' Knight said, confused.

'Special prosecutor for Balkan War Crimes Tribunal,' Hooligan said as Jack rushed in, looking pale and drawn. 'The print belongs to a woman wanted for genocide.'

It was all coming at Knight so fast that his mind was awhirl with disjointed thoughts. Daring and Farrell had both worked with NATO in some capacity at the end of the Balkan war, right? But war crimes? Genocide?

'Let's hear it,' Jack said.

Hooligan went to a laptop computer and gave it several commands. On a large screen at one end of the lab, a grainy black and white photograph of a young teenage girl appeared. Her hair was chopped short in a bowl cut and she wore a white, collared shirt. Knight could not tell much more about her because the photograph was so blurry.

'Her name is Andjela Brazlic,' Hooligan said. 'This picture was taken approximately seventeen years ago, according to the war-crimes prosecutor, which puts her in her late twenties now.'

'What did she do?' Knight asked, trying to match the girl's blurry face with the charge of genocide.

Hooligan gave his computer another command and the screen jumped to an overexposed snapshot of three girls wearing white shirts and dark skirts, standing with a man and a woman whose heads were out of frame. Knight recognised the bowl-cut hairdo on one and realised he'd been looking at a blow-up of this picture. Glaring sunlight obliterated the faces of the other two girls, who had longer hair and were taller. He guessed them to be fourteen and fifteen.

Hooligan cleared his throat and said, 'Andjela and her two sisters there – Senka, the oldest, and Nada, the middle girl – were indicted on charges that they participated in genocidal acts in and around the city of Srebrenica in late 1994 and early 1995, near the end of the civil war that exploded on the break-up of the former Yugoslavia. Allegedly the sisters were part of the kill squads Ratko Mladic oversaw that executed eight thousand Bosnian Muslim men and boys.'

'Jesus,' Pope said. 'What makes three young girls join a kill squad?'

'Gang rape and murder,' Hooligan replied. 'According to the special prosecutor, not long after this photograph was taken in April 1994 Andjela and her sisters were raped repeatedly over the course of three days by members of a Bosnian militia that also tortured and murdered their parents in front of them.'

'That would do it,' Jack said.

Hooligan nodded grimly. 'The sisters are alleged to have executed more than one hundred Bosnian Muslims in retaliation. Some were shot. But most were struck through the skull, and post-mortem through the genitals, with a pickaxe – the same sort of weapon that was ultimately used to kill their mother and father.'

'It gets worse,' Private London's chief scientist pressed on. 'The war-crimes prosecutor told me that eyewitnesses testified that the sisters took sadistic delight in killing the Bosnian boys and desecrating their bodies, so much so that the terrified mothers of Srebrenica came up with an apt nickname for them.'

'What was that?' Knight asked.

'The Furies.'

'Jesus,' Jack said. 'It's them.'

A moment of silence passed before Jack said to the reporter, 'Karen, would you excuse us for a moment? We have to discuss something that has nothing to do with this case.'

Pope hesitated, and then nodded awkwardly, saying, 'Oh, of course.'

When she'd gone, Jack looked back at Knight and Hooligan. 'I have something to tell you that's going to be tough to hear.'

'We've been fired from the Olympic security team?' Knight asked.

Jack shook his head. He looked pale. 'Far from it. No, I just left a meeting with investigators from the Air Accident Investigative Branch, the ones looking into the plane crash.'

'And?' Hooligan said.

Jack swallowed hard. 'They've found evidence of a bomb aboard the jet. There was no mechanical malfunction. Dan, Kirsty, Wendy and Suzy were all murdered.'

Chapter 69

'THIS BETTER BE good, Peter,' Elaine Pottersfield grumbled. 'I'm under insane pressure, and I'm not in much of a mood for a fine-dining experience.'

'We're both under insane pressure,' Knight shot back. 'But I have to talk to you. And I need to eat. And you need to eat. I figured why not meet here and kill three birds with one stone.'

'Here' was a restaurant near Tottenham Court Road called Hakkasan. It had been Kate's favourite Chinese restaurant in London. It was also the inspector's favourite Chinese restaurant in London.

'But this place is packed,' Pottersfield said, taking a seat with some reluctance. 'It will probably take an hour to . . .'

'I've already ordered,' Knight said. 'The dish Kate liked best.'

His sister-in-law looked down at the table. At that angle she looked every bit Kate's older sister. 'Okay,' she said at last. 'Why am I here, Peter?'

Knight gave her the rundown on the Brazlic sisters – the Furies – and their alleged war crimes. As he was finishing his summary, their dinner, a double order of Szechuan Mugyu beef, arrived.

Pottersfield waited until the waiter left before asking, 'And when were these sisters last heard of?'

'July 1995, not long after the NATO-supervised ceasefire expired,' Knight replied. 'They were supposedly apprehended by Bosnian police officers after the mother of two of their victims recognised the Furies when they tried to buy food in a local produce market. According to that same mother, the girls were taken at night to a police station in a small village south-west of Srebrenica where they were to be turned over to NATO forces who were investigating the atrocities.'

Pottersfield said, 'And what? They escaped?'

Knight nodded. 'Villagers heard automatic-weapon fire coming from inside the police station in the dead of night. They were too frightened to investigate until the following morning when the bodies of seven Bosnians, including the two police officers, were found massacred. The Brazlics have been hunted ever since, but none of them surfaced until today.'

'How did they get out of the police station?' Pottersfield asked. 'I'm assuming they'd been placed in restraints.'

'You would think so,' Knight agreed. 'But here's the other strange thing. Mladic's kill squads used, for the most part, Soviet-era full-copper-jacket ammunition. So did the Bosnian police. It was Red Army surplus and found in all their unfired weapons. But the seven Bosnian men in the station were killed by 5.56-millimetre rounds throwing a very different kind of bullet – the kind given to NATO peacekeepers, in fact.'

Pottersfield picked at her meal with chopsticks, thinking. After several bites, she said, 'So maybe one of the men who were killed that night had a NATO weapon and the sisters got hold of it and fought their way out.'

'That's one plausible scenario. Or a third party helped them, someone who was part of the NATO operation. I'm leaning towards that explanation.'

'Evidence?' she asked.

'The bullets, primarily,' Knight said. 'But also because James Daring and Selena Farrell were in the Balkans in the mid-1990s attached to that NATO mission. Daring was assigned to protect antiquities from looters. But apart from that photo I saw of Farrell holding an automatic weapon in front of a NATO field truck, her role in the operation remains a mystery to me.'

'Not for long,' Pottersfield said. 'I'll petition NATO for her files.'

'The war-crimes prosecutor is already on it,' Knight said.

The Scotland Yard inspector nodded, but her focus was far away. 'So what's your theory: that this third entity in the escape – Daring or Farrell or both – could be Cronus?'

'Perhaps,' Knight said. 'It follows, anyway.'

'In some manner,' she allowed while still managing to sound sceptical.

They ate in silence for several minutes before Pottersfield said: 'There's only one thing that bothers me about this theory of yours, Peter.'

'What's that?' Knight asked.

His sister-in-law squinted and waved her chopsticks at him. 'Let's say you're right and Cronus was the person or persons who helped the sisters escape, and let's say that Cronus managed to turn these war criminals into anarchists, Olympics haters, whatever you want to call them.

'The evidence to date reveals people who are not only brutal, but brutally effective. They managed to penetrate some of the toughest security in the world twice, kill, and escape twice.'

Knight saw where she was going: 'You're saying they're detail-orientated, they've planned to the last factor, and yet they make mistakes with these letters.'

Pottersfield nodded. 'Hair, skin, and now a fingerprint.'

'Don't forget the wig,' Knight said. 'Anything on that?'

'Not yet, though this war-crimes angle should help us if DNA samples were ever taken from the sisters.'

Knight ate a couple more bites, and then said, 'There's also a question as to whether Farrell, Daring or both of them had the wherewithal, the financial means to concoct a deadly assault on the Olympics. It has to cost money, and lots of it.'

'I thought of that too,' Pottersfield replied. 'This morning we took a look at James Daring's bank accounts and credit-card statements. That television show has made him wealthy. And his accounts show several major cash withdrawals lately. Professor Farrell, on the other hand, lives more modestly. Except for hefty purchases at expensive fashion boutiques here and in Paris, and getting her hair done at trendy salons once a month, she leads a fairly austere life.'

Knight recalled the dressing table and the high-end clothes in the professor's bedroom and tried again to make it fit with the dowdy woman he'd met at King's College. He couldn't. Was she dressing up to meet Daring? Was there something between them that Knight and his colleagues weren't aware of?

He glanced at his watch. 'I'll pay and take my leave, then. The new nanny is working overtime.'

Pottersfield looked away as he put his napkin on the table and raised his hand for the bill. 'How are they?' she asked. 'The twins?'

'They're fine,' Knight said, and then gazed sincerely at his sister-in-law. 'I know they would love to meet their Aunt Elaine. Don't you think they deserve to have a relationship with their mother's sister?'

It was as if invisible armour instantly enclosed the Scotland Yard inspector. Her posture went tight and she said, 'I'm simply not there yet. I don't know if I could bear it.'

'Their birthday's a week from Saturday.'

'Do you honestly think I could ever forget that day?' Pottersfield asked, getting up from the table.

'No, Elaine,' Knight replied. 'And neither will I. Ever. But I have hope that at some point I'll be able to forgive that day. I hope you will, too.'

Pottersfield said, 'You'll settle the bill?'

Knight nodded. She turned to leave. He called after her, 'Elaine, I'll probably be having a birthday party for them at some point. I'd like it if you came.'

Pottersfield looked over her shoulder at him, her voice raspy when she replied. 'Like I said, Peter, I don't know if I'm there yet.'

Chapter 70

IN THE TAXI on the way home to Chelsea, Knight wondered if his sister-in-law would ever forgive him. Did it matter? It did. It depressed him to think that his kids might never get to know their mother's last living relative.

Rather than sink into a mood, however, he forced his mind to other thoughts.

Selena Farrell was a *fashionista*?

It bothered him so much that he called Pope. She answered, sounding as if she was in a bad temper. They'd had an argument in Hooligan's lab earlier in the day about when and how she should deal with the war-crimes information. She'd wanted to publish immediately, but Knight and Jack had argued that she should wait to get independent corroboration from The Hague and from Scotland Yard. Neither man wanted the information attributed to Private.

Pope said, 'So did your sister-in-law corroborate the fingerprint match?'

'I think that will probably be tomorrow at the earliest,' Knight said.

'Brilliant,' the reporter said sarcastically. 'And the prosecutor at The Hague is not returning my calls. So I've got nothing for tomorrow.'

'There's something else you could be looking into,' Knight offered as the taxi pulled up in front of his home. He paid the driver and stood out on the pavement, describing the dressing table and clothes at Selena Farrell's home.

'High fashion?' Pope asked, incredulous. 'Her?'

'Exactly my reaction,' Knight said. 'Which means a lot of things, it seems to me. She had to have had sources of money outside academia. Which means she had a secret life. Find it, and you just might find her.'

'All well and good for you to say,' Pope began.

God, she irritated him. 'It's what I've got,' he snapped. 'Look, Pope, I have to tuck my kids in. I'll talk to you tomorrow.'

He hung up, feeling as though the case had consumed him the way the mythical Cronus had consumed his own children. That thought left him supremely frustrated. If it wasn't for the Olympics he'd be working full-time to find out who had killed his colleagues at Private and why. When this was over he told himself he would not stop until he solved that crime.

Knight went inside and climbed the stairs, hearing a door slide over carpet, followed by footsteps. Marta was leaving the nursery. She saw Knight, and held her index finger to her lips.

'Can I say goodnight?' he whispered.

'They're already asleep,' Marta said.

Knight glanced at his watch. It was just eight. 'How do you do that? I can never get them down before ten.'

'An old Estonian technique.'

'You'll have to teach it to me sometime,' Knight said. 'Eight a.m.?'

She nodded. 'I will be here.' Then she hesitated before moving past him and going down the stairs. Knight followed her, thinking he'd have a beer and then get to sleep early.

Marta put on her jacket and started to open the front door before looking back at him, 'Have you caught the bad people?'

'No,' Knight said. 'But I feel like we're getting awfully close.'

'That's good,' she said. 'Very, very good.'

Chapter 71

SITTING AT HER desk in the *Sun*'s newsroom later that evening, half-watching the highlights of England's remarkable victory over Ghana in the final round of group-stage football, Pope fumed yet again over the fact that she could not reveal the link between Cronus and the Furies and war crimes in the Balkans.

Even her editor, Finch, had told her that, amazing as it was, she did not have enough to publish the story; and might not have for two, maybe even three days, at least until the prosecutor in The Hague agreed to talk to her on the record.

Three days! she moaned to herself. That's Saturday. They'll never publish that kind of story on a Saturday. That means they'll wait for Sunday. Four days!

Every hard-news journalist in London was working the Cronus case now, all of them chasing Pope, trying to match or better her stories. Until today she'd been way out ahead of the curve. Now, however, she feared that the war-crime angle might leak before she could lay full claim to it in print.

And what was she to do in the meantime? Sit here? Wait for the war-crimes prosecutor to call? Wait for Scotland Yard to run the print against their database and confirm it to the world?

The situation was driving her batty. She should go home. Get some rest. But she was unnerved by the fact that Cronus knew where she lived: she felt afraid to go home. Instead, she started poring over every angle of the story, trying to figure out where she could best push it forward.

At last her thoughts turned grudgingly to Knight's advice that she should look more closely into Selena Farrell. But it had been four days since the professor's DNA had been matched to the hair found in the first letter from Cronus, and three days since MI5 and Scotland Yard had launched the manhunt for her, and there'd been nothing. She'd vanished.

Who am I to look if *they* can't find her? Pope thought before her pugnacious side asserted itself: Well, why *not* me?

The reporter chewed on her lip, thinking about Knight's revelation that Farrell was a fashion connoisseur, and then remembered the full list of evidence taken from the professor's house and office that he had sent her the day before at the Aquatics Centre. She'd looked through the list, of course, searching for the evidence of anti-Olympics sentiment, checking the essays denouncing the Games, and the recording of the flute music.

But she hadn't been looking for clothes, now had she?

Pope called up the evidence list and began scrolling. It didn't take her long to find references to cocktail dresses from Liberty of London and skirts and blouses from Alice by Temperley. Big-money frocks. Hundreds of pounds, easy.

Knight said she'd had a secret life. Maybe he was right.

Excited now, Pope began scouring her notebook, looking for a phone number for the professor's research assistant, Nina Langor. Pope had talked to the assistant several times during the past four days, but Langor had consistently claimed that she was baffled by her boss's sudden disappearance and had no idea why Farrell's DNA would have surfaced in the Cronus investigation.

The research assistant answered her phone guardedly, and sounded shocked when Pope told her about Farrell's haute-couture lifestyle.

'What?' Langor said. 'No. That's impossible. She used to make fun of fashion and hairdos. Then again, she used to wear a lot of scarves.'

'Did she have any boyfriends?' Pope asked. 'Someone to dress up for?'

Langor got defensive. 'The police asked the same thing. I'll tell you what I told them. I believe she's gay, but I don't know for sure. She's a private person.'

The assistant said she had to go, leaving Pope at eleven o'clock that Wednesday evening feeling as if she'd run multiple marathons in the past six days and was suddenly exhausted. But she forced herself to return to the evidence list and continued on, finding nothing until the very end, when she saw reference to a torn pink matchbook with the letters *CAN* on it.

She tried to imagine a pink matchbook bearing the letters *CAN*. Cancer institute? Breast cancer awareness? Wasn't pink the colour of that movement? Something else?

Stymied by her inability to make the evidence talk, Pope made a last-ditch effort around midnight, using a technique that she'd discovered quite by accident a few years before when she'd been presented with disparate facts that made no sense.

She started typing strings of words into Google to see what came up.

'PINK CAN LONDON' yielded nothing of interest. 'PINK CAN LONDON OLYMPICS' got her no further.

Then she typed: 'LONDON PINK CAN GAY FASHION DESIGN LIBERTY ALICE'.

Google gnawed at that search query and then spat out the results.

'Oh,' Pope said, smiling. 'So you are a lipstick lesbian, professor.'

Chapter 72

AT TEN THE following evening Pope turned along Carlisle Street in Soho.

It had been an insanely aggravating and fruitless day. The reporter had called the war-crimes prosecutor ten times and had been assured each time by a saccharine, infuriatingly polite secretary that he would be returning her call soon.

Worse, she'd had to follow a story in the *Mirror* that described the intense global manhunt for Selena Farrell and James Daring. Worse still, she'd had to follow a story in *The Times* about initial autopsy and toxicology reports on the dead Chinese gymnastics coaches. Holes the size of bee stings had been found in both their necks. But they had not died of anaphylactic shock. They'd succumbed to a deadly neurotoxin called *calciseptine* derived and synthesised from the venom of a black mamba snake.

A black mamba? Pope thought for the hundredth time that day. Every paper in the world was going loony over that angle, and she'd missed it.

It only made her more determined when she went through the doors of the Candy Club, submitted to a security search of her bag by a very large Maori woman, and then entered the ground-floor bar. The club was surprisingly crowded for a Thursday night, and the reporter instantly felt uncomfortable when she noticed several glamorous women watching her, evaluating her.

But Pope walked right up to them, introduced herself, and showed them a photograph of Selena Farrell. The bar staff hadn't seen her, nor had the next six women the reporter asked.

She went back to the bar then, spotting a pink matchbook that looked like the one described in the evidence list. One of the bartenders came over to her, and Pope asked what she'd recommend for a cocktail.

'Candy Nipple?' the bartender said. 'Butterscotch schnapps and Baileys?'

The reporter wrinkled her nose. 'Too sweet.'

'Pimm's, then,' said a woman on the barstool next to Pope. Petite, blonde, late thirties, and extremely attractive, she held up a highball glass with a mint sprig sticking out from the top. 'Always refreshing on a hot summer's night.'

'Perfect,' Pope replied, smiling weakly at the woman.

Pope had meant to show the picture of Farrell to the bartender, but she'd already walked away to prepare her Pimm's. Pope set the photo on the bar and turned to the woman who'd recommended the drink. She was studying the reporter in mild amusement.

'First time at the Candy Club?' the woman asked.

Pope flushed. 'Is it that obvious?'

'To the trained eye,' the woman said, a hint of lechery crossing her face as she held out a well-manicured hand. 'I'm Nell.'

'Karen Pope,' she said. 'I write for the *Sun*.'

Nell's eyebrows rose. 'I do so enjoy Page 3.'

Pope laughed nervously. 'Unfortunately, I don't.'

'Pity,' Nell said, her face falling. 'Not even a wee bit?'

'A pity, but no,' Pope replied, and then showed Nell the photograph.

Nell sighed and leaned closer to Pope to study the picture of Farrell with no make-up, and wearing a matching peasant skirt and scarf.

'No,' Nell said, with a dismissive gesture. 'I know I've never seen *her* here. She isn't exactly the type. But *you*, I must say, most definitely fit in here.'

Pope laughed again before gesturing at the picture and saying, 'Think of her in a tight cocktail dress from Liberty of London or Alice by Temperley, and her hair done by Hair by Fairy, and, well, you can't see it from this angle, but she has this tiny mole on her jaw.'

'A mole?' Nell sniffed. 'You mean with little hairs sticking out of it?'

'More like a beauty spot. Like Elizabeth Taylor used to have?'

Nell looked confused, and then she studied the photograph again.

A moment later, she gasped, 'My God – it's Syren!'

Chapter 73

Friday, 3 August 2012

KNIGHT HEARD FEET padding around at seven-thirty that morning. He opened his eyes and saw Isabel holding her Pooh Bear blanket.

'Daddy,' she said in high seriousness. 'When am I three?'

'August the eleventh,' Knight grumbled, and glanced at that picture of Kate on the moor in Scotland. 'A week from tomorrow, honey.'

'What's today?'

'Friday.'

Isabel thought about that. 'So one more Saturday and one more Friday, and then the next one?'

Knight smiled. His daughter always fascinated him with the out-of-the box way her mind worked. 'Yes,' he replied. 'Give me a kiss.'

Isabel kissed him. Then her eyes widened. 'We get presents?'

'Of course, Bella,' Knight replied. 'It will be your birthday.'

She got wildly excited, clapping her hands and dancing in a tight circle before stopping dead in her tracks. 'What presents?'

'What presents?' Luke asked from the doorway. He was yawning as he came into the room.

'I can't tell you that,' Knight said. 'It won't be a surprise.'

'Oh,' Isabel said, disappointed.

'Lukey three?' his son asked.

'Next week,' Knight assured him, and then heard the front door open. Marta. Early again. The world's first perfect nanny.

Knight put on a tracksuit bottom and a T-shirt, and carried the twins down the stairs. Marta smiled at them. 'Hungry?'

'It's my birthday two Fridays and a Saturday from now,' Isabel announced.

'And Lukey,' her brother said. 'I'm three.'

'You *will* be three,' Knight corrected.

'We'll have to plan a party then,' Marta said, as Knight set the kids down.

'A party!' Isabel cried and clapped.

Luke hooted with delight, spun in circles, and cried, 'Party! Party!'

The twins had never had a birthday party, or at least not on the exact date of their birth. That day had been so bitter-sweet that Knight had moved cake and ice-cream celebrations to a day or two later, and had kept the celebration deliberately low-key. He was torn now over how he should reply to Marta's suggestion.

Luke stopped spinning and said, 'Balloons?'

'Mr Knight?' Marta said. 'What do you think? Balloons?'

Before Knight could answer, the doorbell rang, and then rang again, and again, and again, followed by someone pounding the knocker so hard that it sounded like a mason chipping stone.

'Who the hell is that?' Knight groaned, heading towards the door. 'Can you get them breakfast, Marta?'

'Of course,' she said.

The pounding on the door knocker started again before he looked through the security peephole to see an exasperated Karen Pope on his front step.

'Karen,' he called out to her. 'I don't have time to—'

'Make time,' she barked. 'I've made a break in the case.'

Knight ran his fingers back through his sleep-ravaged hair, and then opened the door. Looking like she'd been up all night herself, Pope barged in while Marta went towards the kitchen with Luke and Isabel.

'Lukey want sausages,' Luke said.

'Sausages it is,' Marta replied as they disappeared.

'What's the break?' Knight asked Pope, heading into the living area and clearing enough toys off the couch for them to sit down.

'You were right,' the reporter said. 'Selena Farrell had a secret life.'

She told Knight that the professor had an alter ego called Syren St James, a name that she would adopt when she went to the Candy Club to pick up women. As Syren, Farrell was everything the professor was not: flamboyant, funny, promiscuous, a party girl of the highest order.

'Selena Farrell?' Knight said, shaking his head.

'Think of that part of her as Syren St James,' Pope replied. 'It helps.'

'And you know all this how?' he asked, smelling sausages frying off in the kitchen.

'From a woman named Nell who frequents the Candy Club and has had several one-night stands with Syren over the past few years. She identified her by that mole at her jawline.'

Knight remembered how he'd thought the professor would have been attractive under the right circumstances. He should have listened to his instincts.

'When was the last time she saw, uh, Syren?' he asked.

'Last Friday, late in the afternoon before the Games opened,' Pope replied. 'She came into the Candy Club dressed to kill, but blew Nell out, saying she already had a date. Later, Nell saw Syren leave with a stranger, a woman wearing a pill hat with a black lace veil that covered the upper part of her face. I'm thinking that woman could be one of the Brazlic sisters, aren't you?'

In Knight's kitchen, something fragile crashed and shattered.

Chapter 74

THE OLYMPIC VILLAGE is well past its first stirring now. Swimmers from Australia are already heading to the Aquatics Centre where the men's 1,500-metre heats will unfold. Cyclists from Spain are going to the Velodrome for a quick ride before the men's team pursuit competition later in the day. A Moldovan handball team just passed me. So did that American basketball player – that one with the name I always forget.

It's irrelevant. What matters is that we're at the end of week one and every athlete in the village is trying not to think of me and my sisters, trying not to ask themselves whether they'll be next. And yet they can't help but think of us, now can they?

As I predicted, the media has gone berserk over our story. For every weepy television tale of an athlete overcoming cancer or the death of a loved one to win a gold medal, there have been three more about the effect we are having on the games.

Tumours, they've called us. Scourges. Black stains on the Olympics.

Ha! The only tumours and black stains are those generated by the Games. I'm just exposing them for what they are.

Indeed, out walking among the Olympians like this – anonymous, earnest, and in disguise, another me – I'm feeling that, except for a few minor glitches, everything has gone remarkably according to plan. Petra and Teagan took vengeance on the Chinese and executed their escape perfectly. Marta has ingratiated herself into Knight's life and monitors his virtual world, giving me an inside view of whatever investigations have been launched and why. And earlier this morning, I retrieved the second bag of magnesium shavings, the one I hid in the Velodrome during its construction almost two years ago. Right where I left it.

The only thing that bothers me is—

My disposable mobile rings. I grimace. Petra and Teagan were given precise orders before they left on their latest assignment at midday yesterday, and those orders forbade them from calling me at all. Marta, then.

I answer and snap at her before she can speak, 'No names, and toss that phone when we're finished talking. Do you know the mistake?'

'Not exactly,' Marta says, with a note of alarm in

her voice that is quite rare and therefore instantly troubling.

'What's wrong?' I demand.

'They know,' she whispers. In the background I hear a little monster crying.

The crying and Marta's whisper hit me like stones and car bombs, setting off a raging storm in my skull that destroys my balance, and I go down on one knee for fear that I'll keel over. The light all around me seems ultraviolet except for a diesel-green halo that pulses in time with the ripping sensations in my skull.

'You all right?' a man's voice asks.

I can hear the crying on the phone, which now hangs in my hand at my side. I look up through the green halo and see a grounds worker standing a few feet from me.

'Fine,' I manage, fighting for control against a rage building in me, making me want to cut the grounds worker's head off for spite. 'I'm just a little dizzy.'

'You want me to call someone?'

'No,' I say, struggling to my feet. Though the green halo is still pulsing and the ripping goes on in my skull, the air around me is shimmering a bit less.

Walking away from the groundsman, I growl into the phone: 'Shut that goddamn kid up.'

'Believe me, if I could, I would,' Marta retorts. 'Here, I'll go outside.'

I hear a door shut and the beeping of a car horn. 'Better?'

Only a little. My stomach churns when I ask, 'What do they know?'

In a halting voice, Marta tells me that they know about the Brazlic sisters, and it all starts again: the ripping, the diesel-green halo, and the ultraviolent rage that so completely permeates me now that I feel like a cornered animal, a monster myself, ready to rip out the throat of anyone who might approach me.

There's a bench ahead on the path and I sit on it. 'How?'

'I don't know,' Marta replies, and then explains how she overheard Pope mention 'Andjela and the other Brazlic sisters', which had so shocked her that she'd dropped a glass bowl, which had shattered on the kitchen floor.

Wanting to throttle her, I say, 'Does Knight suspect?'

'Me? No,' Marta says. 'I acted embarrassed and apologetic when I told him the glass was wet. He told me not to worry about it, and to make extra sure the floor was free of glass before letting his little brats walk around.'

'Where are they now, Knight and Pope? What else do they know?'

'He left with her ten minutes ago, and said he

would not be back until late,' Marta replies. 'I don't know any more than what I've told you. But if they know about the sisters, then they know what the sisters did in Bosnia, and the war-crimes prosecutors know we are in London.'

'They probably do,' I agree at last. 'But nothing more. If they had more, they'd be tracking you by one of your current names. They'd be at our doors.'

After a moment's silence, Marta asks, 'So what do I do?'

Feeling increasingly sure that the gap between who the Furies were and who they have become is wide enough to prevent a connection, I reply, 'Stay close to those children. We may need them in the coming days.'

Chapter 75

BY SEVEN P.M. THE intensity inside the Olympic Stadium was beyond electric, Knight thought from his position in the stands on the west side of the venue, high above the track's finish line. The Private London investigator could sense the anticipation rippling through the ninety thousand souls lucky enough to have won a ticket to see who would be the fastest man on Earth. He could also see and hear fear competing with anticipation. People were wondering whether Cronus would attack here.

The event was certainly high-profile enough. The sprint competition so far had gone down as expected. Both Shaw and Mundaho had been brilliant in the 100-metre qualifying heats the day before, each of them dominating and winning easily. But while the Jamaican was able to rest between races, the Cameroonian had been forced to run in the classifications for the 400-metres.

Mundaho had performed almost superhumanly, turning in a time of 43.22 seconds, four one-hundredths of a second off Henry Ivey's world-record performance of 43.18 at the 1996 Atlanta Games.

Two hours ago, Mundaho and Shaw had won their 100-metre semi-final heats, with the Cameroonian just two one-hundredths off Shaw's world record of 9.58 seconds. The men were getting ready to face each other in the 100-metre dash final. After that, Shaw would rest and Mundaho would have to run in the 400-metre semi-finals.

Gruelling, Knight thought as he scanned the crowd through his binoculars. Could Mundaho do it? Win the 100, 200 and 400 at a single Olympic Games?

In the end, did it matter? Would people really care after all that had happened to London 2012? Aside from the joy that Londoners had expressed earlier in the day when Mary Duckworth won the women's marathon, the past forty-eight hours had seen a dramatic ratcheting-up of the anxiety surrounding the Games. On Saturday, the *Sun* had finally published Pope's story describing the link between the killings and the wanted war-crime suspects, the Serbian Brazlic sisters. She had also detailed how both James Daring and Selena Farrell had served in the Balkans at about the same time as the Brazlics were actively executing innocent men and boys in and around the city of Srebrenica.

Farrell, it turned out, had been a volunteer UN observer assigned to NATO in the war-torn area. There were still not many details of the professor's exact duties on the mission, but Pope had discovered that Farrell had been badly hurt in some kind of vehicular accident in the summer of 1995 and had been sent home. After a short convalescence, she'd resumed her doctoral studies and gone on with her life.

The story had caused an uproar that grew when, late on Saturday evening, the body of Emanuel Flores, a Brazilian judo referee, was discovered near a rubbish skip in Docklands, several miles from the ExCel Arena where he'd been working and not on Olympic grounds. An expert in hand-to-hand combat, Flores had nevertheless been garrotted with a length of cable.

In a letter to Pope completely devoid of forensic evidence, Cronus claimed that Flores had accepted bribes to favour certain athletes in the judo competition. The documentation supported the allegations in some ways, and not others.

In reaction, broadcasters and journalists around the world were expressing uniform outrage that Cronus and his Furies seemed to be acting at will.

The media were demanding action from the British government. This morning, Uruguay, North Korea, Tanzania and New Zealand had decided to pull their teams from the final week of competition. Members of Parliament and the Greater London Authority had reacted by stridently renewing calls for Mike Lancer to resign or be fired, and for the manhunt for Daring and Farrell to be intensified.

For his part a visibly shaken Lancer had been in front of cameras all day, defending his efforts. Around noon, he had announced that he was relieving F7 of its command over the entrances to the Olympic Park, and bringing in Jack Morgan of Private to oversee the effort. Together with Scotland Yard and MI5, they decided to institute draconian measures at the venues, including secondary screenings, more identification checks, and pat-downs.

It had not been enough to calm the Games. Ten countries, including Russia, floated the idea that the Olympics should be halted until security was assured.

But in an immediate and aggressive response, a staggering number of athletes had signed a digital petition drafted and distributed by the American diver Hunter Pierce that not only condemned the murders, but also defiantly and forcefully demanded that the IOC and LOCOG not give in to the idea of suspending the games.

To their credit, Marcus Morris, London's Mayor and the Prime Minister were listening to the athletes and dismissing calls to halt the Olympics, saying that England had never bent to terrorism and wasn't about to start now.

Despite the dramatic increase in security measures, some fans had stayed away from what was supposed to be the biggest event of the games. Knight could see scattered empty seats, something that would have been considered impossible before the start of the Olympics. But then again almost everything that had happened so far would have been considered impossible before the Games.

'Bloody bastards have ruined it, Knight,' Lancer said bitterly. The security chief had come up alongside Knight as he was scanning the crowd. Like Knight, Lancer wore a radio nub in his ear tuned to the stadium's security frequency. 'No matter what happens from now on, 2012 will always be the tainted—'

The crowd around them leaped to their feet and started cheering wildly. The final competitors in the men's 100-metre dash were coming out onto the track. Shaw, the reigning Olympic champion, entered first, making little 'stutter' sprints and moving his hands like chopping tools.

Mundaho came out onto the track last and jogged in an almost sleepy lope before crouching and then hopping like a kangaroo down the track with such explosive energy that many in the crowd gasped, and Knight thought: Is that possible? Has anyone ever done that before?

'That man's a freak,' Lancer remarked. 'An absolute freak of nature.'

Chapter 76

THE OLYMPIC FLAME atop the Orbit burned without disturbance or deflection and the flags around the stadium hung flat; the wind had died to nothing – perfect conditions for a sprint race.

The radio nub in Knight's ear crackled with calls and responses between Jack, the security crew, and Lancer, who'd moved off to get a different view. Knight looked around. High atop the stadium, SAS snipers lay prone behind their rifles. A helicopter passed overhead. The war birds had been circling the park all day, and the number of armed guards around the track doubled.

Nothing bad is going to happen in here tonight, Knight told himself. An attack would be suicidal.

The sprinters went to starting blocks that relied on a state-of-the art fully automated timing – FAT – system. Each block was built around ultra-sensitive pressure plates linked to computers to catch any false starts. At the finish line and linked to those same computers was an invisible matrix of criss-crossing lasers calibrated to a thousandth of a second.

The crowd was on its feet now, straining for better views as the announcer called the sprinters to their marks. Shaw was running in lane three, and Mundaho in lane five. The Jamaican glanced at the Cameroonian pivoting in front of his blocks. Setting their running shoes into the pressure sensors, the speedsters splayed their fingertips on the track, heads bowed.

Ten seconds, Knight thought. These guys spend their whole lives preparing for ten seconds. He couldn't imagine it: the pressure, the expectations, the will and the hardship involved in becoming an Olympic champion.

'Set,' the judge called, and the sprinters raised their hips.

The gun cracked, the crowd roared, and Mundaho and Shaw were like twin panthers springing after prey. The Jamaican was stronger in the first twenty metres, uncoiling his long legs and arms sooner than the Cameroonian. But in the next forty metres, the ex-boy soldier ran as if he really did have bullets chasing him.

Mundaho caught Shaw at eighty metres, but could not pass the Jamaican.

And Shaw could not lose the Cameroonian.

Together they streaked down the track, chasing history as if the other men in the race weren't even there, and appeared to lean and blow through the finish simultaneously with a time of 9.38, two-tenths of a second better than Shaw's incredible performance at Beijing.

New Olympic Record!

New World Record!

Chapter 77

THE STADIUM ROCKED with cheers for Mundaho and Shaw.

But who had won?

Up on the big screens, the unofficial results had Shaw in first place and Mundaho in second, and yet their times were identical. Through his binoculars, Knight could see both men gasping for air, hands on their hips, looking not at each other but up at the screens replaying the race in slow motion while judges examined data from the lasers at the finish line.

Knight heard the announcer say that while there had been ties in judged Olympic events like gymnastics in the past, and a tie between two American swimmers at the Sydney 2000 Games, there had never been a tie in any track event at any modern Olympics. The announcer said that the referees would examine photos as well as take the time down to the thousandth of a second.

Knight watched referees huddling by the track, and saw the tallest of them shake his head. A moment later, the screens flashed 'Official Results' and posted Shaw and Mundaho in a dead tie, with a time of 9:382.

'I decline to run another heat,' the referee was heard saying. 'I consider that to have been the greatest foot race of all time and the timing stands. Both men share the world record. Both men win gold.'

The stadium rocked again with cheers, whistles and yells.

Through his binoculars, Knight saw Shaw gazing up at the results and then over at the referee with scepticism and irritation. But then the Jamaican's expression melted into a grin that spread wide across his face. He jogged to Mundaho, who was smiling back at him. They spoke. Then they clasped hands, raised them, and jogged towards their cheering fans, holding the flags of Jamaica and Cameroon above their heads in their free hands.

The men took their long victory lap around the stadium together, and to Knight it was as if a pleasant summer shower had come along to wash foul smoke from the air. Cronus and the Furies now seemed not as powerful a force at the London Olympics as they had been just a few minutes ago.

The sprinters running together in a grand display of sportsmanship was their way of telling the world that the modern Games were still a force to be reckoned with, still a force for good, a force that could demonstrate shared humanity in the face of Cronus's cruel assault.

Shaw said as much when he and Mundaho returned to the finish line and were interviewed by reporters. Knight saw it all up on the big screens.

'When I saw the tie, I could not believe it,' the Jamaican admitted. 'And to tell you the truth, my first response was that I felt angry. I had beaten my own record, but I had not bested everyone as I did in Beijing. But then, after all that has happened at these Games, I saw that the tie was a beautiful thing: good for sprinting, good for athletics, and good for the Olympics.'

Mundaho agreed, saying, 'I am humbled to have run with the great Zeke Shaw. It is the honour of my life to have my name mentioned in the same breath as his.'

The reporter then asked who would win the 200-metre final on Wednesday night. Neither man needed an interpreter. Both tapped their chests and said, 'Me.'

Then each of them laughed and slapped the other on the back.

Knight breathed a sigh of relief when both men

left the stadium. At least Cronus had not targeted those two.

For the next hour, as the men's 1,500-metre semi-finals and the 3,000-metre steeplechase final were run, Knight's mind wandered to his mother. Amanda had promised that she would not turn bitter and retreat into herself as she had after his father's death.

But Knight's past two conversations with Gary Boss indicated that was exactly what she was doing. She would not take his calls. She would not take anyone's calls, even those who wanted to help arrange a memorial for Denton Marshall. According to her assistant, Amanda was spending every waking hour at her table sketching designs, hundreds of them.

He'd wanted to go to see her yesterday and this morning, but Boss had urged him against coming. Boss felt this was something that Amanda needed to go through alone, at least for a few more days.

Knight's heart ached for his mother. He knew at a gut level what she was going through. He'd thought that his own grief for Kate would never end. And in a sense it never would. But through his children he'd found a way to keep going. He prayed his mother would find her own way apart from through work.

Then he thought of the twins. He was about to

call home to say goodnight when the announcer called for competitors in the men's 400-metre semi-finals.

People were on their feet again as Mundaho appeared in the tunnel from the warm-up track. The Cameroonian jogged out, as confident as he had been before the 100-metre event, moving in his characteristic loose-jointed way.

But instead of taking those explosive kangaroo hops, the Cameroonian began to skip and then to bound, his feet coming way up off the track surface and swinging forward as if he were a deer or a gazelle.

What other man can do that? Knight thought in awe. Where did the idea that he could even do that come from? The bullets flying at his back?

The Cameroonian slowed near his blocks on lane one, at the inside rear of the staggered start. Could Mundaho do it? Run a distance four times longer than what he'd just sprinted in world record time?

Evidently Zeke Shaw wanted to know as well because the Jamaican sprinter reappeared in the entry linking the practice track to the stadium and stood with three of the Gurkhas, all looking north towards the runners about to compete.

'Mark,' the official called.

Mundaho set his race shoes with their tiny metal

stubs against the blocks. He crouched and tensed when the official called: 'Set.'

The gun went off in the near-silent stadium.

The Cameroonian leaped off the blocks.

A thousandth of a second later a blinding silver-white light blasted from the blocks as they exploded and disintegrated, throwing out a low-angle wave of fire and hot jagged bits of metal that smashed into Mundaho's lower body from behind, hurling the Cameroonian off his feet and onto the track where he lay crumpled and screaming.

Part Four

MARATHON

Chapter 78

KNIGHT WAS SO shocked that he was unable to move for several seconds. Like many in the stadium he watched and listened in gut-clenched horror as Mundaho writhed on the track, sobbing and groaning in agony as he reached down to his charred and bleeding legs.

The other sprinters had stopped, looking back in shocked disbelief at the carnage in lane one. The intense metallic flame died, leaving the track where the blocks had been scorched and throwing off a burned chemical odour that reminded Knight of signal flares and tyres burning.

Paramedics raced towards the Cameroonian sprinter and several race officials who'd also been hit by the burning shrapnel.

'I want everyone involved with those starting blocks held for questioning,' Lancer bellowed over the radio, barely in control. 'Find the timing judges, referees, everyone. Hold them! All of them!'

Around Knight, fans were coming out of their initial shock, some crying, some cursing Cronus. Many began to move towards the exits while volunteers and security personnel were trying to maintain calm.

'Can you get me on the field, Jack? Mike?' Knight asked.

'That's a negative,' Jack said.

'Double that negative,' Lancer said. 'Scotland Yard has already ordered it sealed for their bomb-forensics unit.'

Knight was suddenly furious that this had happened to Mundaho and to the Olympics – the Games had been caught up in the festering recesses of a twisted mind and made to suffer for it. He did not care what Cronus was going to claim the sprinter had done. Whatever he had or had not done, Mundaho did not deserve to be lying burned on the track. He should have been blowing the rest of the sprinters away in his quest for athletic immortality. Instead, he was being lifted onto a stretcher.

The stadium around Knight began to applaud as paramedics started to wheel the Cameroonian sprinter towards a waiting ambulance. They had IVs in his arm, and had obviously given him drugs, though Knight could still see through his binoculars that the boy soldier was racked with hideous pain.

Knight heard people saying that London would have to end the Games now, and felt furious that Cronus might have won, that it all might be finished now. But then he heard a cynic in the crowd say that there was no chance the Games would be cancelled. He'd read a story in the *Financial Times* that indicated that while London 2012's corporate sponsors and the official broadcasters were publicly aghast at Cronus's actions, they were privately astounded at the twenty-four-hour coverage the Games were receiving, and the public's seemingly inexhaustible appetite for the various facets of the story.

'The ratings for these Olympics are the highest in history,' the cynic said. 'I predict: no chance they'll be cancelled.'

Knight had no time to think about any of it because Shaw, carrying the Cameroonian flag, suddenly came running out of the stadium's entryway, along with the dozen or so competitors who were still in the 400-metre competition. They ran to the rear of the ambulance, exhorting the crowd to chant 'Mundaho! Mundaho!'

The people remaining in the stadium went crazy with emotion, weeping, cheering – and screaming denouncements of Cronus and the Furies.

Despite the medical personnel around him, despite the agony ripping through his body, and despite the drugs, Mundaho heard and saw what his fellow athletes and the fans were doing for him. Before the paramedics slid him into the ambulance, the Cameroonian sprinter raised his right arm and formed a fist.

Knight and everyone else in the stadium cheered the gesture. Mundaho was injured but not broken, burned but still a battle-hardened soldier. He might never run again, but his spirit and the Olympic spirit were still going strong.

Chapter 79

FEELING AS THOUGH she wanted to puke, Karen Pope swallowed antacid pills and stared uncomprehendingly at the television in the *Sun* newsroom as the medics loaded the stout-hearted Cameroonian sprinter into the back of the ambulance. She and her editor, Finch, were waiting for Cronus's latest letter to arrive. So were the Metropolitan Police detectives who'd staked out the lobby, waiting for the messenger and hoping to trace rapidly where the letter had been collected.

Pope did not want to see what Cronus had to say about Mundaho. She did not care. She went to her editor and said, 'I quit, Finchy.'

'You can't quit,' Finch shot back. 'What are you talking about? This is the story of a lifetime you're on here. Ride it, Pope. You've been bloody brilliant.'

She burst into tears. 'I don't want to ride it. I don't want to be part of killing and maiming people. This isn't why I became a journalist.'

317

'You aren't killing or maiming anyone,' Finch said.

'But I'm helping to!' she shouted. 'We're like the people who published the manifesto of the Unabomber over in the States when I was a kid! We're abetting murder, Finch! I'm abetting murder, and I just won't. I can't.'

'You're not abetting murder,' Finch said, softening his voice. 'And neither am I. We are chronicling the murders, the same way journalists before us chronicled the atrocities of Jack the Ripper. You're not helping Cronus, you're exposing him. That's our obligation, Pope. That's *your* obligation.'

She stared at him, feeling small and insignificant. 'Why me, Finch?'

'I dunno. Maybe we'll find out someday. I dunno.'

Pope could not argue any more. She just turned, went to her desk, sat in her seat and put her head down. Then her BlackBerry beeped, alerting her to an incoming message.

Pope exhaled, picked up the mobile and saw that the message was an e-mail with an attachment from 'Cronus'. She wanted to bash her phone into shards, but she kept hearing her editor telling her it was her duty to expose these insane people for what they were.

'Here it is, Finch,' she called tremulously across the room. 'Somebody better tell the police that there's no messenger coming.'

Finch nodded and said, 'I'll do it. You've got an hour to deadline.'

Pope hesitated. Then she got angry and opened the attachment.

Cronus had expected Mundaho to die on the track.

His letter justified the 'killing' as 'just retribution for the crime of hubris', the greatest of all the sins in the era of myth. Arrogance, vanity, in all things prideful and a challenger to the gods, these were the accusations that Cronus threw at Mundaho.

He attached copies of e-mails, texts and Facebook messages between Mundaho and his Los Angeles-based sports agent, Matthew Hitchens. According to Cronus, the discussions between the men were not about competing for greatness for the sake of greatness and for the approval of the gods, as was the case during the ancient Olympics.

Instead, Cronus depicted the correspondence as grossly focused on money and material gain, with lengthy discussions over how winning the sprint jackpot at the London Olympics could increase Mundaho's global value by several hundred million dollars over a twenty-year endorsement career.

'Mundaho put up for sale the gift that the gods gave him,' Cronus concluded. 'He saw no glory in the simple idea of being the fastest man. He saw only gain, and therefore his arrogance towards the gods shone ever more brilliantly. In effect, Mundaho thought of himself as a god, entitled to great riches and to immortality. For the crime of hubris, retribution must always be swift and certain.'

But Mundaho's not dead, Pope thought with satisfaction.

She yelled to Finch: 'Do we have a number for Mundaho's sports agent?'

Her editor thought a moment and then nodded. 'It's here in a master list we compiled for the Games.'

He gave the number to Pope, who texted a message to the sports agent: KNOW U R WITH MUNDAHO. CRONUS MAKES CLAIMS AGAINST HIM AND U. CALL ME.

Pope sent the text, put the phone down and started framing the story on her computer, all the while telling herself that she wasn't helping Cronus. She was fighting him by exposing him.

To her surprise her phone rang within five minutes. It was an audibly distraught Matthew Hitchens en route to the hospital where they'd taken Mundaho. She expressed her condolences and then hit the sports agent with Cronus's charges.

'Cronus isn't giving you the whole story,' Hitchens complained bitterly when she'd finished. 'He doesn't say why Filatri wanted that kind of money.'

'Tell me,' Pope said.

'His plan was to use the money to help children who've survived war zones, especially those who've been kidnapped and forced to fight and die as soldiers in conflicts they don't understand or believe in. We've already set up the Mundaho Foundation for Orphaned Children of War, which was supposed to help Filatri achieve his dream beyond the Olympics. I can show you the formation documents. He signed them long before Berlin, long before there was any talk of him winning three gold medals.'

Hearing that, Pope saw how she could fight back. 'So you're saying that, in addition to ruining the dreams and life of one ex-boy soldier, Cronus's acts may have destroyed the hopes and chances of war-scarred children all over the world?'

Hitchens got choked up, saying: 'I think that just about sums up this tragedy.'

Pope thought of Mundaho, squeezed her free hand into a fist, and said, 'Then that is what my story will say, Mr Hitchens.'

Chapter 80

Monday, 6 August 2012

A FORCE FIVE typhoon rampages through my brain, throwing daggers of lightning brighter than burning magnesium, and everything around me seems saturated with electric blues and reds that don't shimmer or sparkle so much as sear and bleed.

That stupid bitch. She betrayed us. And Mundaho escaped a just vengeance. I feel like annihilating every monster in London.

But I'll settle for one.

I'm more than aware that this move could upset a careful balance I've struck for more than fifteen years. If I handle this wrong, it could come back to haunt me.

The storm in my skull, however, won't let me consider these ramifications for very long. Instead, like watching a flickering old movie, I see myself stick a knife in my mother's thigh, again and again;

and I remember in a cascade of raw emotion how good, how right it felt to have been wronged, and then avenged.

Petra is waiting for me when I reach my home at around four in the morning. Her eyes are sunken, fearful, and red. We are alone. The other sisters have gone on to new tasks.

'Please, Cronus,' she begins. 'The fingerprint was a mistake.'

The typhoon spins furiously again in my mind, and it's as though I'm looking at her down this whirling crackling funnel.

'A mistake?' I say in a soft voice. 'Do you realise what you've done? You've called the dogs in around us. They can smell you, Andjela. They can smell your sisters. They can smell *me*. They've got a cage and gallows waiting.'

Petra's face twists up in an anger equal to my own. 'I believe in you, Cronus. I've given you my life. I killed both Chinese coaches for you. But yes, I made a mistake. One mistake!'

'Not one,' I reply in that same soft voice. 'You left your wig in the wall at the lavatory at the gymnastics venue. They've got your DNA now too. It was impetuous. You did not follow the plan.'

Petra begins to shake and to cry. 'What do you want me to do, Cronus? What can I do to make it right?'

For several moments I don't reply, but then I sigh and walk towards her with open arms. 'Nothing, sister,' I say. 'There's nothing you can do. We fight on.'

Petra hesitates. Then she comes into my arms and hugs me so fiercely that for a moment I'm unsure what to do.

But then my mind seizes on the image of an IV line stuck in my arm and connected to a plastic bag of liquids, and for a fleeting instant I consider what that image has meant to me, how it has consumed me, driven me, made me.

I am much taller than Petra. So when I return her hug, my arms fall naturally around the back of her neck and press her cheek tightly to my chest.

'Cronus,' she begins, before she feels the pressure building.

She begins to choke.

'No!' she manages in a hoarse whisper and then thrashes violently in my arms, trying to punch and kick me.

But I know all too well how dangerous Petra is, how viciously she can fight if she is given a chance; and my grip on her neck is relentless and grows tighter and stronger before I take a swift step back, and then twist my hips sharply.

The action yanks Petra off her feet and swings her through the air with such force that when I whipsaw my weight back the other way, I hear the vertebrae in her neck crack and splinter as if struck by lightning.

Chapter 81

SHORTLY AFTER TEN that morning, Marcus Morris shifted uncomfortably on the pavement outside the Houses of Parliament. But then he looked out forcefully at the cameras and microphones and the mob of reporters gathered around him. 'Though he remains our respected colleague, someone who worked for more than ten years to see these Games realised, Michael Lancer has been relieved of his duties for the duration of the Olympics.'

'About bloody time!' someone shouted, and then the entire mob around *Sun* reporter Karen Pope exploded, roaring questions at the chairman of the London Organising Committee like losing traders in a stock-market commodity pit.

Most of the questions were ones that Pope wanted answered as well. Would the Games go on? Or would they be suspended? If they went on, who would replace Lancer as the committee's chief of security? What about the growing number of countries withdrawing their teams from competition? Should they be listening to the athletes who steadfastly argued against stopping or interrupting the Games?

'We *are* listening to the athletes,' Morris insisted in a strong voice. 'The Olympics will go on. The Olympic ideals and spirit will survive. We will not buckle under to this pressure. Four top specialists from Scotland Yard, MI5, the SAS, and Private will oversee security for us in the final four days of the Games. I am personally heartbroken that some countries have chosen to leave. It is a tragedy for the Games and a tragedy for the athletes. For the rest, the Games go on.'

Morris followed a phalanx of Metropolitan Police officers who opened a hole in the mob and moved towards a waiting car. The vast majority of the media surged as one after the LOCOG leader, bellowing all manner of questions.

Pope did not follow them. She leaned against the wrought-iron fence that surrounded the Parliament buildings and reviewed her notes from the morning and evening before.

In a journalistic coup, she'd tracked down Elaine Pottersfield and learned that, as well as radically intensifying the manhunt for Selena Farrell and

James Daring, law-enforcement efforts were also focusing on the starting blocks that had exploded, maiming Filatri Mundaho.

Mundaho remained in a critical condition in Tower Bridge Hospital, but was said to be exhibiting a 'tremendous fighting spirit' in the wake of two emergency operations to remove the shrapnel and treat his burns.

The starting blocks were another story. Made by Stackhouse Newton and based on the company's famed 'TI008 International Best' system, the starting blocks that had exploded had been used ten times by ten different athletes in the previous days of qualifying.

The blocks had been conducted to and from the track by IOC officials, and had been set up by a crew of timing specialists who claimed to have observed no issue with the blocks before the explosion. Several of those timing specialists had actually been injured at the same time as Mundaho.

Between competitions, the blocks had been locked away in a special room below ground at the stadium. The Olympic track-and-field official who had locked the blocks away on the Saturday evening before the explosion was the same official who had unlocked the storage room late on Sunday afternoon. His name was Javier Cruz, a Panamanian, and he had been the most grievously injured of the race officials, losing an eye to the flying metal.

Scotland Yard bomb experts said the device was a block of metal machined to replicate exactly Stackhouse Newton standards. Only this block had been hollowed enough for shaved magnesium to be inserted along with a triggering device. Magnesium, an incredibly combustible material, explodes and burns with acetylene intensity.

Pottersfield said, 'The device would have killed a normal man. But Mundaho's superhuman reaction time saved his life if not his limbs.'

Pope flipped her notebook closed and reckoned she had enough material for her piece now. She thought of calling Peter Knight to find out if he could add anything to what she knew, but then she spotted a tall figure leaving the visitors' gate at the side of the Houses of Parliament, shoulders hunched forward as he hurried south on St Margaret Street in the direction opposite to that being taken by the now dissipating mob of reporters.

She glanced back at them, realised that none of them had spotted Michael Lancer, and ran after him. She caught up with Lancer as he entered Victoria Tower Gardens.

'Mr Lancer?' she said, slowing beside him. 'Karen Pope – I'm with the *Sun*.'

The former Olympics security chief sighed and looked at her with such despair that she almost didn't have the heart to question him. But she could hear Finch's voice shouting at her.

'Your firing,' she said. 'Do you think it's fair?'

Lancer hesitated, struggling inside, but then he hung his head. 'I do. I wanted the London Games to be the greatest in history and the safest in history. I know that we tried to think of every possible scenario in our preparations over the years. But the truth is that we simply did not foresee someone like Cronus, a fanatic with a small group of followers. In short, I failed. I'll be held responsible for what happened. It's my burden to bear and no one else's. And now, if you'll excuse me, I have to begin to live with that for the rest of my life.'

Chapter 82

Friday, 10 August 2012

LAST TIME I'LL have to visit this hellhole, Teagan thought five days later as she pushed a knapsack through a hole that had been clipped in a chain-link fence surrounding a condemned and contaminated factory building several miles from the Olympic Park.

She wriggled through after the knapsack, then picked it up and glanced at the inky sky. Somewhere a foghorn brayed. Dawn was not far off and she had much to do before she could leave this wretched place for ever.

The dew raised the scent of weeds as she hurried towards the dark shadow of the abandoned building, thinking how her sister Petra must be settling into her new life on Crete. Teagan had read the story about the fingerprint and had feared that Cronus would be insanely angry with her sister. Instead, his reaction had been practical rather than vengeful: her sister was being sent to Greece early to prepare the house where they would live when all this was over.

Entering the building through a window she'd kicked out months before, Teagan imagined the house where Petra was: on a cliff above the Aegean, whitewashed walls dazzling against a cobalt sky, filled with all they could ever want or need.

She turned on a slim red-lensed torch, clipped it to the cap she wore, and used the soft glow to navigate through what had once been the production floor of a textile mill. Wary of loose debris, she made her way to a staircase that descended into a musty basement.

A stronger odour came to her soon enough, so eye-wateringly foul that she stopped breathing through her nose and put the knapsack up on a bench that had only three legs. Bracing her weight against the bench to stop it from rocking, she took out eight IV bags.

Teagan arranged them in their proper order, and then used a hypodermic needle to draw liquid from a vial before shooting equal amounts into four of the bags. Finished, she took the key that hung on a chain around her neck and picked up the eight IV bags, four in each hand.

When she reached the door where the stench was worse, she set the bags on the floor and slid the key into the padlock. The hasp freed with a click. She pocketed the lock and pushed the door open, knowing that if she were to breathe in through her nose now she'd surely retch.

A moan became a groan echoing up out of the darkness.

'Dinner time,' Teagan said, and closed the door behind her.

Fifteen minutes later, she left the storage room feeling confident in the steps she had taken, the work she had done. Four days from now the—

She heard a crash from above her on the old production floor. Voices laughed and jeered before another crash echoed through the abandoned factory. She froze, thinking.

Teagan had been in the factory a dozen times in the last year, and she'd never once encountered another human being inside and did not expect to. The building was contaminated with solvents, heavy metals and other carcinogens, and the exterior fence carried multiple hazardous-waste warning signs to that effect.

Her initial reaction was to go on the attack. But Cronus had been explicit. There were to be no confrontations if they could be avoided.

She switched off her torch, spun around, felt for the door of the storeroom and shut it. She groped in her pocket for the padlock, found it finally, and set the hasp through the iron rings on the door and the jamb. A bottle bounced down the staircase behind her and shattered on the basement floor. She heard footsteps coming and drunken male voices.

Teagan reached up in the darkness to snap the lock shut and felt the hasp catch before she ran a few steps and then paused, unsure. Had it locked?

A torch beam began to play back towards the staircase. She took off without hesitation this time, up on her toes the way sprinters run. She had long ago committed the layout of the factory to memory and dodged into a hall that she knew would take her to a stone stairway and a bulkhead door.

Two minutes later, she was outside. Dawn threw its first rosy fingers of light across the London sky. She heard more crashing and hooting inside the factory and decided it was probably a mob of drunken yobs bent on vandalism. She told herself that once they got a whiff of that basement they wouldn't be doing any further exploring. But as she crawled back through the hole in the fence, all Teagan could think about was the padlock, and whether it had clicked shut after all.

Chapter 83

MID-AFTERNOON THAT second Friday of the Games, the third from last day of competition, Peter Knight entered the lab at Private London and hurried gingerly to Hooligan, holding out a box wrapped in brown paper and parcel tape.

'Is this a bomb?' Knight asked, dead serious.

Private London's chief scientist tore his attention away from one of the *Sun*'s sports pages, which featured a piece on England's chances in the Olympic football final against Brazil. He looked uneasily at the package. 'What makes you think it's a bomb?'

Knight tapped a finger on the return address.

Hooligan squinted. 'Can't read that.'

'Because it's ancient Greek,' Knight said. 'It says, "Cronus".'

'Fuck.'

'Exactly,' Knight said, placing the box on the table

beside the scientist. 'Just picked it up at the front desk.'

'Hear anything inside?' Hooligan asked.

'No ticking.'

'Could be rigged digitally. Or remote-controlled.'

Knight looked queasy. 'Should we clear out? Call in the bomb squad?'

The scientist scratched at his scruffy red beard. 'That's Jack's call.'

Two minutes later, Jack was standing inside the lab, looking at the box. The American appeared exhausted. This was one of the few breaks he'd had from running security at the Olympic Park since taking over on Monday. There had been no further attacks after the Mundaho incident; and that was, in Knight's estimation, largely due to Jack's herculean efforts.

'Can you X-ray the box without blowing us up?' Jack asked.

'Can always try, right?' Hooligan said, picking up the box as if it had teeth.

The scientist took the box to a work table at the far end of the lab. He started up a portable scanner similar to those being used at the Olympic venues, set the box outside the scanner, and waited for it to warm up.

Knight watched the box as if it could seal his fate. Then he swallowed hard – suddenly wanting to leave the lab in case there actually was a bomb in it. He had two children who would be three years old tomorrow. Somehow, he felt, he still had his mother. So could he risk being in a closed room with a potentially explosive device? To get his mind off the danger, he glanced at the screen showing the news highlights and image after image of gold medal-winning athletes from all over the world taking their victory laps, waving the flags of their nations and that of Cameroon.

It had all been spontaneous, the athletes showing their respect to Mundaho and defiance of Cronus. Scores of them had taken up the Cameroonian flag, including the English football team after it won its semi-final against Germany two evenings before. The media was eating it up, selling the gesture as a universal protest against the lunatic stalking the Games.

The American diver Hunter Pierce remained at the forefront of the protest against Cronus. She had been interviewed almost every day since Mundaho's tragedy, and each time she had spoken resolutely of the athletes' solidarity in their refusal to allow the Games to be halted or interrupted.

Mundaho's condition had been upgraded to 'serious': he had third-degree burns and wounds over much of his lower body. But he was said to be alert, well aware of the protests, and taking heart from the global outpouring of support.

As encouraging as that all was, Knight still tore his attention away from the screen in Private London's lab, believing that the assault would not stop simply because of the athletes' protests. Cronus would try to attack again before the end of the Games.

Knight was sure of it. But where would he strike? And when? The relay races tomorrow afternoon? The football final between England and Brazil at Wembley Stadium on Saturday evening? The men's marathon on Sunday? Or the closing ceremony that night?

'Here we go,' Hooligan said, pushing the box received from Cronus onto a small conveyor belt that carried it through the scanner. He twisted the scanner's screen so that they all could see.

The box came into view and so did its contents.

Knight flinched.

'Jesus Christ,' Jack said. 'Are those real?'

Chapter 84

THE WOMAN'S DEATHLY-PALE hands had been severed at the wrists with a blade and a saw that had left the flesh smooth and the bones ragged and chipped.

Hooligan asked, 'Should I fingerprint her?'

'Let's leave that to Scotland Yard,' Jack said.

'No matter,' Knight said, 'I'm betting those hands belong to a war criminal.'

'Andjela Brazlic?' Jack asked.

Hooligan nodded. 'The odds are definitely there, eh?'

'Why send them to you?' Jack asked Knight.

'I don't know.'

The question continued to haunt Knight on his way home later that evening. Why him? He supposed that Cronus was sending a message with the hands. But about what? The fingerprint she'd left on the box? Was this Cronus's way of displaying his ruthlessness?

Knight called Elaine Pottersfield and told her that Hooligan was bringing the hands to Scotland Yard. He laid out his suspicions about their identity.

'If they are Andjela Brazlic's, it shows dissension in Cronus's ranks,' the inspector said.

'Or Cronus is simply saying that it's fruitless to track this particular war criminal. She made a mistake. And now she's dead.'

'That all?' Pottersfield asked.

'We're going to Kate's forest in the morning,' Knight said. 'And the party is at five-thirty.'

The silence was brief. 'I'm sorry, Peter,' she said, and hung up.

Knight reached home around ten, wondering if his sister-in-law would ever come to terms with him – or with Kate's death. It wasn't until he was standing at his front door that he allowed himself to realise that three years before, right about this time, his late wife had gone into labour.

He remembered Kate's face after her waters had broken – no fear, just sheer joy at the impending miracle. Then he recalled the ambulance taking her away. Knight opened the door of his home and went inside, as deeply confused and heartbroken as he'd been thirty-six months before.

The house smelled of chocolate, and two brightly wrapped presents sat on the table in the hallway. He grimaced, realising that he hadn't yet had the chance to go shopping for the kids. Work had been all-consuming. Or had he just let it be all-consuming so that he would not have to think about their birthday and the anniversary of their mother's death?

With no good answer to any of it, Knight examined the presents and was surprised to see that they were from his mother, the gift tags signed: 'With love, Amanda'.

He smiled and tears brimmed in his eyes; if his mother had taken the time from her isolation, grief, and bitterness to buy her grandchildren presents, then maybe she was not allowing herself to retreat as completely as she had after his father's death.

'I'll go home, then, Mr Knight,' Marta said, coming out of the kitchen. 'They are asleep. Kitchen is clean. Fudge made. Luke made an unsuccessful attempt at the big-boy loo. I bought party bags, and ordered a cake too. I can be here all day tomorrow through the party. But I will need Sunday off.'

Sunday. The men's marathon. The closing ceremony. Knight had to be available. Perhaps he could talk his mother or Boss into coming one more time.

'Sunday off, and you really don't need to be here before noon tomorrow,' Knight said. 'I usually take them to Epping Forest and High Beach Church on the morning of their birthday.'

'What's there?' Marta asked.

'My late wife and I were married at the church. Her ashes are scattered in the woods out there. She was from Waltham Abbey and the forest was one of her favourite places.'

'Oh, I'm sorry,' Marta said uncomfortably, and moved towards the door. 'Noon, then.'

'Noon sounds good,' Knight said and shut the door behind her.

He shut off the lights, checked on the kids, and went to his bedroom.

Knight sat on the edge of his bed, gazing at Kate looking out from the photo at him, and remembering in vivid detail how she'd died.

He broke down, sobbing.

Chapter 85

Saturday, 11 August 2012

'I'M THREE!' ISABEL yelled in her father's ear.

Knight jerked awake from a nightmare that featured Kate held hostage by Cronus – not the madman stalking the Olympics, but that ancient Greek figure carrying a long scythe and hungering to eat his children.

Dripping in sweat, his face contorted with dread, Knight looked in bewilderment at his daughter who now appeared upset and was stepping back from her father, holding her blanket tight against her cheek.

His senses came back to him, and he thought: She's fine! Luke's fine! It was just a horrible, horrible dream.

Knight breathed out, smiled, and said, 'Look at how big you are!'

'Three,' Isabel said, her grin returning.

'Lukey three, too!' his son announced from the doorway.

'You don't say,' Knight said as Luke bounced up onto the bed and into his arms. Isabel climbed up after him and cuddled him.

His children's smells surrounded him and calmed him and made him realise again what a lucky, lucky person he was to have them in his life, part of Kate that would live on and grow and become themselves.

'Presents?' Luke asked.

'They're not here yet,' Knight said, too quickly. 'Not until the party.'

'No, Daddy,' Isabel protested. 'That funny man bring presents yesterday. They're downstairs.'

'Mr Boss brought them?' he asked.

His son nodded grimly. 'Boss no like Lukey.'

'His loss,' Knight said. 'Go and get the presents. You can open them up here.'

That set off a stampede as both children scrambled off the bed. Twenty seconds later they were running back into the room, gasping and grinning like little fools.

'Go ahead,' Knight said.

Giggling, they tore into the wrapping and soon had the presents from Amanda open. Isabel's gift was a beautiful silver locket on a chain. They opened the locket to find a picture of Kate.

'That mummy?' Isabel asked.

Knight was genuinely touched at his mother's thoughtfulness. 'Yes – so you can take her with you everywhere,' he said in a hoarse voice.

'What this, Daddy?' Luke asked, eyeing his present suspiciously.

Knight took it, examined it, and said, 'It's a very special watch, for a very big boy. You see – it has Harry Potter, the famous wizard, on the dial, and there's your name engraved on the back.'

'Big-boy watch?' Luke asked.

'Yes,' Knight said, and then teased: 'We'll put it away until you're bigger.'

Outraged, his son shoved out his wrist. 'No! Lukey big boy! Lukey three!'

'I completely forgot,' Knight said, and put the watch on his son's wrist, pleasantly surprised that the strap was a near-perfect fit.

While Luke paraded around admiring his watch, Knight hung the locket around Isabel's neck, closed the chain clasp and oohed and aahed when she looked at herself in the mirror, the spitting image of Kate as a little girl.

He changed Luke's nappy, then bathed and fed them both before getting Isabel into a dress and his son into blue shorts and a white collared shirt. With admonitions not to get their clothes dirty, Knight set himself a record time showering, shaving and dressing. They left the house at nine, went to the garage nearby, and retrieved a Range Rover that they rarely used.

Knight drove north through the streets with Isabel and Luke in their car seats behind him, listening to the news on the radio. It was the last full day of Olympic competition with many relay-race finals to be decided that afternoon.

The announcers talked of the heavy criticism being heaped on Scotland Yard and MI5 over their inability to make any kind of a major breakthrough in the Cronus investigations. No mention was made of the war-criminal's hands though. Pottersfield had asked that it should be kept quiet for the time being.

Many athletes who were finished with the competition were already leaving. Most others, like Hunter Pierce, had vowed to remain at the Olympic Park until the end, no matter what Cronus and his Furies might try.

Knight drove to Enfield, then east and south of Waltham Abbey towards High Beach and Epping Forest.

'Lots of trees,' Isabel said when they'd entered the forest proper.

'Your mummy liked lots of trees.'

The dappled sunlight shone through the foliage that surrounded High Beach Church, which sat in a clearing not far into the woods. There were several cars parked, but Epping Forest was a popular place to walk, and Knight did not expect anyone else to be here specifically for Kate. His mother was lost in her own grief, and Kate's parents had both died young.

They went into the empty church where Knight got the children each to light a candle in their mother's memory. He lit one for Kate, and then lit five more for his colleagues who had died in the plane crash. Holding Isabel and Luke's hands, he led them from the church and out along a path that led into the woods.

A light breeze rustled the leaves. Six or seven minutes later, the vegetation thinned and they passed through a tumbledown stone wall into a sparse grove of ancient oaks growing in long untamed grass that sighed in the summer wind.

Knight stood a while looking at the scene, hugging his children to him, and struggling to control his emotions for their sake.

'Your mummy used to go to that church as a little girl, but she liked to come out here,' he told them softly. 'She said the trees were so old that this was a blessed place where she could talk to God. That's why I spread her . . .'

He choked up.

'It was a perfect choice, Peter,' a woman's emotion-drenched voice said behind them. 'This was Kate's favourite place.'

Knight turned, wiping tears from his eyes with his sleeve.

Holding tight to his trouser leg, Isabel asked, 'Who's that lady, Daddy?'

Knight smiled. 'That's your Aunt Elaine, darling. Mummy's older sister.'

Chapter 86

'I KNEW I couldn't make the party,' Knight's sister-in-law explained quietly on the ride back into London while the children slept in the back of the car. 'And, anyway, I thought meeting them there would make me feel better.'

They were nearing the garage where Knight kept the Range Rover.

'Did it?' Knight asked.

Pottersfield nodded and her eyes got glassy. 'It seemed right, as if I could feel her there.' She hesitated and then said, 'I'm sorry. The way I treated you. I know it was all Kate's decision to have the twins at home. I just . . .'

'No more talk of that,' Knight said, parking. 'We're beyond all that. My children are lucky to have you in their lives. *I'm* lucky to have you in my life.'

She sighed, and smiled sadly. 'Okay. Need any help?'

Knight looked over his shoulder at his sleeping

children. 'Yes. They're getting too big to carry that far by myself.'

Pottersfield took Isabel and Knight hoisted Luke, and they walked the short distance to his house. He heard the television playing inside.

'The new nanny,' he said, fishing for his keys. 'She always arrives early.'

'You don't hear that much any more.'

'It's brilliant, actually,' Knight admitted. 'She's a miracle, the only one ever to tame them. She's got them helping to clean up their room and going to sleep at a snap of her fingers.'

He opened the door and Marta appeared almost instantly. She frowned to see Luke fast asleep on her father's shoulder. 'Too much excitement, I think,' she said, took him from Knight and looked curiously at Pottersfield.

'Marta, this is Elaine,' Knight said. 'My sister-in-law.'

'Oh, hello,' Pottersfield said, studying Marta. 'Peter speaks highly of you.'

Marta laughed nervously, and bobbed her head, saying, 'Mr Knight is too kind.' She paused and asked, 'Did I see you on the television?'

'Maybe. I work at Scotland Yard.'

Marta looked ready to reply when Isabel woke up grumpily, looked at her aunt, and whined, 'I want my daddy.'

Knight took her from Pottersfield, saying, 'Daddy has to go to work for a few hours, but he'll be back in time for the party.'

Marta said, 'We'll go and get cake soon. And balloons.'

Isabel brightened and Luke woke up. Pottersfield's mobile rang.

The inspector listened closely, began nodding, and then said, 'Where are they taking her?'

She listened while Marta came and took Isabel from Knight and shepherded the children down the hall towards the kitchen, saying, 'Who wants apple juice?'

Pottersfield snapped shut her phone, looked at Knight and said, 'A constable just picked up Serena Farrell wandering incoherent, filthy, and covered in her own excrement somewhere inside the ruins of the old Beckton Gas Works. They're bringing her to St Thomas's Hospital.'

Knight glanced back over his shoulder at Marta, who held Isabel and Luke's hands tightly.

'I'll be back by five to help you put up decorations,' he promised.

'Everything will be under control by then,' she replied confidently. 'Leave everything to me, Mr Knight.'

Chapter 87

'ARE YOU SURE?' I demand, doing everything in my power not to scream into my mobile.

'Positive,' Marta hisses back at me. 'She was found wandering around the Beckton Gas Works, not far from the factory. Who was there last?'

First Petra and now you, Teagan, I think murderously as I glance at Marta's sister next to me behind the wheel of her car. My thoughts are boiling again. But I reply cryptically to Marta: 'Does it matter?'

'I'd go and clean that factory out if I were you,' Marta says. 'They're right behind us.'

It's true. Over the homicidal buzz I've got going in my ears, I can almost hear the baying of dogs.

What a blunder! What a colossal blunder! Farrell wasn't supposed to be freed until tomorrow morning, a diversion that would draw all police attention to her while I completed my revenge. I should have just killed Farrell when I had the chance. But no, I had to be clever. I had to pile deception upon deception upon deception. But this one has backfired on me.

My fingers go to that scar on the back of my head and the hatred ignites.

My hand has been forced. My only hope is ruthlessness.

'Take the children,' I say. 'Now. You know what to do.'

'I do,' Marta replies. 'The little darlings are already fast asleep.'

Chapter 88

THE SIGHTS, SOUNDS, and smells of St Thomas's Hospital unnerved Knight in a way he did not expect. He hadn't been back in a medical facility of any sort since Kate's body had been taken to one and it made him feel disorientated by the time he and Pottersfield reached the intensive-care unit.

'This is what she looked like when they found her,' the Metropolitan Police officer guarding the room said, showing them a picture.

Farrell was dressed as Syren St James, filthy in the extreme, and looking as dazed as a lobotomy patient. An IV line hung from one hand.

'She talking?' Pottersfield asked.

'Babbled about a body with no hands,' the officer said.

'No hands?' Knight said, glancing at Pottersfield.

'Not much of what she said made sense. But you might have a better chance now that they've given her an anti-narcotic.'

'She was on narcotics?' Pottersfield asked. 'We know that for certain?'

'Powerful doses, mixed with sedatives,' he replied.

They entered the intensive-care unit. Professor Selena Farrell lay asleep in a bed surrounded by monitoring equipment, her skin a deathly grey. Pottersfield went to her side and said, 'Professor Farrell?'

The professor's face screwed up in anger. 'Go away. Head. Hurts. Bad.' Her words were slurred and trailed off at the end.

'Professor Farrell,' Pottersfield said firmly. 'I'm Inspector Elaine Pottersfield of the Metropolitan Police. I have to speak with you. Open your eyes, please.'

Farrell's eyes blinked open and she cringed. 'Turn off lights. Migraine.'

A nurse closed the unit's curtains. Farrell opened her eyes again. She gazed around the room, saw Knight, and looked puzzled. 'What happened to me?'

'We were hoping *you* could tell *us*, professor,' Knight said.

'I don't know.'

Pottersfield said, 'Can you explain why your DNA – from your hair, to be exact – was found in one of the letters from Cronus to Karen Pope?'

The information was slow to penetrate Farrell's

fogged brain. 'Pope? The reporter?' she said to Knight. 'My DNA? No, I don't remember.'

'What *do* you remember?' Knight demanded.

Farrell blinked and groaned, and then said: 'Dark room. I'm on a bed, alone. Tied down. Can't get up. My head is splitting open, and they won't give me anything to stop it.'

'Who are "they"?' Knight demanded.

'Women. Different women.'

Pottersfield was beginning to look irritated. She said, 'Selena, do you understand that your DNA links you to seven murders in the last two weeks?'

That shocked the professor and she became more alert. 'What? Seven . . .? I haven't killed anyone. I never . . . What, what day is it?'

'Saturday, 11 August 2012,' Knight replied.

The professor moaned, 'No. It felt like I was only there overnight.'

'In the dark room with women?' Pottersfield asked.

'You don't believe me?'

'No,' Pottersfield said.

Knight said, 'Why did you fake getting sick and flee your office when Karen Pope played the flute music to you?'

Farrell's eyes widened. 'It made me sick, because . . . I'd heard it before.'

Chapter 89

I TERMINATE THE call to Marta and look over at Teagan, feeling as if I'd like to rip her head off right now. But she's behind the wheel and an accident is out of the question at this late stage of the game.

'Turn around,' I say, struggling for calm. 'We've got to go to the factory.'

'The factory?' Teagan replies nervously. 'It's broad daylight.'

'Farrell escaped. She was picked up inside the gasworks. Knight and the Scotland Yard inspector Pottersfield is with her at the hospital right now.'

Teagan loses colour.

'How could that have happened?' I demand softly. 'She wasn't supposed to be freed until tomorrow morning. It was your responsibility to see to that, sister.'

Panic-stricken, she says, 'I should have told you, but I knew how much pressure you were under. There were drunken lads inside the factory when I was there yesterday morning. I figured the smell would keep them from the room. They must have broken the lock and let her go or something. I don't know.'

'We've got to clean the place,' I say. 'Get us there. Now.'

We don't talk during the rest of the drive, or during our entry into the toxic factory grounds, or as we sneak inside the basement. I have only been here once before, so Teagan leads. We both carry rubbish bags.

The smell coming from the open storage room door is obscenely foul. But Teagan goes inside without hesitation. I glance at the iron rings on the door and the frame, unbroken, and then let my gaze travel across the floor.

The lock's in the corner, its hasp open but not busted.

I crouch, pick it up, and loop the hasp around my middle finger like a brass knuckle, hiding the lock inside my palm. Inside, Teagan is already gloved and stuffing used IV equipment into the rubbish bag.

'Let's get this done,' I say, and move towards her before squatting down to pick up a used syringe with my left hand.

Rising, feeling the urge to vengeance enfolding me like an old lover, I move the needle towards the rubbish bag as a feint before letting go with an uppercut, with the hasp leading.

Teagan never has a chance. She never sees the blow coming.

The impact crushes her larynx.

She staggers backward, choking, purple-faced, her eyes bulging right out of her head, staring at me in disbelief. The second blow breaks her nose, hurls her against the wall, and makes her understand that I am an infinitely superior being. My third strike connects with her temple and she crumples in the grime.

Chapter 90

'OF COURSE YOU'D heard that music before,' Pottersfield shot back. 'It was all over your computer. So was a program used to take control of the Olympic Stadium's electronic billboard on the night of the opening ceremony.'

'What?' the professor cried, struggling to sit upright and wincing in pain. 'No, no! Someone began sending me that music about a year ago on my phone machine and in attachments to e-mails from blind accounts. It was like I was being stalked. After a while, any time I heard it I got sick.'

'Convenient nonsense,' Pottersfield snapped. 'What about the program on your computer?'

'I don't know what program you're talking about. Someone must have put it on there – maybe whoever was sending me the music.'

Knight was incredulous. 'Did you report this cyber-stalking to anyone?'

The classics professor nodded firmly. 'Twice, as a matter of fact, at Wapping police station. But the detectives said flute music was not a crime, and I had no other proof that someone was stalking me. I said I had suspicions about who was behind the music, but they didn't want to hear any of it. They advised me to change my phone number and my e-mail address, which I did. It stopped. And the headaches stopped, too – until you played the music again in my office.'

Knight squinted, trying to make sense of this explanation. Was it possible that Farrell had been set up as a diversion of some sort? Why hadn't she just been killed?

Pottersfield must have been thinking along the same lines because she asked, 'Who did you think was behind the music?'

Farrell gave a little shrug. 'Well, I've only known one person in my life who plays a Pan flute.'

Knight and Pottersfield said nothing.

'Jim Daring,' the professor said. 'You know, the guy at the British Museum? The one who has the television show?'

That changed things, Knight thought, remembering how Daring had spoken highly of Farrell and repeatedly told him and Pope to go and see her. Was it all part of an attempt to frame her?

Pottersfield still sounded sharply sceptical. 'How

do you know he played a Pan flute and why ever would he use the music to harass you?'

'He had a Pan flute in the Balkans in the 1990s. He used to play it for me.'

'And?' Knight said.

Farrell looked uncomfortable. 'He, Daring, was interested in me romantically. I told him I wasn't interested, and he got angry and then obsessed. He stalked me back then. I reported him, too. In the end it didn't matter. I was injured in a truck accident and airlifted out of Sarajevo. I haven't seen him personally since.'

'Not once in how many years?' Knight asked.

'Sixteen? Seventeen?'

'And yet you suspected him?' Pottersfield said.

The professor's expression turned stony. 'I had no one else to suspect.'

'I imagine not,' the police inspector said. 'Because he's missing, too. Daring, I mean.'

The confusion returned to Farrell's face. 'What?'

Knight said, 'You claim you were held in a dark room and tended by women. How did you get out?'

The question threw Farrell for several moments, before she said, 'Boys, but I'm not . . . No, I definitely remember I heard boys' voices, and then I passed out again. When I woke up I could move my arms and legs. So I got up and found a door and . . .' She hesitated and looked off into the distance. 'I think I was in some kind of old factory. There were brick walls.'

Pottersfield said, 'You told the officer about a dead body without hands.'

There was fear on the professor's face as she looked back and forth between Knight and Pottersfield. 'There were flies on her. Hundreds.'

'Where?'

'I don't know,' Farrell said, grimacing and rubbing at her head. 'Somewhere in that factory, I think. I was dizzy. I fell a lot. I couldn't think straight at all.'

After a long pause, Pottersfield seemed to come to some sort of conclusion. She pulled out her mobile, got up, and took several steps away from Farrell's hospital bed. A moment later she said, 'It's Pottersfield. You're looking for an abandoned factory of some sort near the Beckton gasworks. Brick walls. There could be a body in there with no hands. Maybe more.'

In the meantime, Knight thought of the reporting that Karen Pope had done on Farrell, and asked, 'How did you get into that room in the factory?'

The professor shook her head. 'I don't remember.'

'What's the last thing you *do* remember?' Pottersfield said, shutting her phone.

Farrell blinked, then tensed up and replied, 'I can't say.'

Knight said, 'Would Syren St James know?'

363

The name clearly confused the professor, who asked softly, 'Who?'

'Your alter ego among the elite lesbians of London,' Pottersfield said.

'I don't know what you're—'

'—Everyone in London knows about Syren St James,' Knight said, cutting her off. 'She's been in all the papers.'

The professor looked crushed. 'What? How?'

'Karen Pope,' Knight replied. 'She found out about your secret life and wrote about it.'

Farrell cried weakly, 'Why would she do that?'

'Because the DNA linked you to the killings,' Pottersfield said. 'It still does. The DNA says that you're involved somehow with Cronus and his Furies.'

Farrell went hysterical, shouting: 'I am not Cronus! I am not a Fury! I've had another life, but that's no one's business but my own. I've never had anything to do with any killings!'

The attending nurse burst into the room and ordered Knight and Pottersfield out.

'One more minute,' Pottersfield insisted. 'You were in the Candy Club the last time you were seen, two weeks ago last night, on Friday, 27 July.'

That seemed to puzzle the professor.

'Your friend Nell said she saw you there,' Knight said. 'She told Pope you were with a woman wearing a pill-box hat with a veil that hid her face.'

Farrell grasped at the memory, and then nodded slowly. 'Yes, I went with her to her car. She had wine in the car and poured me some and . . .' She gazed at Pottersfield. 'She drugged me.'

'Who is *she*?' Pottersfield demanded.

Farrell, embarrassed, said, 'Her real name? I couldn't tell you. I assume she was like me, operating under an alias. But she told me to call her Marta. She said she was from Estonia.'

Chapter 91

VIOLENT THUNDERSTORMS STRUCK London late that Saturday afternoon.

Lightning brought rain that pelted off the windscreen as Pottersfield's unmarked police car sped towards Chelsea, its siren wailing. The inspector kept glancing furiously at Knight who looked as if he was fighting a ghost as he punched in Marta's mobile number yet again.

'Answer,' he kept saying. 'Answer, you bitch.'

Pottersfield shouted: 'How could you not have checked her out, Peter?'

'I *did* check her out, Elaine!' Knight shouted back. 'You did, too! She was just so perfect for what I needed.'

They screeched to a halt in front of Knight's place where several other police cars were already parked, their lights flashing. Despite the rain, a crowd was gathering. Uniformed officers were already starting to put up barriers.

Knight leaped from Pottersfield's vehicle, feeling as if he were tottering on the edge of a dark and unfathomable abyss.

Bella? Little Lukey? It was their birthday.

Inspector Billy Casper met Knight at the door, his expression sombre. 'I'm sorry, Peter. We got here too late.'

'No,' he cried, rushing inside. 'No.'

Everywhere Knight looked he saw the things that surrounded his children: toys, baby powder, and packages of balloons, streamers and candles. He walked numbly past it all and into the kitchen. Luke's cereal bowl from breakfast still had milk in it. Isabel's blanket lay on the floor beside her high chair.

Knight picked it up, thinking that Bella must be lost without it. The enormity of his predicament suddenly threatened to crush him. But he refused to collapse, and fought back in the only way he knew how: he kept moving.

He found Pottersfield and said, 'Check her flat. Her address is on her C.V. And her prints have to be everywhere in here. Can you track her mobile number?'

'If she's got it turned on,' Pottersfield said. 'In the meantime, call your friend Pope, and I'll get to the media people I know. We'll get the twins' faces everywhere, Peter. Someone will have seen them.'

Knight began to nod, but then said, 'What if that's what they want?'

'What?' Pottersfield asked. 'Why?'

'A sideshow,' he said. 'A diversion. Think about it. If you put their faces everywhere and tell the public that they've been kidnapped by a woman believed to be an associate of Cronus, law-enforcement manpower and media attention go to Isabel and Luke, leaving the Olympics open to a final attack.'

'We've got to do something, Peter.'

Knight couldn't believe he was saying it, but he replied, 'We can wait them out for a few hours at least, Elaine. See if they get nervous. See if they call. If they don't by, say, eight, then by all means, put their faces everywhere.'

Before Pottersfield could reply, Knight pulled out his mobile and punched in Hooligan's number.

Knight heard cheering in the background and Hooligan crowed: 'Did you catch that, Peter? It's 1-1. We're tied!'

'Come to my house,' Knight said. 'Now.'

'Now?' Hooligan cried, sounding a little drunk. 'Have you gone crazy? This is for the bloody gold medal and I've got midfield seats.'

'Cronus has my kids,' Knight said.

Silence, then: 'No! Fuck. I'll be right there, Peter. Right there.'

Knight hung up. Elaine held out her hand for his mobile. 'I'll need it for a few minutes while we put on a trace.'

He handed her the phone and went upstairs. He got Kate's picture and brought it with him into the nursery as thunder shook the house. He sat on the couch, looked at the empty cots and the wallpaper that Kate had picked out and wondered if he had been destined for tragedy and loss.

Then he noticed the bottle of children's liquid antihistamine on the changing table. He set Kate's picture down and went over, noticing that the bottle was almost empty. At that he felt duped and enraged. Marta had been drugging his kids right under his nose.

Pottersfield came in. She glanced at the photograph of Kate on the couch, and then handed Knight his phone. 'You're now linked to our system. Any call coming in to your number we should be able to trace. And I just got an alert. We found two bodies in a condemned factory contaminated with hazardous waste not far from the gasworks. Both women in their thirties. One was beaten to death within the last few hours – no ID. The other died earlier this week and was handless. We're assuming it's Andjela Brazlic and her older sister, Nada.'

'Two Furies gone. It's just Marta and Cronus now,' Knight said dully, putting down the children's cold-medicine bottle. 'Do you think Daring could be Cronus? After what Farrell told us. The stalking in the Balkans? The flute?'

'I don't know.'

Knight suddenly felt gripped by doubt, intense and claustrophobic. 'Does it matter where I am when a call comes in?'

'It shouldn't,' Pottersfield replied.

He set Kate's photograph down on the changing table and said, 'I can't just sit here, Elaine. I feel like I have to move. I'm going to take a walk. Is that okay?'

'Just keep your mobile on.'

'Tell Hooligan to call me when he gets here. And Jack Morgan should be notified. They're at the stadium for the relays.'

She nodded and said, 'We'll find them.'

'I know,' he said with wavering conviction.

Knight put on his raincoat and left by the rear door in case the media were already camped outside. He walked down the alley, trying to decide whether to wander aimlessly or to get the car and drive back to High Beach Church to pray. But then he understood that he really had just one place to go, and only one person he wanted to see.

Knight altered direction and trudged through the rainy city, passing pubs and hearing cheering coming from inside. It sounded as though England was winning football gold while he was losing everything that ever mattered to him.

His hair and his trouser legs were soaking wet when he reached the door on Milner Street and rang the bell and pounded the knocker while looking up at the security camera.

The door opened, revealing Boss. 'She can't be seen,' he said sharply.

'Get out of my way, little man,' Knight said in a tone so threatening that his mother's assistant stood aside without further protest.

Knight opened the door of his mother's studio without knocking. Amanda was hunched over her design table, cutting fabric. A dozen or more original new creations hung on mannequins around the room.

His mother looked up icily. 'Haven't I made it abundantly clear that I wish to be left alone, Peter?'

Walking towards her, Knight said, 'Mother—'

But she cut him off: 'Leave me alone, Peter. What in God's name are you doing here? It's your children's birthday. You should be with them.'

It was the final straw. Knight felt dizzy and then blacked out.

Chapter 92

KAREN POPE HURRIED through the drizzling rain and the dimming light towards Knight's house in Chelsea. She'd been tipped off by the *Sun*'s police reporter that something big was going on at the Private investigator's home, and she'd gone there immediately, dialling Knight's number constantly on the way.

But Pope kept getting an odd beeping noise and then a voice saying that his number was 'experiencing network difficulties'. She could see the police barrier ahead and . . .

'Oi, Peter call you in too, then?' Hooligan asked, trotting up beside her. His eyes were red and his breath smelled of cigarettes, garlic and beer. 'I came from the bloody gold-medal game. I missed the winning goal!'

'Missed it for what?' she demanded. 'Why are the police here?'

He told her and Pope felt like crying. 'Why? Why his kids?'

It was the same thing she asked Pottersfield when they got inside.

'Peter believes that it's a diversionary tactic,' the inspector said.

Hooligan could not hide the slight slur in his voice, saying, 'Maybe. I mean this Marta was here for the past fortnight, right?'

'Give or take, I think,' Pope said.

'Right, so I'm asking myself why?' Hooligan replied. 'And I'm thinking Cronus sends her in as a spy. He can't get someone inside Scotland Yard, but he can get this Marta inside Private, right?'

'So?' Pottersfield said, squinting.

'Where are Peter's computers? His phones?'

'He's got his mobile with him,' Pottersfield said. 'House phone is in the kitchen. I saw the computer upstairs in his room.'

Twenty minutes later, Hooligan found Pottersfield and Pope talking with Billy Casper. 'Thought you'd want to see this, inspector,' he said, holding up two small evidence bags. 'Picked up the bug on the phone and the keystroke recorders on the DSL cable. I'm betting his mobile's bugged as well. Maybe more.'

'Call him,' Pottersfield said.

'I tried,' Hooligan said. 'And texted him. I'm getting no answer, other than something about network difficulties.'

Chapter 93

DARKNESS WAS FALLING outside Amanda's studio. Knight's mobile lay on the coffee table. He sat on the couch, looking at the phone, his brain feeling scalded and his stomach emptier than it had ever been.

Why hadn't they called?

His mother sat beside him, saying, 'It's more than anyone as good as you should have to bear, but you can't give up hope, Peter.'

'Absolutely not,' Boss said emphatically. 'Those two barbarians of yours are fighters. You have to be as well.'

But Knight felt as beaten as he had while holding his newborns and watching his wife's body rushed to the ambulance. 'It's their birthday,' he said softly. 'They were expecting what any three-year-old expects. Cake and ice cream and . . .'

Amanda reached out and stroked her son's hair. It was such a rare and unexpected gesture that Knight looked at her with a feeble smile on his face. 'I know how horrid life's been for you lately, Mother, but I wanted to thank you for caring about them. The only presents they got to open were from you.'

She looked surprised. 'Is that so? I didn't think they'd get there so soon.'

'I took them over,' Boss said. 'I thought they should be there.'

Knight said, 'Thank you, Boss. They loved them. And I must say, Amanda, that putting the pictures of Kate in the locket was one of the kindest and most thoughtful things you've ever done.'

His mother, normally stoic, got tears in her eyes. 'Boss and I worried because they weren't toys.'

'No, no, they loved them,' Knight insisted. 'Luke was wearing that watch as if it was a gold medal. And the necklace fits Isabel perfectly. I don't think she'll ever take it off.'

Amanda blinked several times, and then glanced at Boss before asking, 'You think they're wearing them now, Peter? The watch and the necklace?'

'I would assume so,' Knight replied. 'I didn't see them in the house.'

Amanda looked at Boss who was grinning. 'Did you activate them?'

Boss replied: 'Even before I registered the warranties!'

'What are you two talking about?' Knight said.

376

'Didn't you look at the boxes they came in, Peter?' Amanda cried. 'The necklace and watch were manufactured by Trace Angels, a company I've invested in. There are tiny GPS transmitters embedded in the jewellery so that parents can track their children!'

Chapter 94

KNIGHT BOLTED OUT the door of his mother's house, watching two tiny heart-shaped icons pulsing and moving slowly on a map on the screen of his iPhone.

According to the map, Luke and Isabel were less than two miles away! That realisation had caused Knight to run from his mother's without a moment's hesitation, going out into the street to find a cab and to see why his phone was having trouble connecting inside.

Knight punched in Elaine Pottersfield's number again, and got nothing but a message about network problems. He was about to turn and rush back into Amanda's home when he saw a taxi coming.

He hailed it, and jumped inside. 'Lancaster Gate Tube station,' he said.

'Yah, mon,' the driver said. 'Hey, it's you!'

Knight did a double take, realising it was the same driver who'd chased the taxi that had tried to run him and Lancer down.

'Cronus has my kids.'

'De crazy guy who blew up Mundaho?' the Jamaican cried.

'Go like hell, man,' Knight said.

They roared north-west towards Brompton Road while Knight tried Pottersfield's number again. It did not go through, but he'd no sooner ended the attempt than the iPhone buzzed, alerting him to a text.

It was from Hooligan and read: 'AT YOUR HOUSE. YOUR COMPUTER AND PHONE BUGGED. ASSUME YOUR MOBILE BUGGED 2. MAYBE TRACEABLE. CALL.'

Traceable? Knight thought. They've been tracking *me*?

'Pull over,' he yelled.

'But your kids, mon!' the taxi driver said.

'Pull over,' Knight said, forcing himself to calm down. He glanced at the beating hearts on his screen. They'd gone into an address on Porchester Terrace.

'Do you have a mobile?'

'My old lady's phone died this morning,' the driver said, stopping at the kerb. 'I gave her mine to use while hers be fixed.'

'Son of a . . .' Knight said. He looked at the screen one last time and memorised the address where the twins were being held.

Then he handed the phone to the driver along with two fifty-pound notes. 'Listen carefully, mate. I'm going to leave this phone with you, and you're going to drive it out to Heathrow.'

'What?'

'Don't argue,' Knight said, now scribbling on a business card. 'Drive it to Heathrow and then circle back to this address in Chelsea. You'll see police there. Ask for Inspector Pottersfield or Hooligan Crawford – he's with Private. Give them the phone. There'll be a reward in it for you.'

'What about your kids, mon?'

But Knight was already gone, running across Brompton Road towards Montpelier Street, heading north towards Hyde Park, thinking that the last thing he wanted was to have police arrive in force, surround the place, and force Marta's hand – or Cronus's hand, for that matter. It could cost Luke and Isabel their lives and Knight could not survive that. He'd scout the place out, and then find a phone to alert Elaine, Jack, Hooligan, Pope, and everyone else in London.

Knight was gasping for air by the time he reached the trail that paralleled the west shore of The Serpentine. His lungs were on fire when he left the park ten minutes later and crossed Bayswater Road, across from Lancaster Gate Tube station.

He went west along Bayswater Road, passed a

crowd of revellers at the Swan Pub still celebrating England's' come-from-behind victory over Brazil, and finally took a right onto Porchester Terrace. The address he sought was on the west side of the street towards Fulton Mews.

Knight stayed on the east pavement, moving methodically north until he'd got as close to the address as he dared in case the street was being monitored. He desperately wished he'd had his binoculars with him, but could see that the white apartment building had balconies on every floor and iron bars on the ground-floor windows.

There were identical apartment buildings on either side of the building Knight was targeting. Every window in the building was dark except for a light that glowed from French doors leading to the balcony of a flat on the north-east corner of the third floor. Was this where Marta was holding his children?

Rain began to fall again, hard enough for Knight to decide he would not look out of place if he put up the hood on his raincoat and walked past the building on the east side of the street.

Were Isabel and Luke inside? Cronus? Was this their hideout? Knight walked past, taking what he hoped would look like casual glances at the doorway, wondering if he should risk crossing to the other side for a closer look before he went to one of the hotels over on Inverness Terrace to call Elaine.

Then he noticed how close that balcony was to the balcony immediately to the north, which was attached to a wholly separate building. It appeared to Knight that anyone would almost certainly be able to see from that balcony on the adjacent building into the apartment where he thought Luke and Isabel might be being held.

Hell, you could probably jump from one balcony to the other.

Knight slowed and studied the facades of the apartment buildings, trying to figure out how to climb up there. But then lights went on behind the French windows of the adjacent balcony. Someone was home there.

Instantly a plan hatched in Knight's mind. He'd ring their bell, explain what was going on, and ask to use their phone to call Pottersfield and to access the balcony for surveillance purposes. But then he thought to go to the rear of the two buildings to see if any other lights were on. It took him three minutes. No other lights. He returned to Porchester Terrace just as a woman came out through the front door of the apartment building he wished to enter.

Knight bolted past her, smiled at her as if they were old friends, bounded up the steps, and caught the security door before it could shut. Even better.

He'd go straight up and knock at the door of the flat on the south-east corner of the third floor. When they saw his Private badge they were sure to let him in.

He ran up the two flights of stairs and came out into a centre hallway that smelled of frying sausages. The third floor was divided into four separate flats. Knight went to the south-east-facing flat, number 3B, heard a television inside, and knocked sharply before holding up his Private badge and ID to the peephole.

He heard footsteps approach and then a pause before locks were thrown and the apartment door opened to reveal a puzzled Michael Lancer who said, 'Knight? What are you doing here?'

Chapter 95

LANCER WORE A tracksuit and looked as though he had not shaved in days. And his eyes were sunken and hollow as if he'd slept little since being fired from his position with the London Organising Committee.

'*You* live here, Mike?' Knight asked incredulously.

'Past ten years,' Lancer replied. 'What's going on?'

Puzzled now, Knight said. 'Can I come in?'

'Uh, sure,' Lancer said, standing aside. 'Place is a mess, but . . . why are you here?'

Knight walked down a hallway into a well-appointed living area. Beer bottles and old Chinese takeaway containers littered the coffee table. The southern wall was exposed brick. Pressed against it was an open armoire that held a television tuned to the BBC's wrap-up of the last full day of Olympic competition. Beside it was a desk and on top of it a glowing laptop computer. A blue cable came out from the side of the computer and was plugged into a wall socket.

Seeing that cable, it all suddenly seemed to make some sense to Knight.

'What do you know about your neighbours on the other side of that wall?' he asked, spotting the French window that led out onto the balcony.

'You mean in the other building?' Lancer asked, puzzled.

'Exactly,' Knight said.

The LOCOG member shook his head. 'Nothing. It's been empty for almost a year, I believe. I mean, I haven't seen anyone on the balcony for almost that long.'

'Someone's in there now,' Knight said, and then gestured at the blue cable. 'Is that a CAT 5e line linked to the Internet?'

Lancer seemed to be struggling to understand where Knight was going with all these questions. 'Yes, of course.'

'No Wi-Fi?' Knight asked.

'The CAT has much higher security. Why are you so interested in the flat in the building next door?'

'Because I believe that Cronus or one of his Furies has rented it so they could tap into your computer line.'

Lancer's jaw dropped. 'What?'

'That's how they were able to crack the Olympic

security system,' Knight went on. 'They tapped into your line, stole your passwords, and in they went.'

The former decathlon athlete looked at his computer, blinking. 'How do you know all this? How do you know they're next door?'

'Because my children are in there.'

'Your children?' Lancer said, shocked.

Knight nodded, his hands balled into fists. 'A woman named Marta Brezenova, a nanny I hired recently, kidnapped them on Cronus's behalf. She doesn't know that the twins are wearing pieces of jewellery fitted with a GPS transmitter. Their signals are coming from that flat.'

'Jesus,' Lancer said, dumbstruck. 'They were right next to me the whole . . . we've got to call Scotland Yard, MI5. Get a special-weapons unit in here.'

'You do that,' Knight said. 'I'm going to see if I can look into that flat from your balcony. And tell them to come in quiet. No sirens. I don't want my kids getting killed on a knee-jerk reaction.'

Lancer nodded emphatically, pulled out his mobile, and began punching in numbers as Knight slipped out through the French window onto the rain-soaked balcony. He moved past wet patio furniture and tried to see into the other flat.

The other balcony was less than six feet away, featured an iron balustrade, and was empty, apart from some old wet leaves. The French window had gauzy white curtains hanging over it that let light out, but gave Knight no clear idea of the interior layout. To his right, Knight could hear Lancer talking on his phone, explaining what was going on.

A wind came up. The French window on the far balcony blew open several inches, revealing a stark white carpet and a white country-style table on which several computers stood glowing, all connected to blue CAT 5e lines.

Knight was about go back into Lancer's apartment to tell him what he'd seen when he heard his son whine from somewhere in the adjacent flat: 'No, Marta! Lukey want to go home for birthday party!'

'Shut up, you spoiled little bastard,' Marta hissed before Knight heard a loud slap and Luke went hysterical. 'And learn to use the loo!'

Chapter 96

THE PRIMAL INSTINCT of a father wanting to protect his child seized Knight so completely that without considering the consequences he climbed up on Lancer's railing thirty feet above the ground, crouched, and dived forward.

As Knight pushed off from the wet rail his shoes slipped ever so slightly, and he knew in an instant that he wasn't going to make it onto the floor of the balcony next door. He wasn't even going to reach the railing, and he thought for sure that he was going to plunge and break every bone in his body.

But somehow his fingers snagged the bottom of the iron balustrade where it met the balcony floor and he grabbed at it for dear life, dangling and wondering how long he could hold on.

'Shut up!' Marta snapped inside, and slapped Luke again.

The little boy's sobs turned bitter, and that was enough to trigger a massive surge of adrenalin in

Knight. He swung his body left and right like a pendulum, feeling the iron biting into his hands, but not caring because on the third swing he was able to catch the edge of the balcony floor with the toe of his right shoe.

Seconds later he was over the railing and onto the balcony itself, his muscles trembling and a chemical taste in his mouth. Luke's crying had become muffled and nasal, as if Marta had gagged Knight's son.

Ignoring the stinging in his hands, Knight gripped his Beretta and eased up to the half-open French window. He peeked inside and saw that the living area was similar in layout to Lancer's place. The furnishings were wildly different, however, with a much colder touch. Everything in the room, except a gold and red tapestry that hung on the right-hand wall, was the same stark white as the carpet. Luke's muffled cries were coming from a hallway by the kitchen.

Knight pushed open the French window and stepped inside. He kicked off his shoes and stalked quickly to the hallway. He had no illusions about what he was doing now. Marta was a part of the death of Denton Marshall. She'd helped destroy his mother's happiness. She had tried to destroy the Olympics, and she'd taken his children. He would not hesitate to kill her to save them.

Luke's cries softened enough for Knight to be able to hear Isabel weeping too, and then a deeper groaning. All of it was coming from a room on the left, its door open and lights on. Knight hugged the wall and reached the doorway. He looked down the hallway beyond and saw two doors, both open, lights off.

It was all going down in the room right next to him. He thumbed the Beretta's safety.

Gun held out in front of him, Knight stepped into the doorway, sweeping his weapon around the room. He spotted Isabel lying on her side on a bare mattress on the floor to his right, tied up, tape across her mouth, looking towards Marta.

The nanny was about fifteen feet from Knight, her back turned to the door, and she was changing Luke's nappy on a table against the wall. She had no idea that he was standing in the doorway behind her, searching for a clear shot.

But James Daring did.

The museum curator and television star was staring at Knight, who understood much of the situation in a heartbeat. Knight stepped forward, aiming the pistol, and said, 'Get away from my son, you war-criminal bitch, or I will head-shoot you and enjoy doing it.'

The nanny pivoted in disbelief towards Knight, her attention darting to a black assault rifle standing in the corner several feet away.

'Don't even think about it,' Knight said, taking another step towards her. 'Get down on your belly, hands up behind your head, or I will kill you. Right now.'

Marta's eyes went dead and vacant, but she started to comply slowly, lowering her centre, watching Knight the way a cornered lioness might.

Knight took another step forward, gripping the Beretta two-handed, seeing her framed in his pistol sights. 'I said get down!' he yelled.

Marta went flat, and put her hands up behind her head.

Glancing at Daring, Knight said, 'Cronus?'

The television personality's eyes glazed before Knight heard a nearby thudding noise and something viciously hard hit his head.

It was like storms he'd seen come up over dry lowlands in Portugal: thunder boomed so loud that it deafened Knight even as heat lightning crackled, sending electric tentacles through his brain, so brilliant that they blinded him into darkness.

Chapter 97

THE SOUNDS OF hydraulic doors opening and shoes slapping on tile stirred Karen Pope from an edge-of-consciousness sleep.

The *Sun* reporter lay on a sofa in Private London's lab, feeling wrecked by a fatigue that was compounded with worry. No one had heard from Knight since he'd walked out the rear door of his house. Not Pottersfield, not Hooligan, not Pope, not Morgan, nor anyone else at Scotland Yard or Private.

They'd waited for him at his home until shortly after dawn when Pottersfield had left to examine the bodies of the two dead women found in the abandoned factory. Pope and Hooligan returned to Private to run the fingerprints that Hooligan had taken at Knight's house through the Balkan War Crimes database.

They'd got a hit almost immediately: Senka, the oldest of the Brazlic siblings, had been all over the place. When Hooligan informed Pottersfield, the inspector told them that preliminary fingerprint work on the more recently slain woman positively identified her as Nada, the middle Brazlic sister.

At that point, around eight a.m. that Sunday, Pope had hit a wall of exhaustion and had lain down on the couch, using one of Hooligan's lab coats for a blanket. How long had she slept?

'Hooligan, wake up,' she heard Jack say. 'There's a beat-up Rasta at the front desk looking for you. He says he's got something that he was supposed to hand-deliver to you for Knight. And he refuses to give it to me.'

At that Pope opened an eye to see the American standing at Hooligan's desk and Private London's chief scientist rousing from a nap. Above him, the clock read 10:20.

Two hours and twenty minutes? Pope sat up groggily, then got to her feet and stumbled after Hooligan and Jack out of the lab to the reception area, where a Jamaican sat painfully in a chair by the lift. A large bandage covered his grossly swollen cheek. His arm was in a cast and secured by a sling.

'I'm Hooligan,' the scientist said.

The Rasta struggled up and held out his good hand, saying, 'Ketu Oladuwa. I drive de cab.'

Hooligan gestured at the cast and bandage. 'Crash?'

Oladuwa nodded. 'Big time, mon. On my way to Heathrow. Broadsided by a panel van. I been in hospital all night.'

Pope said, 'What about Knight?'

'Ya, mon,' the Rasta said, digging in his pocket and coming up with a smashed iPhone. 'He gimme dis one here last night and tell me to drive it to Heathrow and then back to his home to find you or some inspector with da police. I went to Knight's home when I got out of hospital dis morning, and police told me you gone, so I came here.'

'To give us a smashed phone?' Jack asked.

'Wasn't smashed before da accident,' the Rasta said indignantly. 'He said something on dat phone help you find his kids.'

'Fuck,' Hooligan grunted. He snatched the remains of Knight's phone from Oladuwa, spun around and took off for the lab with Pope and Jack close on his heels.

'Hey!' Oladuwa yelled after them. 'Him say I get reward!'

Chapter 98

KNIGHT SURFACED FROM oblivion slowly, starting deep in the reptilian part of his brain with a sense of the smell of meat frying. At first he had no notion of who he was, or where he was, just that odour of meat frying.

Then he understood that he was lying prone on something hard. His hearing returned next, like pounding surf that cleared to static and then to voices, television voices. Knight knew who he was then, and dimly recalled being in the bedroom with his children, Marta, and Daring before it had all gone blank. He tried to move. He couldn't. His wrists and hands were bound.

The flute began, airy and trilling, and Knight forced his eyes open, seeing blurrily that he was not in that bedroom in the white flat any more. The floor below him was hardwood, not carpeted. And the walls around him were dark-panelled and heaved to and fro like the sea churning.

Knight felt nauseated and shut his eyes, still hearing the flute music, and the broadcast announcers arguing before he moved his head and felt a terrible throbbing at the back of his skull. After several seconds he opened his eyes a second time, finding that his focus was now better. He spotted Isabel and Luke unconscious on the floor not far away, still bound and gagged.

Then he twisted his head, trying to locate the source of the music, seeing the side of a four-poster bed at the centre of the room and, on it, James Daring.

Dazed as he was, Knight understood Daring's predicament at a glance. It was the same predicament in which he'd seen the museum curator before it had all gone to blackness: the television star lay spread-eagle on the mattress, lashed to the bedposts and wearing a hospital gown. His mouth was taped shut. An IV line ran into his wrist from a bag hanging on a rack by the bed.

The flute music stopped and Knight saw someone backlit by brilliant sunlight coming towards him across the room.

Mike Lancer carried a black combat shotgun loosely in his left hand, and a glass of orange juice in his right. He set the juice down on a table and squatted down near Knight, gazed at him in amusement, and said, 'Awake at last. Feel like things got rearranged upstairs, did you?' He laughed and displayed the weapon. 'Brilliant, these old riot guns. Even air-driven, the beanbags really pack a wallop, especially if delivered to the head at close range.'

'Cronus?' Knight said, still hazy. He could smell alcohol on Lancer's breath.

Lancer said, 'You know, I had a feeling about you right from the beginning, Knight, or at least since Dan Carter's untimely death: a premonition that you would come closest to figuring me out. But I took the necessary precautions, and here we are.'

Deeply confused, Knight said: 'The Olympics were your life. Why?'

Lancer rested the riot gun against the inside of his knee and reached back to scratch the side of his head. As he did, Knight saw his face flush with anger. He stood up, grabbed the juice glass, and drank from it before saying, 'The modern Games have been corrupt since the beginning. Bribed judges. Genetic freaks. Drug-fuelled monsters. It needed to be cleaned up, and I was the one to . . .'

Even in Knight's blurry state, it didn't sound right, and he said, 'Bullshit. I don't believe you.'

Lancer glared at him before whipping the glass at Knight. It missed and shattered against the wall behind him. 'Who are you to question my motives?' Lancer roared.

Concussion or not, threat or not, things were

becoming clearer to Knight, who said, 'You didn't do this just to expose the Games. You sacrificed them in front of a world audience. There has to be a warped sense of rage behind that.'

Lancer got angrier. 'I am an emanation of the Lord of Time.' He looked over at the twins. 'Cronus. Devourer of children.'

The implied threat terrified Knight. How far gone was the man?

'No,' Knight said, following his foggy instincts. 'Something happened to you. Something that filled you with hatred and made you want to do all this.'

Lancer's voice rose. 'The Olympics are supposed to be a religious festival, one where honourable men and women compete in the eyes of heaven. The modern Games are its exact opposite. The gods were offended by the arrogance of men, the hubris of mankind.'

Knight's vision blurred slightly, and he felt sickened again, but his brain was working better with each passing second. He shook his head. 'The gods weren't offended. *You* were offended. Who were they? The arrogant men?'

'The ones that have died in the last two weeks,' Lancer retorted hotly. Then he smiled. 'Including Dan Carter and your other dear colleagues.'

Knight stared at him, unable to comprehend the depths of the man's depravity. 'You bombed that plane?'

'Carter was getting a little too close,' Lancer replied. 'The others were collateral damage.'

'Collateral damage!' Knight shouted, feeling like he wanted to kill the man standing before him, ripping him limb from limb. But then his head began to throb again and he lay there panting, looking at Lancer.

After several moments he said, 'Who offended you?'

Lancer's expression went hard as he stared off into the past.

'Who?' Knight demanded again.

The former decathlon champion glared at Knight in utter fury, and said, 'Doctors.'

Chapter 99

IN BROAD, BITTER strokes, I tell Knight a story that no one except the Brazlic sisters has ever heard in its entirety, starting with the hatred I was born with, right through stabbing my mother and killing the monsters who stoned me after I went to live with Minister Bob in Brixton, the roughest neighbourhood in all of London.

I tell Knight that after the stoning, in the spring of my fifteenth year, Minister Bob had me enter for a track meet because he thought I was stronger and faster than most boys. He had no idea what I was capable of. Neither did I.

During that first meet I won six events: the 100, 200, javelin, triple jump, long jump and discus. I did it again in a regional competition, and a third time at a junior national meet in Sheffield.

'A man named Lionel Higgins approached me after Sheffield,' I tell Knight. 'Higgins was a private decathlon coach. He told me I had the talent to be the greatest all-around athlete in the world and to win the Olympic gold medal. He offered to help me figure out a way to train full-time, and filled my head with false dreams of glory and a life lived according to Olympic ideals, of competing fairly, may the best man win, and all that nonsense.'

Snorting scornfully, I say: 'The monster slayer in me bought the phoney spiel hook, line and sinker.'

I go on to tell Knight how I lived the Olympic ideals for the next fifteen years of my life. Despite the headaches that would lay me low at least once a month, Higgins arranged for me to join the Coldstream Guards, where in return for a decade of service I'd be allowed to train. I did so, furiously, single-mindedly, some say maniacally for a shot at athletic immortality that finally came for me at the Games in Barcelona in 1992.

'We expected the oppressive heat and humidity,' I say to Knight. 'Higgins sent me to India to train for it, figuring that Bombay would be worse than Spain. He was right. I *was* the best prepared, and I was mentally ready to suffer more than anyone else.'

Wrapped in the darkest of my memories, I shake my head like a terrier breaking a rat's spine, and say, 'None of it mattered.'

I describe how I led the Barcelona decathlon after the first day, through the 110-metre hurdles, high jump, discus, pole vault, and the 400. Temperatures were in the upper nineties and the oppressive, saturated air took its toll on me: I cramped up and collapsed after placing second in the 400.

'They rushed me to a medical tent,' I tell Knight. 'But I wasn't concerned. Higgins and I figured I would need a legal electrolytic boost after day one. I kept calling for my coach, but the medical personnel wouldn't let him in. I could see they were going to put me on an IV. I told them I wanted my own coach to replenish the fluids and minerals I lost with a mixture we'd fine-tuned to my metabolism. But I was in no condition to fight them when they put the needle in my arm and connected it to a bag of God only knows what.'

Looking at Knight, feeling livid, I'm reliving the aftermath all over again. 'I was a ghost of myself the next day. The javelin and the long jump were my best events, and I cratered in both. I didn't finish in the top ten and I was the reigning world champion.'

The anger in me is almost overwhelming when I say, 'No dream realised, Knight. No Olympic glory. No proof of my superiority. Sabotaged by what the modern Games have become.'

Knight stares at me with the same distrustful and fearful expression that Marta gave me when I offered to save her and her sisters in that police station in Bosnia.

'But you were world champion,' Knight says. 'Twice.'

'The immortals win Olympic gold. The superior wins gold. I was robbed of my chance by monsters. It was premeditated sabotage.'

Knight gazes at me in disbelief now, 'And so you started plotting your revenge right then – eighteen years ago?'

'The scope of my revenge grew over time,' I admit. 'It began with the Spanish doctors who doped me. They died of supposedly natural causes in September '93. The referees who oversaw the event were killed in separate car crashes in '94 and early '95.'

'And the Furies?' Knight asks.

I sit on a stool a few feet from him. 'Hardly anyone knows that after my regiment ended its service in the Queen's Guard, we were sent into Sarajevo for a rotation with the NATO peacekeeping mission. I lasted less than five weeks due to a roadside bomb that cracked my head for the second time in my life.'

Knight's words were less slurred now, and his eyes less glassy when he said 'Was that before or after you helped the Brazlic sisters escape from that police station near Srebrenica?'

I smile bitterly. 'After. With new passports and new identities, I brought the Furies to London and set them up in a flat next door. We even cut a secret door behind my armoire and their tapestry so we could appear to live separate lives.'

'Dedicated to destroying the Olympics?' Knight asks acidly.

'Yes, that's right. As I said, the gods were behind this, behind me. It was fate. How else do you explain that very early on in the process I was asked to be a member of the organising committee and, lo and behold, London won the bid. Fate allowed me to be on the inside from the start, hiding things where I needed them, altering them if they suited my purpose, given full access to every inch of every venue. And now with everyone hunting you and your children, fate will allow me to finish what I've begun.'

Knight's face contorts. 'You're insane.'

'No, Knight,' I reply. 'Just superior in ways you can't understand.'

I stand up and start to walk away. He calls after me, 'So are you going to wipe out all the Furies before your big finale? Kill Marta and then escape?'

'Not at all,' I chuckle. 'Marta's out putting your daughter's necklace and your son's watch on trains to Scotland and France respectively. When she's done, she'll return here, release Mr Daring and then kill your children. And then you.'

Chapter 100

KNIGHT'S POUNDING HEAD felt battered, as if it had been struck again. His attention lurched to his sleeping children. The necklace and wristwatch *were* gone. There was no way to trace them now. And what about the taxi driver? Why hadn't he given the phone to Hooligan or Pottersfield? Why hadn't they come for him? Were they tracking Marta to the trains?

Knight looked back to Lancer, who was gathering up a bag and some papers.

'My kids have done nothing,' Knight said. 'They're just three years old. Innocent.'

'Little monsters,' Lancer said flatly, turning for the door. 'Goodbye, Knight. It was nice competing with you, but the better man has won.'

'No, you haven't!' Knight shouted after him. 'Mundaho proved it. You haven't won. The Olympic spirit lives on whatever you do.'

That hit a nerve because Lancer turned and

marched back towards Knight – only to flinch and stop at the sound of a gunshot.

It came from the television and caused Lancer to relax, a smirk on his face.

'The men's marathon has started,' he said. 'The final game has begun. And you know what, Knight? Because I'm the superior man, I'm going to let you live to see the ending. Before Marta kills you, she's going to let you witness exactly how I snuff out that Olympic spirit once and for all.'

Chapter 101

A HALF-HOUR LATER, approaching noon, Pope glanced nervously from coverage of the men's marathon to Hooligan, who was still hunched over the shards of the iPhone, trying to coax Knight's whereabouts from them.

'Anything?' the reporter asked, feeling completely stymied.

'Sim card's pretty fuckin' hammered, eh?' Private London's chief scientist replied without looking up. 'But I think I'm getting close.'

Jack had left to oversee security at the finish line of the men's marathon. Elaine Pottersfield was in the lab, however. The police inspector had arrived only a few moments before, agitated and exhausted by the pressures of the preceding twenty-four hours.

'Where did this cabbie say he picked up Peter?' she asked impatiently.

Pope said, 'Somewhere in Knightsbridge, I think.

If Oladuwa had a mobile we could call him, but he said his wife's got it.'

Pottersfield thought a moment. 'Milner Street in Kensington, perhaps?'

'That was it,' Hooligan grunted.

'Knight was at his mother's, then,' the inspector said. 'Amanda must know something.' She yanked out her phone and started scrolling for her number.

'Here we are,' Hooligan said, raising his head from two sensors clipped to a surviving piece of Knight's sim card to look at the screen, which was covered with the gibberish of code.

He leaned over to a keyboard and began typing even as Pope heard Pottersfield say hello, identify herself as both a police detective and the sister of Knight's dead wife, and ask to speak with Amanda Knight. Then the inspector left the lab.

Two minutes later, Hooligan's screen mutated from electronic hieroglyphics to a blurry screen shot of a website. Pope said, 'What is that?'

'Looks like a map of some sort,' Hooligan replied as the inspector burst back into the lab. 'Can't read the URL, though.'

'Trace Angels!' Pottersfield shouted. 'It says Trace Angels!'

Chapter 102

THE CROWD ALONG the south side of Birdcage Walk, facing St James's Park, is bigger and deeper than I had anticipated. But then again, the men's marathon is one of the final competitions of the Games.

It's beastly hot, half-past eleven, and the leaders are coming around to start the second of four long laps that constitute the racetrack. I hear the crowd's roar, and spot the runners heading west towards the Victoria Memorial and Buckingham Palace.

Carrying a small shoulder sack, I push to the front of the crowd, holding aloft my Olympic security pass, which was never taken from me. It's critical that I be seen now, here, at this moment. I'd planned to find any policeman I could. But when I look down the side of the course, I see someone familiar. I duck the tape and walk towards him, holding up the pass.

'Inspector Casper?' I say. 'Mike Lancer.'

The inspector nodded. 'Seems to me you got a raw deal.'

'Thank you,' I say, then add, 'I'm no longer official, of course, but I was wondering if I could cut across the street when there's a gap in the runners. I wanted to watch from the north side if I could.'

Casper considered the request, then shrugged and said, 'Sure, why not?'

Thirty seconds later, I'm across the street, pushing back through the crowd and into the park. Inside, I move east, glancing at my watch and thinking that Marta will release Daring in ninety minutes or so, right around the end of the marathon, a move that should attract heavy police attention and give me enough of an edge to ensure that I can't possibly be beaten.

I won't be defeated today, I think. Not today. And never again.

Chapter 103

FOR THE LAST thirty minutes, his mouth taped shut, his head pounding and painful, Knight had alternated between trying to break free of his bonds, gasping in frustration, and looking longingly at his comatose children, dully aware of the marathon coverage blaring from the television in Lancer's spare bedroom.

It was 11:55. In mile eleven – kilometre nineteen – just shy of an hour into the race, runners from the UK, Ethiopia, Kenya and Mexico had broken away from the main pack along the Victoria Embankment. They were using each other to chew up ground as they headed past the London Eye towards Parliament at sub-Olympic-record pace despite the blistering heat.

Knight wondered grimly what atrocity Lancer had waiting somewhere along the marathon route. But he refused to contemplate what Marta might have in store for him and the twins in the aftermath of the last race of the Games.

He closed his eyes and began to pray to God and to Kate, pleading with them to help him save their children. He told them he'd be fine about dying if that meant he'd be with Kate again. But the children, they deserved to . . .

Marta walked into the room, carrying the black assault weapon that Knight had seen the night before as well as a plastic bag containing three litre-sized Coke bottles. Her dark locks had been chopped and dyed, leaving her hair a violent blonde tipped with silver highlights that somehow matched the black leather skirt, tank top and calf-length boots she wore. Her heavy make-up changed her appearance still further. If Knight hadn't spent so much time around her in the last two weeks he might never have recognised her as the plain nanny who'd first approached him at the playground.

Marta paid Knight no mind, as if he and everyone else in the room were afterthoughts. She set the Coke bottles on a dresser, then cradled the gun and went to Daring's side. She set the gun down, picked up a hypodermic needle and shot it into the IV line that had been inserted into the museum curator's arm.

'Time to wake up,' she said, and gathered up the gun again.

She fished an apple from her pocket and bit into

it. Her attention shifted lazily to the marathon coverage.

Luke stirred and opened his eyes, looking right at his father. His eyes went wide. Then his brows knitted, his face grew beet-red and he began making whining noises, not of fear but as if he desperately wanted to tell his father something. Knight recognised that red-faced expression and understood the meaning behind the stifled cries immediately.

At the noise, Marta looked over with such a cold expression on her face that Knight's pounding brain screamed at him to make her look at him and not at his son.

Knight began to moan behind his tape. Marta glanced over, chewing her apple, and said, 'Shut up. I don't want to hear you cry like your little boy.'

Instead of complying, Knight moaned louder and smashed his feet against the floor, trying not only to alert someone below but to bother Marta. He wanted to get her talking. He knew enough about hostage negotiation to understand how crucial it was to get a captor talking.

Isabel woke up and started to cry.

Marta took up the gun, stomped over to Knight, and laughed. 'We own the flat below, too. So go ahead, make noise. No one hears you.'

With that she kicked him in the stomach. Knight doubled up and rolled over on his back, gasping and feeling glass from the shattered fruit-juice tumbler crunch beneath him. Luke began to wail. Marta glared at the children. Knight was sure that she was going to kick them. But then she squatted down and ripped the tape off Knight's mouth. 'Tell them to shut up or you're all dead right now.'

'Luke wants to use the loo,' Knight said. 'Take the tape off. Ask him.'

Marta shot him a foul look, then scuttled across to his son and peeled off the tape over his mouth. 'What?'

Knight's son shrank away from Marta, but looked at his father and said, 'Lukey need go poop. Big-boy loo.'

'Crap in your pants for all I care.'

'Big-boy loo, Marta,' the boy insisted. 'Lukey go big-boy. No nappy.'

'Give him a chance,' Knight said. 'He's just three.'

Marta's expression turned into a disgusted sneer. But she got out a knife and cut free Luke's ankles. Gun in one hand, she hauled Knight's son to his feet and snarled, 'If this is another false alarm, I'll kill you first.'

They moved past Daring and disappeared through the door into the hallway. Knight glanced all around, rolled back slightly, and heard glass crunch again, felt tiny shards of it pricking his arms and back.

The pain jolted his brain into realising his opportunity, and he began frantically arching his back and moving around, fingers groping desperately beneath him. Please, Kate. Please.

The index finger of his right hand felt the keen edge of a larger shard of glass, perhaps two inches long, and tried to coax it into his hand. But he fumbled and dropped it. Cursing under his breath, Knight groped again. But he hadn't found it when he heard Luke cry, 'See, Marta? Big boy!'

A second later, he heard a toilet flush. Knight's fingers searched in a frenzy. Nothing. He heard footsteps, arched his hips one more time and pushed himself back closer to where the glass had shattered. Then Luke walked in, wrists still taped in front of him, beaming at his father.

'Lukey big boy now, Daddy,' he said. 'Lukey three. No nappies.'

Chapter 104

'GOOD JOB, LAD,' Knight said, lying back, smiling at his son, glancing at Marta – who was still cradling the gun – and feeling a thick chunk from the bottom of the juice glass lying on the floor just below the small of his back.

The fingers of his right hand closed round it just as Marta said to Luke, 'Go and sit down next to your sister – and don't move.' She turned to inspect Daring, who was now shifting on the bed.

'Wake up,' she said again. 'We have to go soon.'

Daring moaned as Knight twisted the chunk of glass into the duct tape around his wrists and began to saw at it. Luke came dutifully towards his father, smiling and saying, 'Lukey big boy.'

His attention jumping back to Marta, Knight said, 'Brilliant. Now sit down like Marta told you too.'

But his son didn't budge. 'We go home, Daddy?' Luke said, and Bella began to whine in agreement behind her gag. 'We go and have party?'

'Soon,' Knight said, feeling the tape begin to part. 'Very soon.'

But then Marta snatched up the gun and a roll of duct tape and started towards Luke. His son took one look at the tape and cried, 'No, Marta!'

Luke ducked and started to run. Marta became infuriated. Pointing the gun at Knight's son, she barked, 'Sit down. Now. Or you die.'

But Knight's son was too young to understand fully the implications of having a loaded weapon aimed at him. 'No!' Luke said impudently, and jumped onto the mattress beside Isabel, his eyes darting around, looking for escape.

'I'll teach you, then,' Marta said, stalking towards Luke, her stare fully on the boy and not on Knight who felt his wrists come free.

As she passed him, looking to corner his son, Knight lashed out with his bound feet.

They connected hard with Marta's Achilles tendons. She cried out as her legs buckled and she fell sideways to the floor. The gun clattered away.

Knight twisted around, clutching that chunk of glass, and tried to slash her with it. But her reaction time was stunningly fast and practical. She threw up her forearm, taking the cut there before kneeing Knight hard in the chest.

The wind knocked out of him, Knight let go of the glass shard.

Insane with fury, Marta jumped to her feet and snatched up the gun. She marched over to one of the Coke bottles, opened it, and stuffed the muzzle inside and down into the liquid before saying, 'I don't care what Cronus wants. I have had enough of you, and your bastard children.'

Marta deftly wrapped duct tape around her bleeding arm, and then around the gun barrel and the mouth of the bottle before swinging around the crudely silenced weapon. Her eyes had gone dark and dead, and Knight had a glimpse of what all those Bosnian boys must have seen when the Brazlic sisters had come calling. With grim intent, Marta marched towards Luke who still sat beside his sister. She said to Knight, 'The boy goes first. I want you to see how it's done.'

'Lancer is going to kill you!' Knight shouted at her. 'Just like he killed your sisters!'

That stopped her progress. She turned to him and said, 'My sisters are very much alive. They have already escaped from London.'

'No,' Knight said. 'Lancer killed them both. He broke Andjela's neck, and then cut off her hands and sent them to me. Nada's throat was cut from ear to ear.'

'That's a lie!' Marta snarled as she came at him, raising the gun.

'They were found in the same abandoned factory

near the gasworks where you kept Selena Farrell.'

That information made Marta pause briefly. 'How come it hasn't been on the news?'

'They probably haven't alerted the media,' Knight said, fumbling for an answer. 'They do that, you know – hide things.'

'You're lying,' she said. Then she shrugged. 'And even if it is true, so much the better for me. I am sick of them. I think of killing them myself from time to time.'

Marta clicked off the rifle's safety catch.

Chapter 105

SUDDENLY SIRENS WAILED nearby, coming closer, and Knight's spirits surged with renewed hope.

'They're coming for you now,' he said, grinning insanely at Marta and the bottom of the Coke bottle. 'You're going to the gallows, no matter what you do to me and my children.'

'No.' She laughed caustically. 'If they go anywhere, they go next door, not here. In the meantime, I kill you and then use the tunnel to escape.'

She tried to press the Coke bottle against Knight's head. But he batted at it with his hand and jerked around as the sirens came closer and louder. He thought: Buy time. At least the twins will be saved.

But then Marta stepped on the side of Knight's neck with her boot, choking him as she lowered the silenced gun.

He looked up at her cross-eyed and grabbed at her

ankles, trying to upset her balance. But she just ground her boot deeper and harder into his neck until his strength was gone.

Marta peered down at him. 'Goodbye, Mr Knight. Too bad I don't have a pickaxe.'

Chapter 106

KNIGHT THOUGHT OF Kate in the instant before Marta's eyes snapped wide open. She screamed in agony, yanked the Coke bottle away from his head and her boot off his neck, and fired the rifle. With a weird wet thud, the silenced gun blew a hole in the wall just above Knight's head. Coke and plastic fragments showered down on him as Marta screamed in agony once more. Frenzied, she spun away from Knight, groping wildly behind her.

Luke had bitten into Marta's hamstring, and was holding on like a little bulldog while his nanny furiously pounded against him, screaming again and again. Knight kicked her hard in the shin and she dropped the gun before ramming her elbow hard into Luke's side.

The boy slammed against the wall and lay still.

Knight crawled after the gun while Marta glared at Luke and felt down her leg for the gaping wound he'd left. She didn't notice his father until he was inches from the rifle.

She cursed and lunged towards Knight as his finger found the trigger and he tried to swing the gun to point it at her. She swept her other arm round and struck the side of the barrel, deflecting his aim even as the now unsilenced rifle went off again, this time with a deafening boom that disorientated Knight for a second. He looked around, dizzy, praying that he'd managed to shoot Marta somehow.

But then the oldest Fury kicked him in the ribs and ripped the gun from his hands. Gasping – and grinning in triumph – she aimed the muzzle at Knight's unconscious son.

'Watch him die,' she snarled.

The shot this time sounded distant and otherworldly to Knight, but it was aimed perfectly at his breaking heart. He fully expected Luke's small body to jump at the bullet's impact.

Instead, Marta's throat exploded in a slurry of blood before the war-criminal nanny crumpled and sprawled dead between Knight and his son.

Dumbfounded and slack-jawed, Knight twisted his head around and saw Kate's older sister rising from a shooting crouch.

Part Five

THE FINISH LINE

Chapter 107

TWENTY-FIVE MINUTES AFTER Pottersfield had shot and killed the wanted war criminal Senka Brazlic, the police inspector and Knight were in her car, sirens and lights on, racing through the streets of Chelsea and heading towards The Mall where the top runners were well into their fourth and final lap of the marathon route.

Ordinarily, the men's marathon, the final event of the summer Games, would end in the host city's Olympic stadium. But the London organisers – largely at Lancer's urging, it turned out – had decided that sending the runners through the scruffy East End was not the best way to sell the city's stunning attributes to the world.

Instead, the organisers opted to have the marathon contestants run four 6.5-mile laps, each of them featuring some of London's most notable landmarks as telegenic backdrops for the race: from Tower Hill to the Houses of Parliament along the

Thames, past the London Eye and Cleopatra's Needle. The start and finish would take place on The Mall, well in sight of Buckingham Palace.

'I want his picture in everyone's mobile, iPhone, BlackBerry,' Pottersfield shouted into her radio. 'Find him! Having the marathon here was his idea!'

Knight was thinking about how bloody brilliant she was at her job. She'd called up the Trace Angels site, seen that the children had been put on trains, but then thought to look at their whereabouts earlier and saw the address on Porchester Terrace.

After contacting the trains and getting word from conductors that there was no one matching the Knight children's description aboard, she'd led the police contingent to the building near Lancaster Gate. They'd been in the Furies' flat when the crudely silenced gun had gone off next door and they'd heard it. They'd discovered the entrance to Lancer's place behind that tapestry on the wall, and had then thrown a stun grenade a moment after Knight had fired the weapon.

Setting down her radio, Pottersfield said shakily, 'We'll get him. Everybody's hunting him now.'

Knight grunted, staring out the window into the glaring sunlight, still feeling dizzy and sore from the blows he'd taken. 'You okay, Elaine? Having to shoot?'

'Me? You shouldn't even be here, Peter,'

Pottersfield scolded. 'You should be back there in that ambulance with your kids, going to hospital. You need to be looked at yourself.'

'Amanda and Boss are on their way to meet Luke and Bella. I'll get examined when Lancer's stopped.'

Pottersfield changed down and shot out onto Buckingham Palace Road. 'You're sure Lancer said the attack was on the marathon?'

Knight struggled to remember before replying: 'Before he left, I told him that no matter what he might do, the Olympic spirit would never die. I told him that Mundaho had proved it, and Shaw, and Dr Pierce. That got him insanely angry, and I was certain he would kill me. But then the starting gun for the marathon went off. And he said something like: "The men's marathon. The final game has begun. And because I'm the superior man, I'm going to let you live to see the ending. Before Marta kills you, she's going to let you witness exactly how I snuff out that Olympic spirit once and for all." '

Pottersfield skidded the car to a stop in front of the police barrier opposite St James's Park and got out, holding up her badge to the officers guarding it. 'He's with Private and with me. Where's Inspector Casper?'

The policeman who looked miserable in the stifling heat, pointed north towards the roundabout in front of Buckingham Palace, and said, 'You want me to call him?'

Knight's sister-in-law shook her head before vaulting the barrier and battling her way through the crowd onto Birdcage Walk with Knight following somewhat woozily right behind her. Runners who were well behind the leaders were heading painfully towards the Queen Victoria Memorial at the centre of the roundabout.

Billy Casper was already hustling towards Knight and Pottersfield. 'Sweet Jesus, Elaine,' he said. 'I had the bastard right in front of me not an hour ago. He went into St James's Park.'

'Did you get Lancer's picture?'

'Everyone in the force got it ten seconds ago,' Casper replied, and then looked grim. 'The route is more than ten kilometres long. There's half a million people – maybe more – lining the route. How the hell are we going to find him?'

'At the finish, or somewhere near it,' Knight said. 'It fits his flair for the dramatic. Have you seen Jack Morgan?'

'He's way ahead of you, Peter,' Casper said. 'As soon as he heard Cronus was Lancer and that he was still on the loose, he went straight to the finish arena. Smart guy for a Yank.'

But twenty-six minutes later, as roars went up from back along the marathon route south of St

James's Park, Lancer had still not been sighted, and every aspect of the timing system had been re-examined for possible booby traps.

Standing high atop stands erected along The Mall, Knight and Jack – who had shown up minutes after Knight had asked after him – were using binoculars to look up into the trees to see if Lancer had climbed one and taken up position as a sniper. Casper and Pottersfield were doing much the same on the other side of the street. But their views were hampered by scores of large Union Jack and Olympic flags fluttering on poles running westward towards Buckingham Palace.

'I checked him out myself,' Jack said sombrely, lowering his binoculars. 'Lancer, I mean. When he did some work for us a few years back in Hong Kong. He was squeaky clean, nothing but raves from everyone who'd ever known him. And I don't remember ever seeing that he'd served in the Balkans. I'm sure I would have remembered that.'

'He was there for less than five weeks,' Knight said.

'Long enough to recruit bloodthirsty bitches as mad as he is,' Jack said.

'Probably why he left the deployment off his C.V.,' Knight said.

Before Jack could reply, the roar of the crowd came closer and people in the stands around the

Queen Victoria Memorial leaped to their feet as two policemen on motorcycles appeared about a hundred yards in front of the same four runners who'd broken free of the main pack back at mile twelve.

'The motorcyclists,' Knight said, and threw up his binoculars, trying to see the faces of the officers. But he could tell quickly that neither man was Lancer.

Behind the motorcycles, the top four runners appeared – the Kenyan, the Ethiopian, the barefoot Mexican, and that lad from Brighton – each of them carrying Olympic and Cameroonian hand flags.

After twenty-six miles, three hundred and eighty-five yards, after forty-two thousand, one hundred and ninety-five metres, the Kenyan and the Brit were leading, sprinting side by side. But at the two-hundred-yard mark and hard behind the leaders, the Ethiopian and the Mexican split and sprinted to the leaders' flanks.

The crowd went wild as the whippet-thin runners churned down the final straight towards gold and glory, four abreast and none of them giving ground.

Then, twenty yards from the finish, the lad from Brighton surged forward, and it looked as if the UK was going to have its first men's-marathon gold to go with the historic win by Mary Duckworth in the women's race the previous Sunday.

Astonishingly, however, mere feet from the finish

line, the Brighton lad slowed, the runners raised their flags, and the foursome went through the tape together.

For a second, the crowd was stunned and Knight could hear broadcasters braying about the unprecedented act and what it was supposed to mean. And then everyone on The Mall saw it for what it was and started lustily to cheer the gesture, Peter Knight included.

He thought: You see that, Lancer? Cronus? You can't snuff out the Olympic spirit because it doesn't exist in any one place; it's carried in the hearts of every athlete who's ever striven for greatness, and it always will be.

'No attack,' Jack said when the cheering died down. 'Maybe the show of force along the route scared Lancer off.'

'Maybe,' Knight allowed. 'Or maybe he wasn't talking about the end of the marathon at all.'

Chapter 108

THE NAUSEATING ENDING to the men's marathon keeps replaying on the screens around the security stations as I wait patiently in the sweltering heat in the line at the north entrance to the Olympic Park off Ruckholt Road.

My head is shaven and, along with every bit of exposed skin, has been stained with henna to a deep russet tone ten times as dark as my normal colour. The white turban is perfect. So is the black beard, the metal bracelet on my right wrist and the Indian passport, and the sepia-brown contact lenses, the glasses and the loose white Kurta pyjamas and tunic that together with a dab of patchouli oil complete my disguise as Jat Singh Rajpal, a tall Sikh textile trader from Punjab lucky enough to hold a ticket to the closing ceremony.

I'm two feet from the screeners when my face, my normal face, appears on one of the television screens that had been showing the finish of the marathon.

At first I feel panicky. But then I quickly compose myself and take several discreet glances at the screen, hoping it's just some kind of recap of the events of the Olympics including my dismissal from the organising committee. But then I see the banner scrolling beneath my image and the news that I'm wanted in connection with the Cronus murders.

How is it possible! Many voices thunder in my head, triggering one of those insanely blinding headaches. It's everything I can do to stay composed when I step towards an F7 guard, a burly woman, and a young police constable who are inspecting tickets and identification.

'You're a long way from home, Mr Rajpal,' the constable says, looking at me expressionlessly.

'One is willing to make the journey for an event as wonderful as this,' I say in a practised accent that comes through flawlessly despite the pounding in my skull. I have to fight not to reach up under my turban to touch that scar throbbing at the back of my head.

The F7 guard glances at a laptop computer screen. 'Have you been to any other events during the games, Mr Rajpal?' she asks.

'Two,' I say. 'Athletics this past Thursday evening, and field hockey earlier in the week. Monday afternoon. The India-Australia game. We lost.'

She scans the screen and nods. 'We'll need to put

your bag and any other metal objects through the screener.'

'Without hesitation,' I say, putting the bag on the conveyor belt and depositing coins, my bracelet, and my mobile in a plastic tray that follows it.

'No kirpan?' the constable asks.

I smile. Clever lad. 'No, I left the ceremonial dagger at home.'

The constable nods. 'Appreciate that. We've had a few of your blokes try to come in with them. You can go on through now.'

Moments later my headache recedes. I've retrieved my bag, which contains only a camera and a large tube of what appears to be sunscreen. Moving quickly past Eton Manor I cross an elevated pedestrian bridge that leads me onto the north-east concourse. Skirting the Velodrome, the basketball arena and the athletes' village, I make my way continuously south past the sponsors' hospitality area. I pause to look at them, realising that I've overlooked many possible violators of the Olympic ideals.

No matter, I decide. My final act will more than compensate for the oversight. At that thought, my breath quickens. So does my heart, which is hammering when I smile at the guards at the bottom of the loose spiral staircase that climbs between the legs of the Orbit. 'The restaurant?' I say. 'Still open?'

'Until half-past three, sir,' one of them replies. 'You've got two hours.'

'And if I wish for food after that?' I ask.

'The other vendors down here will all be open,' he says. 'Only the restaurant is closing.'

I nod and start the long climb, barely giving heed to the nameless monsters descending the staircase, all of them oblivious to the threat I represent. Twelve minutes later, I reach the level of the slowly turning restaurant, and go up to the maître d'.

'Rajpal,' I say. 'Table for one.'

She frowns. 'Would you be willing to share?'

'It would be a great pleasure,' I reply.

She nods. 'It will still be ten or fifteen minutes.'

'Might I use the gents' while I wait?' I ask.

'Of course,' she says and stands aside.

Other prospective patrons press in behind me, leaving the woman so busy that I'm sure she's already begun to forget about me. When she calls my name, she'll figure I got tired of waiting and left. Even if she has someone check the toilet, they won't find me. Rajpal is already gone.

I go to the gents', and take the stall I need, which is luckily vacant. Five minutes go by before the rest of the facility empties. Then, as quickly as I can, I pull myself up to a sitting position on the stall dividers and push up one of the ceiling tiles to reveal a reinforced crawl-way built so that maintenance workers can easily get at the electrical and cooling systems.

A few moments of struggle and I'm laying up there in the crawl-way, the ceiling tile back in place. Now all I have to do is calm myself, prepare myself, and trust in fate.

Chapter 109

KNIGHT AND JACK were inside the Olympic Park by four that afternoon. The sunlight was still glaring and the heat shimmered off the track. According to Scotland Yard and MI5, which had together seized control of security under orders from the Prime Minister, Mike Lancer had made no effort to get inside the park with his security pass, which someone had smartly flagged immediately after the warning about him had been issued.

Around four-thirty, Knight's head was still aching as he followed Jack into the empty stadium where teams with sniffer dogs were patrolling. At the moment, his thoughts were less about finding Lancer than they were about his children. Were they all right in hospital? Was Amanda by their side?

Knight was about to make a call to his mother when Jack said, 'Maybe he did get spooked at the marathon. Maybe that was his last chance: he saw it wasn't going to work, and he's making his escape.'

'No,' Knight said. 'He's going to try something here. Something big.'

'He'll have to be Houdini,' Jack observed. 'You heard them, they've gone to war-zone security levels. They're putting double teams of SAS snipers up high and every available cop in the halls and stairways.'

'I'm hearing you, Jack,' Knight said. 'But given what the insane bastard has done so far, we can't be sure that *any* security level is going to work. Think about it. Lancer oversaw a billion and a half dollars in security spending for the Olympics. He knows every contingency that Scotland Yard and MI5 provided for in their plans. And for much of the past seven years that lunatic has had access to every inch of every venue as it was built. Every goddamn inch.'

Chapter 110

AT THREE-THIRTY THAT afternoon, echoing through the fourteen-inch gap between the restaurant ceiling and the roof of the Orbit, I hear hydraulic gears being braked and halted, and feel the slow rotation of the observation deck stop. Closing my eyes and calming my breathing, I prepare for what lies ahead. My fate. My destiny. My just and final due.

At ten minutes to four I squeeze the tube of special skin cream onto the turban cloth and use it to turn my skin near-black. A maintenance crew enters and cleans the room below me. I can hear their mops sluicing the floor for several minutes, followed by half an hour of silence that is interrupted only by the soft sounds of the movement it takes to stain my head, neck and hands.

At twelve minutes past four, the first sniffer dog team enters the gents', and I have the sudden terrible thought that the monsters might have been clever enough to bring an article of my clothing to prime their beasts. But the patrol is in and out in under a minute, fooled no doubt by the smell of the patchouli oil.

They return at five and again at six. When they leave after the third time, I know that my hour is at hand. Cautiously, I grope around under a strip of insulation, finding a loaded ammunition clip put there seven months ago. Pocketing the clip, I lower myself into the stall and then strip off my remaining clothes, leaving me two-tone, black and white, and a terror to behold in the mirror.

Naked now except for my wristwatch, I rip a length of the turban fabric and wrap the two ends around my hands, leaving an eighteen-inch section dangling slack. Taking a position tight to the wall next to the gents' door, I settle down to wait.

At six forty-five, I hear footsteps and men's voices. The door opens and comes right up against my face before it swings back the other way to reveal the back of a tall, athletic black monster in a tracksuit and carrying a large duffel bag.

He is big. I assume he's skilled. But he is no match for a superior being.

The slack turban fabric flicks over his head and settles below his chin. Before he can even react, I've got my knee in his back and I'm throttling the life out of him. Seconds later, still feeling the quivering and soft nasal whining of his death, I drag the monster's body to the farthest stall, and then move to his duffel bag, glancing at my watch. Thirty minutes until showtime.

It takes me less than half that to don the parade uniform of the Queen's guardsman and set the black bearskin hat on my head, feeling its familiar weight settle above my eyebrows and tight to my ears. After a minor adjustment, I've got the leather chinstrap taut and snug against my jaw. Last, I pick up his automatic rifle, knowing very well that it's empty. I don't care. The ammo clip is full.

Then I return to the middle stall and wait. At a quarter past seven, I hear the door open and a voice growl, 'Supple, we're up.'

'On it in two,' I reply, disguising my voice with a cough. 'Go to the hatch.'

'See you topside,' he says.

I hope not, I think before I hear the door close behind him.

Out of the stall now, I go to the door, tracking the sweep second hand of my watch. At exactly ninety seconds, I take a deep breath and step out through the door and into the hallway, carrying the duffel bag.

At a quick pace, eyes gazing straight ahead, my face expressionless, I walk through the restaurant to the glass doors on the right-hand side of the dining room. Two SAS men are already unlocking the doors. As they swing them open, exposing me to the heat, I set my dufflel bag to one side next to another identical one, and charge past them onto the observation platform and towards a narrow doorway that is open and guarded by yet another SAS man.

I've timed it perfectly. The guard hisses, 'Cutting it bloody close, mate.'

'Shaving it close is what the Queen's Guard do, mate,' I say, ducking past him and into a tight stairwell with a narrow steel staircase that rises to a retracting hatch door and open air.

I can see the early-evening sky and clouds racing above me. Hearing distant trumpets calling, I climb towards my fate, so close now that I can feel it like a muscle burn and taste it like sweet sweat on my lips.

Chapter 111

THE TRUMPETERS STOOD to either side of the stage down on the floor of the Olympic Stadium, blowing a plaintive melody that Knight did not recognise.

He stood high in the stands at the north end of the venue, using binoculars to scan the crowd. He was tired, his head aching, and was feeling overly irritated by the lingering heat and the sound of the trumpets launching the closing ceremony. As it stopped, the screens around the stadium jumped to a feed showing a medium-range view of the Olympic cauldron high atop the Orbit and flanked as it had been since the opening ceremony by the ramrod-straight Queen's guardsmen.

The guardsmen on the raised platform above the roof shouldered their guns, pivoted through forty-five degrees and marched stiff-legged, their free arms pumping, in opposite directions towards two new guardsmen who climbed up onto the roof from hatches on either side of the observation deck and moved towards the platform and cauldron. The guards passed each other exactly halfway between the cauldron and the stairwell. The guards who were being relieved of duty disappeared from the roof and the new pair climbed the platform from either side to stand rigidly at attention beside the Olympic flame.

Knight roamed the crowd for the next hour and a half. As the summer sky began to darken and breezes began to stir, he was buoyed by the fact that despite the threat Lancer still posed, an incredible number of athletes, coaches, judges, referees and fans had decided to attend the closing ceremony when they could just as easily have gone home to more certain safety.

The affair had originally been planned as a celebration as joyous as the opening ceremony had been before the death of the American shot-putter. But the organisers had tweaked the ceremony in light of the murders, and had made it more sombre and meaningful by enlisting the London Symphony Orchestra to back Eric Clapton who delivered a heart-wrenching version of his song 'Tears in Heaven'.

In that same vein, as Knight moved south inside the stadium, Marcus Morris was now giving a speech that was part elegy to the dead and part celebration of all the great and wonderful things that had happened at the London Games in spite of Cronus and his Furies.

Knight glanced at the programme and thought: We've got a few more speeches, a spectacle or two, the turning over of the Olympic flag to Brazil; and then a few words by the mayor of Rio and . . .

'Anything, Peter?' Jack asked over the radio. They'd changed security frequencies in case Lancer was trying to monitor their broadcasts.

'Nothing,' he replied. 'But it still doesn't feel right.'

That thought was paramount in Knight's mind until the organisers broke from the scheduled programme to introduce some 'special guests'.

Dr Hunter Pierce appeared on the stage along with Zeke Shaw and the four runners who'd won marathon gold. They pushed Filatri Mundaho in a wheelchair before them, a sheet over his legs. Medical personnel followed.

Mundaho had suffered third-degree burns over much of his lower body, and had endured several excruciating abrasion procedures during the past week. The co-world-record holder in the 100 metres should have been in agony, unable to rise from his hospital bed. But you'd never have known it.

The orphaned ex-boy soldier's head was up, proud and erect. He was waving to the crowd, which leaped to its collective feet and began cheering for him. Knight's eyes watered. Mundaho was showing incredible, incredible courage, along with an iron will and a depth of humanity that Lancer could not even begin to fathom.

They gave the sprinter his gold-medal ceremony, and during the playing of the Cameroonian national anthem Knight was hard pressed to find someone in the stadium who wasn't teary-eyed.

Then Hunter Pierce began to talk about the legacy of the London Games, arguing that it would ultimately signify a rekindling of and rededication to Pierre de Coubertin's original Olympic dreams and ideals. At first Knight was held enraptured by the American diver's speech.

But then he forced himself to tune her out, to try to think like Lancer and like Lancer's alter ego Cronus. He thought about the last few things that the madman had said to him. He tried to see Lancer's words as if they were printed on blocks that he could pick up and examine in detail: AT THE END, JUST BEFORE YOU DIE, KNIGHT, I'M GOING TO MAKE SURE THAT YOU AND YOUR CHILDREN WITNESS HOW I INGENIOUSLY MANAGE TO SNUFF OUT THE OLYMPIC SPIRIT FOR EVER.

Knight considered each and every word, exploring their meaning in every sense. And that's when it hit him, the seventh to last word in the sentence.

He triggered his radio microphone, and said, 'You

don't snuff out a spirit, Jack.'

'Come back with that, Peter?' Jack said.

Knight was already running towards the exit, saying, 'Lancer told me he was going to "snuff out the Olympic spirit forever".'

'And?'

'You don't snuff out a spirit, Jack. You snuff out a flame.'

Chapter 112

LOOK AT ME now, hiding in plain sight of a hundred thousand people and cameras linked to billions more.

Fated. Chosen. Gifted by the gods. I am clearly a being superior in every way, certainly superior to pathetic Mundaho and Shaw and that conniving bitch Hunter Pierce, and the other athletes down there on the stage inside the stadium, all of them condemning me as a . . .

The wind is picking up. I shift my attention into the wind: north-west, far beyond the stadium, far beyond London. Out there on the horizon dark clouds are boiling up into thunderheads. What could be more fitting as a backdrop?

Fated, I think, before I hear a roar go up in the stadium.

What's this? Sir Elton John and Sir Paul McCartney are coming onto the stage and taking seats at opposite white pianos. Who's that with them? Marianne Faithfull? Oh, for pity's sake, they're singing 'Let it Be' to Mundaho.

At their monstrous screeching, you can't begin to understand how much I want to abandon my stance of attention, rub my scar and end this hypocritical pap right now. But, with my eyes locked dead ahead into the approaching storm, I tell myself to stay calm and follow the plan to its natural and fated ending.

To keep the infernal singing from getting to me, I focus on the fact that, just a few minutes from now, I *will* reveal myself. And when I do I'll be able to rejoice in their shared horror: McCartney, John, and Faithfull too. I'll watch them all trampling over Mundaho as they run for the exits and I joyously make one final sacrifice in the name of every true Olympian who ever lived.

Chapter 113

HEARING THE CROWD in the stadium singing 'Let it Be', Knight raced towards the base of the Orbit, seeing Jack already there ahead of him, interrogating the Gurkhas guarding the staircase that wound its way up the tower's DNA-like superstructure towards the circular observation deck.

When Knight arrived, legs cramping and head splitting, he gasped, 'Was Lancer up there?'

'They say the only people who went up after three-thirty were some SAS snipers, a dog team, and the two Queen's guardsmen protecting the—'

'Can we alert them, the men on the roof?' Knight said, cutting Jack off.

'I don't know,' Jack said. 'I mean, I don't think so.'

'I think Lancer plans to blow up the cauldron, maybe this entire structure. Where's the propane tank and feeder line that keep the flame alight?'

'It's over this way,' called the strained voice of a man hurrying them.

Stuart Meeks was head of facilities at the Olympic Park. A short man in his fifties who sported a pencil-thin moustache and slicked-back hair, he carried an iPad and sweated profusely as he used an electronic code to open a door set flush in the concrete floor. The steps beneath the door led down into a massive utility basement that ran beneath the western legs of the Orbit and out under the river and the plaza towards the stadium.

'How big is the tank down there?' Knight asked as Meeks lifted the door.

'Huge – five hundred thousand litres,' Meeks said, holding out the iPad, which showed a schematic of the gas system. 'But as you can see here it serves all the propane needs in the park, not just the cauldron. The gas is drawn from the main reservoir here into smaller holding tanks at each of the venues – and in the athletes' village, of course. It was designed, like the electrical station, to be self-sufficient.'

Knight gaped at him. 'Are you saying if it blows, everything blows?'

'No, I don't . . .' Meeks stopped. He turned pale. 'I honestly don't know.'

Jack said, 'Peter and I were with Lancer ten days ago up on the observation deck shortly after he'd finished inspecting security on the cauldron. Did Lancer go down into this basement during that inspection, Stu?'

Meeks nodded. 'Mike insisted on looking at everything one last time. From the tank and up the line, all the way to the coupling that connects the piping to the cauldron. It took us more than an hour.'

'We don't have an hour,' Knight said.

Jack was already on the steep ladder, preparing to climb down to inspect the giant propane tank. 'Call in the dogs again, Stu. Send them down as soon as they get here. Peter, trace the gas line up to the roof.'

Knight nodded before asking Meeks if he had any tools with him. The facilities director unsnapped a Leatherman from a pouch on his hip and told Knight he'd send the schematic of the gas-line system to his phone. No more than twenty yards up the spiral staircase that climbed the Orbit, Knight felt his phone buzz, alerting him to the arrival of the schematic.

He was about to open the link when he thought of something that made the diagram seem irrelevant at this point. He keyed his microphone and said, 'Stuart, how is the gas line to the cauldron controlled? By that I mean is there a manual valve up there that controls the gas flow that will have to be moved for the flame in the cauldron to go out, or will it be done electronically?'

'Electronically,' Meeks replied. 'Before it connects to the cauldron the line runs through a crawl space that's part of the ductwork in the ceiling above the restaurant and below the roof.'

Despite the pounding in his skull and his general sense of irritability, Knight was picking up the pace as he climbed. The wind was strong now. In the distance he thought he heard the rumble of thunder.

'Any way to get on the roof?' he asked.

'There are two hatches with retractable doors and staircases on opposite sides of the roof,' Meeks said. 'That's how the guardsmen have been climbing up and down for their shifts. There's also an exhaust grate in the ductwork several feet from that valve you asked about.'

Before Knight could think about that, he heard Jack say, 'Main tank appears clear. Stuart, we know the max volume and what it's holding?'

There was long pause before the Olympic Park's facility supervisor said in a hoarse voice, 'It was filled again at dawn, day before yesterday, Jack.'

Two hundred feet above the Olympic Park, Knight now understood that underground between the Orbit and the stadium was a mega-explosive device certainly capable of toppling the tower, but also of causing tremendous damage to the south end of the stadium and everyone seated there. Not to mention what might happen if a central explosion set off other detonations around the venue.

'Evacuate, Jack,' Knight said. 'Tell security to stop

the ceremony and get everyone out of the stadium, and out of the park.'

'But what if he's watching?' Jack said. 'What if he can trigger it remotely?'

'I don't know,' Knight said, feeling torn. His personal inclination was to turn around and get the hell out of there. He was a father. He'd already almost died once today. Could he dare tempt fate twice?

Still climbing, Knight toggled on the schematic on his phone, looking for the digitally controlled cauldron valve that was somewhere between the roof and the restaurant ceiling. At a glance, he felt almost sure that that control valve was the most likely place for Lancer to attach a triggering device to the main gas line.

If he could reach it, he could defuse it. If he couldn't . . .

Chapter 114

LIGHTNING FLASHED IN the near distance and the wind began to gust as Knight reached the entrance to the observation deck of the Orbit. Samba music blared from inside the Olympic stadium as part of Brazil's tribute to the 2016 games.

Though they'd been warned that he was coming, the Gurkhas at the entry insisted on checking Knight's ID before allowing him to enter. Inside he was met by the senior SAS man, a guy named Creston, who said that he and his team and the skeleton television camera crew had been on the deck since roughly five o'clock when the restaurant had been closed to everyone but the Queen's guardsmen who were using the gents' inside to change in and out of uniform.

Queen's Guard, Knight thought. Lancer's regiment served in the Guard. Hadn't he said that?

'Get me in that restaurant,' Knight said. 'There

might be a triggering device tied into the gas line above the kitchen.'

In seconds, Knight was running through the restaurant towards the kitchen with the SAS man in tow. Knight looked over his shoulder at him. 'Are the roof hatches open?'

'No,' Creston said. 'Not until the end of the ceremony. They're timed.'

'No way to talk to the guardsmen up there?'

He shook his head. 'They aren't even armed. It's a ceremonial bit.'

Knight pressed his microphone. 'Stuart, where do I go up through the ceiling?'

'In the kitchen, left of the oven hood,' Meeks replied. 'The kitchen is past the toilets and through the double doors.'

As Knight went into the hallway towards the kitchen, he saw the gents', remembered that the guardsmen got changed there, and had a sudden strange intuition. 'When did the relieved guards leave?' he asked the SAS man.

Creston shrugged. 'Right after their shift. They had seats inside the stadium.'

'They changed and left?'

He nodded.

Still, rather than barge on into the kitchen, Knight stopped and pushed on the door of the ladies' toilet.

'What are you doing?' Creston asked.

'Not sure,' Knight said, seeing it empty and then squatting to peer under the stalls. All empty.

He quickly crossed to the gents' and did the same, finding a black man's naked body stuffed into the farthest stall.

'We have a dead guardsman in the men's loo up here,' Knight barked into his radio as he headed towards the kitchen. 'I believe Lancer has taken his uniform and is now on the roof.'

He looked at the SAS man. 'Figure out how to get those hatch doors open.'

Creston nodded and took off, with Knight going in the opposite direction, bursting into the kitchen and quickly spotting the trapdoor in the ceiling left of the restaurant's oven hood and vent. Dragging a stainless steel food-preparation table over beneath the trapdoor, he triggered his mike and said, 'Can we get a visual on the guards to confirm that one of them is Lancer?'

Listening to Jack relay the request to snipers high atop the stadium, Knight noticed the padlock on the trapdoor for the first time. 'I need a combination, Stuart,' he said into his radio.

Meeks gave it to him, and with shaking hands Knight spun the dial and felt the lock give. He used a broom to push the trapdoor open, then looked around the kitchen one last time to see if there was anything he might be able to use or might need to shut down a gas line. A self-igniting blowtorch of the kind that chefs use to caramelise sugar caught his eye. He snatched it up.

Knight tossed the torch up into the crawl space, and then swung his arms twice to loosen them before jumping up and grabbing the sides of the trapdoor frame. He hung there a second, took a deep breath, and raised his legs in front of him before driving them backward with enough force for him to be able to lurch his way up into the cavity between the restaurant ceiling and the roof of the Orbit.

Knight pulled out a slim torch, flipped it on and, pushing the blowtorch in front of him, wriggled towards a piece of copper pipe that bisected the ductwork about six feet away. Knight didn't have to get much closer to see the bumpy black electrical tape wrapped around it, securing a mobile phone and something else to the gas line.

'I've got the trigger. It's a small magnesium bomb taped to the gas line,' he said. 'It's not on a timer. He's going to blow it remotely. Shut down the entire gas system. Put out the Olympic flame. Now.'

Chapter 115

BLOW, WINDS, BLOW.

Lightning flashes and thunder blasts north-west towards Crouch End and Stroud Green, not far at all from where my drug-addled parents gave birth to me. It is fitting. It is fated.

Indeed, as the jackass who runs the International Olympic Committee prepares to have the flags lowered, declare the Games over, and order the flame extinguished, I fully embrace my destiny. Breaking from my stance of rigid attention, I gaze into the black wall of the oncoming storm, thinking how remarkable it is that my life has been like a track oval, starting and finishing in much the same place.

Pulling out a mobile phone from my pocket, I hit a number on speed dial and hear it connect. Pocketing the phone, I take up my rifle, take two strides forward and pivot to my right. Towards the cauldron.

Chapter 116

A FEW MINUTES earlier, Karen Pope trudged out into the west stands of the Olympic Stadium just as IOC President Jacques Rogge, looking haggard and grave, walked to the lectern on the stage. The reporter had just filed her latest update to the *Sun*'s website, describing the escape of Knight and his children, the death of Marta and her sisters, and the global manhunt for Mike Lancer.

As Rogge spoke over the noise of a rising wind and against the building rumour of thunder, Pope was thinking that these cursed Games were finally almost over. Goodbye and good riddance as far as she was concerned. She never wanted to write about the Olympics again, though she knew that was an impossible dream. She felt depressed and lethargic, and wondered if what she was feeling was as much battle fatigue as the desperate need to sleep. And Knight wasn't answering his phone. Neither was Jack Morgan, or Inspector Pottersfield.

What was going on that she didn't know about?

As Rogge droned on, preparing to declare the Games at an end, Pope happened to look up at the cauldron atop the Orbit, seeing the flame billow in the wind. She admitted that she looked forward to seeing it extinguished while feeling somewhat guilty about the—

The Queen's guardsman to the cauldron's left suddenly lifted his gun, threw off his bearskin hat, walked out in front of the Olympic flame, pivoted and opened fire. The other guard jerked, staggered, and fell to his side and off the platform. His body hit the roof, slid and slipped off the Orbit, plunging and then gone.

Pope's gasp of horror was obliterated by the screams of the multitude in the stadium rising into one trembling cry before a booming voice coming over the public address system drowned it out: 'You sorry inferior creatures. You didn't think an instrument of the gods would let you off that easily, did you?'

Chapter 117

I CLUTCH THE mobile phone in my left hand, speaking into it, and hearing the power in my voice echo back to me. 'All you SAS snipers out there in the park, don't be stupid. I'm holding a triggering device. If you shoot me, this entire tower, much of the stadium, and tens of thousands of lives will be lost.'

Below me, the crowd erupts and turns as frenzied as rats fleeing a sinking ship. Seeing them scurry and claw, I smile with utter satisfaction.

'Tonight marks the end of the modern Olympics,' I thunder. 'Tonight we snuff out the flame that has burned so corruptly since that traitor de Coubertin came up with this mockery of the true Games more than a century ago!'

Chapter 118

KNIGHT HEARD THE gunshots and Lancer's booming threat through an exhaust grate in the ceiling of the ductwork several feet beyond the gas line and the triggering device.

He didn't have time to try and defuse the trigger, and for all he knew Lancer had booby-trapped it to go off if it was tampered with.

'How about cutting off the tanks?' he asked over his radio.

'It's a disaster, Peter,' Jack shot back. 'He's welded the valves open.'

Above him, Lancer launched into a longer tirade, beginning with the doctors in Barcelona who had drugged him to prevent him from winning gold in the decathlon, from being named the greatest all-around athlete in the world. And in the background, Knight could hear the petrified crowd trying to escape the stadium. He understood he had only one chance.

He pushed the blowtorch forward and crawled after it, past the gas line and the triggering device, until he lay beneath the exhaust grate.

Through the slats he saw flashes of approaching lightning and the billowing glow of the Olympic flame still burning.

Four bolts held the grate in place. All of them looked sealed in some kind of chemical resin. Maybe he could melt it.

Knight grabbed the blowtorch and ignited it. As fast as he could, he heated the resin until it melted. Then he grabbed the nearest bolt head with the pliers on the Leatherman tool that Meeks had given him and wrenched at it. He felt thrilled when it gave.

Chapter 119

LIGHTNING INSCRIBES THE sky and thunder booms like close cannon fire as I bellow at the crazed crowd trying to escape the stadium, 'For these reasons and a thousand others, the modern Games must end. Surely you understand!'

But instead of screams of terror, or even calls of agreement, I'm hearing something I did not expect in return. The monsters are booing me. They're catcalling, and casting filthy slurs on my genius, my superiority.

These are the final indignities of a martyr for a just cause – stabbing, hurtful. But nothing like a roadside bomb, or even a rock, nothing that can stop me from seeing my fate fulfilled.

Still, this rejection is enough to raise a wave of hatred in me like no other, a tsunami of loathing for all the monsters in the stadium before me.

Looking up into the thundering dark sky that is now spitting lightning and hurling rain, I cry, 'For you, Gods of Olympus. I do this all for you!'

Chapter 120

KNIGHT WAS ALREADY well beyond the exhaust vent, up on the raised platform surrounding the cauldron, and now charging at full tilt through the pouring rain.

Before the madman's thumb could hit the mobile's send button, Knight hit Lancer low, hard, and from the side, a stunning blow that caused the crazed Olympian to lurch and fall to the floor of the platform. His automatic weapon skittered away.

Knight landed on top of Lancer, who was still clutching the mobile phone. The former decathlon champion was some ten years older than Knight. But he quickly proved bigger, stronger, and more skilled as a fighter.

Lancer backhanded Knight so hard that the Private London agent was thrown off, and almost slammed his face against the searing wall of the cauldron. The infernal heat and the drenching rain revived him almost instantly.

He twisted, seeing that Lancer was trying to regain his feet. But Knight kicked viciously at the madman's ankle and connected. Lancer howled, stumbled to one knee and was rising again when Knight got his right forearm around the man's bull neck from behind, trying to get a choke hold on him and seize the mobile before the gas bomb could be triggered.

He squeezed Lancer's throat and grabbed at his thumb, trying to pry loose his grip on the phone. But then Lancer jammed his chin down on Knight's forearm, twisted his torso, and threw elbow punches that struck Knight hard on ribs still bruised from the Fury's attempt to run him down.

The Private London agent grunted in dire pain but held on, thinking of Luke and Isabel before taking a cue from his son. He bit brutally at the back of the insane man's head, feeling a chunk of thick scar tissue tear away from Lancer's scalp. Lancer screamed in agony and rage.

Knight bit again, this time lower, his teeth sinking into neck muscles as a lion might try to cripple a buffalo.

Lancer went berserk.

He swung and bucked, bellowing in blind primal fury and throwing meaty fists over his shoulder, hitting Knight in the head before pummelling his torso with elbow blows again, left and right, blows so hard that several of the Private agent's ribs cracked and broke.

It was too much for him.

Knight's breath was knocked out of him and the pain in his side erupted with such force that he grunted, releasing both his bite and the chokehold that he'd had on Lancer's neck. He fell to the platform in the rain, groaning and fighting for air and a relief from the agony that now consumed him.

Blood dripping from his bite wounds, Lancer turned and glared down at Knight in triumph and in loathing.

'You had no chance, Knight,' he gloated, backing away and raising the mobile phone towards the sky again. 'You were up against an infinitely superior being. You had no—'

Knight flung the Leatherman at Lancer.

It flew end over end before the narrow prongs of the pliers struck Lancer and pierced deep into his right eye.

Staggering backwards, still clutching the mobile, reaching futilely for the tool that had sealed his fate, Lancer let out a series of blood-curdling screams worthy of some mythical creature of doom, like Cronus after Zeus threw him deep into the darkest and deepest pit in Tartarus.

For a second, Knight feared Lancer would find his balance and manage to trigger the bomb.

But then thunder exploded directly over the Orbit, throwing a single white-hot jagged bolt that ignored the lightning rods fixed high above the observation deck and struck the butt end of the Leatherman tool protruding from Lancer's eye, electrocuting the self-described instrument of the gods and hurling him back and over into the cauldron where he was engulfed and consumed by the roaring Olympic flame.

Epilogue

Monday, 13 August 2012

ON THE THIRD floor of St Thomas's Hospital, sitting in a wheelchair, Knight smiled stiffly at the people gathered around the beds that held Luke and Isabel. While the effects of what turned out to be a concussion had mellowed to a dull thumping in his head, his broken and bruised ribs were killing him, making each breath feel like saws working in his chest.

But he was alive. His kids were alive. The Olympics had been saved and avenged by forces far beyond Knight's understanding. And Inspector Elaine Pottersfield had just entered the room carrying two small chocolate cakes, each adorned with three lit birthday candles.

Never one to miss the chance to sing, Hooligan broke into 'Happy Birthday' and was joined by the twins' nurses and doctors, and by Jack Morgan,

Karen Pope, and Knight's mother. Even Gary Boss, who'd arrived early to decorate the hospital room with bright balloons and bunting, joined in.

'Close your eyes and make a wish,' the twins' aunt said.

'Dream big!' their grandmother cried.

Isabel and Luke closed their eyes for a second, and then opened them, took deep breaths and blew out every one of the candles. Everyone cheered and clapped. Pottersfield cut the cakes.

Ever the journalist, Pope asked, 'What did you wish for?'

Knight's son got annoyed. 'Lukey not telling you. It's secret.'

But Isabel looked at Pope matter-of-factly and said, 'I wished we could have a new mummy.'

Her brother's face clouded. 'No fair. That's what Lukey wished for.'

There were soothing sounds of sympathy all around and Knight felt his heart break once again.

His daughter was staring at him. 'No more nannies, Daddy.'

'No more nannies,' he promised, glancing at his mother. 'Right, Amanda?'

'Only if they are under my direct and constant supervision,' she said.

'Or mine,' Boss said.

Cake and ice cream were served. After several

bites, Pope said, 'You know what threw me about Lancer, kept me from ever considering him as a suspect?'

'What's that?' Hooligan asked.

'He had one of his Furies try to run him down on day one,' she said. 'Right?'

'Definitely,' Knight said. 'I'll bet he had that planned from the beginning. I just happened to be there.'

'There was another clue if you think about it,' Hooligan said. 'Cronus never sent you a letter detailing the reasons why Lancer should die.'

'I never thought of that,' Knight said.

'Neither did I,' Jack said, getting up from his chair and dumping his paper plate into the wastebasket.

After they had finished eating and had unwrapped the presents that everyone seemed to have brought, Knight's children were soon drowsy. When Isabel's eyes closed, and Luke started to rock and suck his thumb, Amanda and Boss left with whispered promises to return in the morning to help see home Knight and the twins.

His sister-in-law was next to depart, saying, 'Hiring a war criminal as your nanny was not your finest hour, Peter, but ultimately you were brilliant. Absolutely brilliant. Kate would have been so proud of how hard your fought for your children, for the Olympics, for London, for everyone.'

Knight's heart broke yet again. 'I'd hug you, Elaine, but—'

She blew him a kiss, said she was going to check up on Selena Farrell and James Daring, and walked out the door.

'I've got a present for you before I leave, Peter,' Jack said. 'I want you to have an obscene raise, and I want you to take your kids to somewhere tropical for a few weeks. It's on Private. We'll work out the details after I get back to LA. Speaking of which, I've got a jet to catch.'

After Private's owner had gone, Pope and Hooligan got up to leave as well. 'We are off to the pub, then,' Hooligan said. 'Highlights of the entire Olympic football tournament to watch.'

'We?' Knight said, arching his eyebrow at Pope.

The reporter slipped her arm around Hooligan's waist and smiled. 'Turns out we share a lot in common, Knight. My brothers are all football-mad lads as well.'

Knight smiled. 'There's a certain symmetry there.'

Hooligan grinned and threw his arm around Pope's shoulder. 'Think you're right about that, Peter.'

'Bloody right,' Pope said and they departed, laughing.

The nurses followed and Knight was left alone in the hospital room with his children. He looked up at the television for a moment and saw a shot of the Olympic flame still burning over London. After Lancer's death, Jacques Rogge had asked that the flame should burn on a while longer, and the government had immediately agreed.

It was, Knight decided, a good thing.

Then he let his attention dwell on Luke and Isabel, thinking how beautiful they were, and thanking the gods for saving them from a cruel ending.

He sighed, thinking of how his heart had fallen apart when Isabel and Luke had both wished for a new mother, and again when Elaine had told him how proud Kate would have been of him.

Kate. He missed her still and thought morosely that maybe she had been his singular mate, the one and only love that fate had in store for him. Maybe it was his destiny to go on alone. To raise the children and . . .

A knock came at the door and an American woman's cheery voice called softly from out in the hall, 'Mr Knight? Are you in there?'

Knight looked towards the door. 'Yes?'

A very beautiful and athletic woman slipped in. He knew her immediately and tried to get to his feet, whispering, 'You're Hunter Pierce.'

'I am,' the diver said, smiling brightly now and studying him closely. 'Don't get up. I heard you were injured.'

'Only a bit,' he said. 'I was lucky. We were all lucky.'

Pierce nodded, and Knight could not help but think that she was dazzling up close and in person.

He said, 'I was there at the Aquatics Centre. When you won gold.'

'Were you?' she said, pressing her fingers to the small of her neck.

Knight's eyes were watering and he did not know why. 'I reckon it was the finest example of grace under pressure that I've ever had the honour of witnessing. And the way you spoke out against Cronus, forcefully, consistently. It was . . . well, simply remarkable, and I hope people have told you that.'

The diving champion smiled. 'Thank you. But all of us – Shaw, Mundaho, all of the athletes – they sent me here to tell you that we thought *your* performance last night outshone us all.'

'No, I . . .'

'No, really,' Pierce said emphatically. 'I was there in the stadium. So were my children. We saw you fight him. You risked your life to save ours, and the Olympics, and we, I . . . I wanted to thank you in person from the bottom of my heart.'

Knight felt emotion welling up in his throat. 'I . . . don't know what to say.'

The American diver looked over at his children.

'And these are the brave twins we read about in the *Sun* this morning?'

'Luke and Isabel,' Knight says. 'The lights of my life.'

'They're beautiful. I'd say you're a blessed man, Mr Knight.'

'Call me Peter,' he said. 'And, honestly, you can't know how grateful I am to be here and to have them here. What a blessing it all is. And, well, to have you here too.'

There was a long moment when they were both looking at each other as if they'd just recognised something both familiar and long forgotten.

Pierce cocked her head, and said, 'I'd only meant to pop in for a bit, Peter, but I just had a better thought.'

'What's that?' he asked.

The American diver smiled again, and then affected a corny British accent, saying: 'Would you fancy me wheeling you out of here down to the café? We can have a spot of tea and catch up while your little lovelies are off sailing in the Land of Nod?'

Knight felt flooded with happiness.

'Yes,' he said. 'Yes, I believe I'd like that very much.'

AVAILABLE IN PAPERBACK FROM JANUARY 2013

Private: No. 1 Suspect

James Patterson
& Maxine Paetro

Jack Morgan is accused of a horrific murder – and not even his own world-class investigators can prove he didn't do it.

Since former US Marine Jack Morgan started Private, it has become the world's most effective investigation firm – sought out by the famous and the powerful to discreetly handle their most intimate problems. Private's investigators are the smartest, the fastest, and the most technologically advanced in the world – and they always uncover the truth.

When his former lover is found murdered in Jack's bed, he is instantly the number one suspect. While Jack is under police investigation and fighting to clear his name, the mob strong-arms him into recovering $30 million in stolen pharmaceuticals for them. And the beautiful owner of a chain of luxury hotels persuades him to quietly investigate a string of murders at her high-class establishments.

With Jack and his team stretched to breaking point, one of his most trusted colleagues threatens to leave Private, and Jack realises he is facing his biggest challenge yet.

arrow books

Turn the page for an extract of

Turn the page for an
extract of

PRIVATE

CHAPTER 1

THE CAR WAS waiting for me at LAX. Aldo was out at the curb, holding a sign reading, 'Welcome Home Mr. Morgan.'

I shook Aldo's hand, threw my bags into the trunk, and slid onto the cushy leather seat in the back. I'd done six cities in three days, the return leg from Stockholm turning into a twenty-five-hour journey through airline hell to home.

I was wiped out. And that was an understatement.

'Your packet, Jack,' Aldo said, handing a folder over the divider. The cover was marked 'Private,' the name of my private investigation firm. Our main office was in LA, and we had branches in six countries with clients all over the map who demanded and paid well for services not available through public means.

I had worried lately that we were growing too big too fast, that if big was the enemy of good, *great* didn't stand a chance. And most of all, I wanted Private to be great.

I tucked the folder from Accounting into my briefcase and as the car surfed into the fast lane, I took out my BlackBerry. Unread messages ran into triple digits, so I chose selectively as I thumbed through the list.

The first e-mail was from Viviana, the stunner who'd sat next to me from London to New York. She sold 3-D teleconferencing equipment, not exactly must-have technology, but it was definitely interesting.

There was a text from Paolo, my security chief in Rome, saying, 'Our deadbeat client is now just dead. Details to follow.' I mentally kissed a two-hundred-thousand-euro fee good-bye and moved to texts from the home team.

Justine Smith, my confidante and number two at Private, wrote, 'We've got some catching up to do, bud. I've left the porch light on.' I smiled, thinking that as much as I wanted to see her, I wanted to shower and hit the rack even more.

I sent Justine a reply, then opened a text from Rick Del Rio. 'Noccia wants to see you pronto, that prick.'

The text was like a gut punch.

Carmine Noccia was the scion of the major Mob family by that name, capo of the Las Vegas branch, and my accidental buddy because of a deal I'd had to make with him six months before.

If I never saw Carmine Noccia again, it would be way too soon.

I typed a four-letter reply, sent it to Del Rio, and put my phone back into my pocket as the car turned into my driveway. I collected my bags and watched Aldo back out, making sure he didn't get T-boned on Pacific Coast Highway.

I swiped my electronic key fob across the reader and went through the gate, pressed my finger to the biometric pad, and entered my home sweet home.

For a half second, I thought I smelled roses, but I chalked it up to the delight of standing again in my own house.

I started stripping in the living room and by the time I'd reached the bathroom, I was down to my boxers, which I kicked off outside the shower stall.

I stood under water as hot as I could stand it, then went into my bedroom and hit the wall switch that turned on the lights on either side of the bed.

For a long moment, I stood frozen in the doorway. I couldn't understand what I saw – because it made no sense. How could Colleen be in my bed? Her sweater was soaked with blood.

What the hell was this?

A tasteless prank?

I shouted her name, and then I was on my knees beside the bed, my hand pressing the side of her neck. Her skin was as warm as life – but she had no pulse.

Colleen was wearing a knee-length skirt and a blue cardigan, clothes I'd seen her wear before. Her rose-scented hair was fanned out around her shoulders and her violet-blue eyes were closed. I gripped her shoulders and gently shook her, but her head just lolled.

Oh, Jesus. No.

Colleen was dead.

How in God's name had this happened?

CHAPTER 2

I'D SEEN COUNTLESS dead while serving in Afghanistan. I've worked murders as part of my job for years, and I've even witnessed the deaths of friends.

None of that protected me from the horror of seeing Colleen's bloody and lifeless form. Her blood spattered the bedspread, soaking through. Her sweater was so bloody I couldn't see her wounds. Had she been stabbed? Shot? I couldn't tell.

The covers were pulled tight and I saw no sign of a struggle. Everything in the room was exactly as I had left it four days ago – everything but Colleen's dead body, right here.

I thought about Colleen's attempted suicide after we'd broken up six months ago – the scars were visible: silver lines on her wrists. But this was no suicide.

There was no weapon on or near the bed.

It looked as if Colleen had come into my bedroom,

put her head on the pillow, and then been killed while she slept.

And that made no sense.

Just then, my lagging survival instinct kicked in. Whoever had killed Colleen could still be in the house. I went for the window seat where I kept my gun.

My hands shook as I lifted the hinged top of the window seat and grabbed the metal gun box. It was light. Empty.

I opened the closet doors, looked under the bed, saw no one, no shells, no nothing. I stepped into jeans, pulled on a T-shirt, then walked from window to window to door, checking locks, staring up at skylights looking for broken panes.

And I backtracked through my mind.

I was certain the front door had been locked when I came home. And now I was sure that every other entry point was secure.

That could only mean that someone had entered my house with an electronic gate key and biometric access – someone who knew me. Colleen had been my assistant and my lover for a year before we'd broken up. I hadn't deleted her codes.

Colleen wasn't the only one with access to my house, but maybe I wouldn't have to guess who had killed her.

My house was watched by the best surveillance

system ever made. There were cameras posted on all sides, over the doorways, sweeping the highway, and taking in 180 degrees of beachfront beyond my deck.

I opened the cabinet doors on the entertainment unit in the living room and flipped the switch turning on the six video monitors stacked in two columns of three. All six screens lit up – and all six screens were blank. I stabbed the buttons on the remote control again and again before I realized the hard drive was gone. Only a detached cord remained.

I grabbed the phone by the sofa and called Justine's direct line at the office. It was almost seven. Would she still be there?

She answered on the first ring.

'Jack, you hungry after all?'

'Justine. Something bad has happened.'

My voice cracked as I forced myself to say it.

'It's Colleen. She's dead. Some *bastard* killed her.'

CHAPTER 3

I OPENED THE front door and Justine swept in like a soft breeze. She was a first-class psychologist, a profiler, smart – hell, brilliant. Thank God she was here.

She put her hand on my cheek, searched my eyes, said, 'Jack. Where is she?'

I pointed to the bedroom. Justine went in and I followed her, standing numb in the doorway as she walked to the bed. She moaned, 'Oh, no,' and clasped her hands under her chin.

Even as I stood witness to this heartbreaking tableau, Colleen was still alive in my mind.

I pictured her in the little house she had rented in Los Feliz, a love nest you could almost hold in cupped hands. I thought about her twitching her hips in skimpy lingerie, big fuzzy slippers on her feet, sprinkling her thick brogue with her granny's auld Irish sayings: 'There'll be caps on the green and no one to fetch 'em.'

'What does that mean, Molloy?' I'd asked her.

'Trouble.'

And now here she was on my bed. Well beyond trouble.

Justine was pale when she came back to me. She put her arms around me and held me. 'I'm so sorry, Jack. So very sorry.'

I held her tight – and then, abruptly, Justine jerked away. She pinned me with her dark eyes and said, 'Why is your hair wet?'

'My hair?'

'Did you take a shower?'

'Yes, I did. When I came home, I went straight to the bathroom. I was trying to wake myself up.'

'Well, this is no dream, Jack. This is as real as real can be. When you showered, had you seen Colleen?'

'I had no idea she was here.'

'You hadn't told her to come over?'

'No, Justine, I didn't. *No.*'

The doorbell rang again.

CHAPTER 4

THE ARRIVAL OF Dr. Sci and Mo-bot improved the odds of figuring out what had happened in my house by 200 percent.

Dr. Sci, real name Seymour Kloppenberg, was Private's chief forensic scientist. He had a long string of degrees behind his name, starting with a PhD in physics from MIT when he was nineteen – and that was only ten years ago.

Mo-bot was Maureen Roth, a fifty-something computer geek and jack-of-all-tech. She specialized in computer crime and was also Private's resident mom.

Mo had brought her camera and her wisdom. Sci had his scene kit packed with evidence-collection equipment of the cutting-edge kind.

We went to my room and the four of us stood around Colleen's dead body as night turned the windows black.

We had all loved Colleen. Every one of us.

'We don't have much time,' Justine said, breaking the silence, at work now as an investigator on a homicide. 'Jack, I have to ask you, did you have anything to do with this? Because if you did, we can make it all disappear.'

'I found Colleen like this when I got home,' I said.

'Okay. Just the same,' said Justine, 'every passing minute makes you more and more the guy who did it. You've got to call it in, Jack. So let's go over everything, fast and carefully. Start from the beginning and don't leave anything out.'

As Mo and Sci snapped on latex gloves, Justine turned on a digital recorder and motioned to me to start talking. I told her that after I got off the plane, Aldo had met me at British Airways arrivals, 5:30 sharp.

I told her about showering, then finding Colleen's body. I said that my gun was missing as well as the hard drive from my security system.

I said again that I had no idea why Colleen was here or why she'd been killed. 'I didn't do it, Justine.'

'I know that, Jack.'

We both knew that when the cops got here, I would be suspect number one, and although I had cop friends, I couldn't rely on any of them to find Colleen's killer when I was so darned handy.

I had been intimately involved with the deceased.

There was no forced entry into my house.

The victim was on my bed.

It was what law enforcement liked to call an open-and-shut case. Open and shut on me.

CHAPTER 5

IF YOU'RE NOT the cops on official business, processing an active crime scene is a felony. It's not just contaminating evidence and destroying the prosecution's ability to bring the accused to trial, it's accessory to the crime.

If we were caught working the scene, I would lose my license, and all four of us could go to jail.

That said, if there was ever a time to break the law, this was it.

Mo said, 'Jack, please get out of the frame.'

I stepped into the hallway and Mo's Nikon flashed.

She took shots from every angle, wide, close-up, extreme close-ups of the wounds in Colleen's chest.

Sci took Colleen's and my fingerprints with an electronic reader while Mo-bot ran a latent-print reader over hard surfaces in the room. No fingerprint powder required.

Justine asked, 'When did you last see Colleen alive?'

I told her that I'd had lunch with her last Wednesday, before I left for the airport.

'Just lunch?'

'Yes. We just had lunch.'

A shadow crossed Justine's eyes, like clouds rolling in before a thunderstorm. She didn't believe me. And I didn't have the energy to persuade her. I was overtired, scared, heartsick, and nauseated. I wanted to wake up. Find myself still on the plane.

Sci was talking to Mo. He took scrapings from under Colleen's nails, and Mo sealed the bags. When Sci lifted Colleen's skirt, swab in hand, I turned away.

I talked to Justine, told her where Colleen and I had eaten lunch on Wednesday, that Colleen had been in good spirits.

'She said she had a boyfriend in Dublin. She said she was falling in love.'

I had a new thought. I spun around and shouted, 'Anyone see her purse?'

'No purse, Jack.'

'She was brought here,' I said to Justine. 'Someone had her gate key.'

Justine said, 'Good thought. Any reason or anyone you can think of who could have done this?'

'Someone hated her. Or hated me. Or hated us both.' Justine nodded. 'Sci? Mo? We have to get out of here. Will you be all right, Jack?'

'I'm not sure,' I said.

'You're in shock. We all are. Just tell the cops what you know,' she said as Sci and Mo packed up their kits.

'Say you took a very long shower,' Sci said, putting his hand on my shoulder. 'Make that a long bath and then a shower. That should soak up some of the timeline.'

'Okay.'

'The only prints I found were yours,' said Mo-bot.

'It's *my* house.'

'I know that, Jack. There were no prints other than yours. Check the entry card reader,' she said. 'I would do it, but we should leave.'

'Okay. Thanks, Mo.'

Justine squeezed my hand, said she'd call me later, and then, as if I had dreamed them up, they were gone and I was alone with Colleen.

JAMES PATTERSON

**To find out more about James Patterson
and his bestselling books, go to
www.jamespatterson.co.uk**

Also by James Patterson

ALEX CROSS NOVELS

Along Came a Spider • Kiss the Girls • Jack and Jill •
Cat and Mouse • Pop Goes the Weasel • Roses are Red •
Violets are Blue • Four Blind Mice • The Big Bad Wolf •
London Bridges • Mary, Mary • Cross • Double Cross •
Cross Country • Alex Cross's Trial (*with Richard DiLallo*) •
I, Alex Cross • Cross Fire • Kill Alex Cross

THE WOMEN'S MURDER CLUB SERIES

1st to Die • 2nd Chance (*with Andrew Gross*) •
3rd Degree (*with Andrew Gross*) • 4th of July
(*with Maxine Paetro*) • The 5th Horseman (*with Maxine Paetro*)
• The 6th Target (*with Maxine Paetro*) • 7th Heaven (*with
Maxine Paetro*) • 8th Confession (*with Maxine Paetro*) •
9th Judgement (*with Maxine Paetro*) • 10th Anniversary
(*with Maxine Paetro*) • 11th Hour (*with Maxine Paetro*)

DETECTIVE MICHAEL BENNETT SERIES

Step on a Crack (*with Michael Ledwidge*) • Run for Your Life
(*with Michael Ledwidge*) • Worst Case (*with Michael Ledwidge*) •
Tick Tock (*with Michael Ledwidge*) • I, Michael Bennett
(*with Michael Ledwidge*)

STAND-ALONE THRILLERS

Sail (*with Howard Roughan*) • Swimsuit (*with Maxine Paetro*) •
Don't Blink (*with Howard Roughan*) • Postcard Killers
(*with Liza Marklund*) • Toys (*with Neil McMahon*) •
Now You See Her (*with Michael Ledwidge*) • Kill Me If You Can
(*with Marshall Karp*) • Guilty Wives (*with David Ellis*)

NON-FICTION

Torn Apart (*with Hal and Cory Friedman*) •
The Murder of King Tut (*with Martin Dugard*)

ROMANCE

Sundays at Tiffany's (*with Gabrielle Charbonnet*) •
The Christmas Wedding (*with Richard DiLallo*)

FAMILY OF PAGE-TURNERS

MAXIMUM RIDE SERIES

The Angel Experiment • School's Out Forever •
Saving the World and Other Extreme Sports •
The Final Warning • Max • Fang • Angel • Nevermore
(*to be published August 2012*)

DANIEL X SERIES

The Dangerous Days of Daniel X (*with Michael Ledwidge*) •
Daniel X: Watch the Skies (*with Ned Rust*) • Daniel X: Demons
and Druids (*with Adam Sadler*) • Daniel X: Game Over
(*with Ned Rust*)

WITCH & WIZARD SERIES

Witch & Wizard (*with Gabrielle Charbonnet*) •
Witch & Wizard: The Gift (*with Ned Rust*) •
Witch & Wizard: The Fire (*with Jill Dembowski*)

MIDDLE SCHOOL SERIES

Middle School: The Worst Years of My Life
(*with Chris Tebbetts and Laura Park*) • Middle School: Get Me
Out of Here! (*with Chris Tebbetts and Laura Park*)

GRAPHIC NOVELS

Daniel X: Alien Hunter (*with Leopoldo Gout*) • Maximum Ride:
Manga Vol. 1 (*with NaRae Lee*) • Maximum Ride: Manga Vol. 2
(*with NaRae Lee*) • Maximum Ride: Manga Vol. 3 (*with NaRae
Lee*) • Maximum Ride: Manga Vol. 4 (*with NaRae Lee*) •
Maximum Ride: Manga Vol. 5 (*with NaRae Lee*)

For more information about James Patterson's novels, visit
www.jamespatterson.co.uk

Or become a fan on Facebook

We support

I'm proud to support the National Literacy Trust, an independent charity that changes lives through literacy.

Did you know that millions of people in the UK struggle to read and write? This means children are less likely to succeed at school and less likely to develop into confident and happy teenagers. Literacy difficulties will limit their opportunities throughout adult life.

The National Literacy Trust passionately believes that everyone has a right to the reading, writing, speaking and listening skills they need to fulfil their own and, ultimately, the nation's potential.

My own son didn't use to enjoy reading, which was why I started writing children's books – reading for pleasure is an essential way to encourage children to pick up a book. The National Literacy Trust is dedicated to delivering exciting initiatives to encourage people to read and to help raise literacy levels. To find out more about the great work that they do, visit their website at www.literacytrust.org.uk.

James Patterson